2⁴⁰

PENGUIN CRIME FICTION
SARATOGA BESTIARY

Stephen Dobyns lives in Syracuse, New York, and teaches at Syracuse University. In addition to six Charlie Bradshaw mysteries (including the most recent, *Saratoga Hexameter*), his novels include *Dancer with One Leg*, *Cold Dog Soup*, *A Boat Off the Coast*, and *The Two Deaths of Señora Puccini*. His sixth book of poems, *Cemetery Nights*, was published to high acclaim in 1987.

SARATOGA BESTIARY

Stephen Dobyns

PENGUIN BOOKS

PENGUIN BOOKS
Published by the Penguin Group
Viking Penguin, a division of Penguin Books USA Inc.,
375 Hudson Street, New York, New York 10014, U.S.A.
Penguin Books Ltd, 27 Wrights Lane, London W8 5TZ, England
Penguin Books Australia Ltd, Ringwood, Victoria, Australia
Penguin Books Canada Ltd, 2801 John Street, Markham, Ontario, Canada L3R 1B4
Penguin Books (N.Z.) Ltd, 182–190 Wairau Road, Auckland 10, New Zealand

Penguin Books Ltd, Registered Offices: Harmondsworth, Middlesex, England

First published in the United States of America by Viking Penguin,
a division of Penguin Books USA Inc., 1988
Published in Penguin Books 1990

10 9 8 7 6 5 4 3 2 1

Grateful acknowledgment is made for permission to reprint an excerpt from
"Triptych, Middle Panel Burning" from *Half-Promised Land* by Thomas Lux.
Copyright © 1986 by Thomas Lux. Reprinted by permission of Houghton
Mifflin Company.

LIBRARY OF CONGRESS CATALOGING IN PUBLICATION DATA
Dobyns, Stephen, 1941–
    Saratoga bestiary/Stephen Dobyns.
        p. cm.
    ISBN 0 14 01.0613 8
    I. Title.
    PS3554.O2S25   1990
    813'.54—dc20   90–30307

Printed in the United States of America
Set in Times Roman

For Thomas Lux and Jean Kilbourne

If there are, each day, terrors
we have to live with
let them be: that we fail to make
something (anything, in whatever
realm: a new lilypad,
a way to line one extra belly
with nutrients, a tool
to scan and receive the vision of God);
and, of course, of course: that we not
be able to love.

—Thomas Lux
"Triptych, Middle Panel Burning"

SARATOGA
BESTIARY

1

The man sitting across the desk from Charlie Bradshaw was one of the wealthiest men in Saratoga Springs. Indeed, he was one of the wealthiest in the United States, and it was a stroke of good fortune that he should be in the market for a private detective and that detective should be Charlie, whose business this January seemed in a state of hibernation. As Charlie kept telling himself, a customer like George Whitman could make the difference between groceries and no groceries. With Whitman's backing, Charlie could become the pet detective of the horse set, and he imagined stretch limousines double-parked outside his door on Phila Street. The sad part was that Whitman also appeared to be crazy.

"And just how long has Man o' War been missing?" asked Charlie. Although his knowledge of racing was not what it should be considering a lifetime in Saratoga, Charlie was positive that Man o' War had died back when he was in third grade.

"Just five days." Whitman sat somewhat stiffly in Charlie's visitor's chair. He was a thin man in his early sixties with gunpowder-gray hair. As he spoke, he picked invisible specks of lint from his immaculate gray tweed suit, slowly moving his long hands as though moving them underwater.

"And do you know how they got him away?"

"We believe it was in a Ford Pinto."

Charlie was unable to keep silent. "They got a horse into a Ford Pinto?"

Whitman's hands stopped moving as, finger to finger, he formed a little cage in front of his chest. "Mr. Bradshaw, we are not talking about a horse. We are talking about the painting of a horse. The actual horse has been dead for forty years."

"Certainly," said Charlie, "but even a picture. It must have been a big picture and a Pinto is a small car. . . ." He stopped. Whitman was staring past him at the framed photograph of Jesse James on the wall behind the desk. He gave the impression of someone who was mentally enunciating the word "idiot" but was too well-bred to say it. At least he's not crazy, thought Charlie.

"Last Monday one of the thieves called the museum," continued Whitman, still eyeing the photograph. "He explained we could have the painting back for $10,000. Otherwise he would destroy it. We had several conversations over several days and on Wednesday we settled on a price of $5,000."

"And what do you want me to do?" asked Charlie. Now that he began to think of it, all sorts of information about Man o' War started springing to mind: how Big Red had had his only loss in twenty-one races right here in Saratoga in the Sanford Memorial Stakes in 1919 to a horse named Upset, how he had been purchased the year before in Saratoga as a yearling for $5,000, which was exactly what the thieves were asking for the painting. How ironic! Charlie wanted to mention these details to Mr. Whitman—who looked like a man who felt he'd made a mistake and was thinking of correcting it—but he kept silent.

Whitman shifted his gaze back to Charlie. He had light gray eyes, as if all the color had been leached from them by the constant counting of money. "We want you to deliver the ransom. This evening I'll get a call as to where the money should be taken and then I'll contact you. For this you'll be paid $250."

"No police?" asked Charlie.

"Mr. Bradshaw, there are many paintings in the Racing Hall of Fame but Voss's painting of Man o' War is one of the most valuable, both as an example of the art and because Man o' War is still, perhaps, the best horse of the century. No police, no investigation, no trickery. We want the painting returned." Mr. Whitman stood up. He was a tall man, nearly half a foot taller than Charlie. "You be here tonight and I'll call you after I hear from the thieves. Ideally, we'll have the painting back tomorrow."

Charlie stood up as well. "How'd they steal the painting from the museum?"

"No, Mr. Bradshaw, your questions are irrelevant. No police, no investigation, no trickery." Whitman walked to the frosted glass door separating Charlie's office from the small waiting room, then turned and lifted his chin slightly as if smelling something unpleasant. "By the way, Mr. Bradshaw, whom do you favor in the Super Bowl?"

The question took Charlie by surprise. He had little interest in football, feeling such an interest was somehow a betrayal of his love of baseball. "Ah, the Eagles, I guess."

"You're not a Patriots fan?" Whitman looked disapproving.

"The Eagles have a pretty good team." Really, he hardly cared, but he remembered the saying that patriotism was the last refuge of a scoundrel and he supposed it adversely influenced him.

"What's the current line?"

Charlie knew no more about point spreads than he did about bedspreads. "I haven't heard it for today," he said. Whitman probably guessed he didn't know the first thing about it, and for a moment Charlie wished he had asked his friend Victor Plotz. On the other hand, he felt irritated with Whitman for thinking that just because he was a private detective in Saratoga Springs he should know the lowdown about point spreads for Sunday's game.

Whitman appeared disappointed. "Expect to hear from me tonight," he said. Then he left, quietly shutting the door behind him. Charlie waited until he heard the outside door close as well, then he exhaled a lungful of air through pursed lips, making a breathy whistling sound.

The $250 would pay the rent and maybe this job could lead to others. But then Charlie began thinking of something a little more grand. What if he did more than just deliver the money? What if he found the painting and even caught the thieves? Anything was possible.

Charlie had a date that night but he would break it. Perhaps he could change it to tomorrow night. As he turned to face the window, he saw his present girlfriend framed in the second-story window across the street. Dressed in white, she was bending over a man, her nose inches from his, as she inserted her fingers into his mouth. She looked kindly and eager. She was a dental hygienist and her name was Grace Washburn. Blond, forty, and slightly overweight, she had a sort of militant good cheer and pink cheeks that turned bright red when she and Charlie made love. They had been dating for three months and already she had cleaned Charlie's teeth fourteen times. Never in his whole life had Charlie's teeth been so clean. His gums ached just to think about it. And Saturday night, if they went out, Charlie could expect to have his teeth cleaned still again.

On several occasions Charlie had asked if they couldn't forget the teeth-cleaning for just once, but Grace's feelings had been hurt. Her great pride was her particular ability to clean teeth. And Charlie had submitted once more, sitting in a straight chair in her kitchen, a goosenecked lamp shining in his eyes, as Grace picked over his teeth with a wide variety of tools, then flossed them, then brushed them. Afterwards, they would go out to eat or watch a movie on Grace's VCR, and after that they would make love. It was a comfortable relationship, except for the teeth-cleaning, and, although they'd only been dating a short time, Charlie had known her since moving into this office several years before. Well, he hadn't actually "known her," but he would often see Grace when he glanced out the window, and after a while they had begun to smile and even wave. It had seemed inevitable they would eventually date.

Charlie continued to watch Grace as he picked up the handset of his black desk phone to call her. Between their two windows a thick leaden sky was letting down fat white flakes. It was supposed to snow all day and nearly a foot was expected. This much of January and most of December had been like that. As Charlie started to dial, he heard the outside door open again. At first he thought it was Whitman, who perhaps had changed his mind and didn't want to hire a private detective who believed that Man o' War was still alive; but then there was a sharp rap on the glass and the door opened to admit a tall man in a brown overcoat whom Charlie had never seen before.

"You're Bradshaw? My name is Moss, Blake Moss." The man crossed the office in three strides and took hold of Charlie's hand, which was stretched toward him across the desk. As Charlie's hand was seized, he could feel his bones crack and the nail of his pinkie dug painfully into the skin of his index finger. Moss released him, then sat down abruptly in the visitor's chair facing the desk. All his movements were quick and determined, as if designed to show the world that he wasn't someone to fool around.

"I'll jump right to the point, Mr. Bradshaw. I've come to you with a proposition."

Charlie sat back down and massaged his hand under the desk where Moss couldn't see it. He hadn't had a customer all week and now he'd had two in a half hour. But perhaps Moss wasn't a customer. "What's on your mind?" asked Charlie.

"You and I are in the same line of work, Mr. Bradshaw. I have a detective agency in Albany, with branch offices in Schenectady, Pittsfield and Kingston. Now I want to open an office in Saratoga." Moss leaned back and placed his large hands on his knees. He was about forty with a round face and small, delicate-looking ears. His blond hair was cut in a perfect flat top. "Military" was the word that came to Charlie's mind. Moss was a big man, even somewhat swollen, and had the look of an ex-football player who needed to exercise more vigorously if he wanted to avoid a future in which he resembled a loaf of soft white bread.

"Saratoga's a nice town," said Charlie, wondering if it could really support two private detectives.

"I don't like competition, Bradshaw." Moss took out a pack of Marlboros and offered one to Charlie, who refused. Lighting one for himself, Moss shook out the match and tossed it into the metal wastebasket. "I don't care to spend my time ducking around trying to get your clients while keeping you from getting mine. What I want is to offer you $20,000 a year to be the Saratoga branch manager of the Moss Security Agency. Apart from your regular investigations, you'll be in charge of about a dozen security guards." Moss paused and glanced around Charlie's office, his eyes settling only briefly on Jesse James, before passing on to the pale green walls, the cracks in the ceiling, the thin brown rug covering the old linoleum, the gray safe in the corner, empty except for Charlie's .38. "And of course," continued Moss, "we'll have to move the office to some more suitable location."

"Suitable?" asked Charlie. Twenty thousand a year was several thousand more than he was making by himself. On the other hand, he wouldn't be his own boss.

"I was thinking of an office in the Pyramid Mall."

"The mall?"

"Where it would have the most visibility. Shoplifting, missing husbands, runaways, bad checks, insurance fraud—you want to be where people can see you."

Charlie rubbed his hand on the back of his neck. He had a scratchy feeling in his chest and he was afraid he was getting a cold. "I like working by myself," he said. "And I like working here."

"Don't tell me about it now," said Moss, standing up. "Don't make any hasty decisions. I've already checked your reputation and you're just the sort of fellow I want. Think about it and I'll talk to you on Monday. Twenty thousand plus health insurance, including dental. I bet you don't even have health insurance."

"Only dental," said Charlie, remaining seated.

Moss stubbed out his cigarette in the green glass ashtray on the desk. "You backing the Pats?" he asked.

Charlie's mind did a few quick flips as he realized that again the subject was football. "Sure," he said.

"I'm an Eagles fan myself."

"What odds?" asked Charlie.

Moss looked at him suspiciously. "You mean the line? Pats by four and a half. But it all depends on Eason's knees. He sees the doc tomorrow." Moss walked to the door. "Monday, Bradshaw. Think hard about this. It would mean a chunk of money. You could buy yourself some clothes."

"I've got plenty of clothes," said Charlie.

Blake Moss gave Charlie a brief nod and left, leaving the door open behind him. After a moment, Charlie went to close it. He looked down at his khaki pants and brown sport coat, his tan chamois cloth shirt. "Plenty of clothes," he repeated to himself. "They're just old, that's all."

2

Standing behind the bar at the Bentley, Victor Plotz took a maraschino cherry from the bowl in front of Charlie and squeezed it between two fingers until its scarlet sides split. Then he popped it in his mouth, stem and all.

"Just a few friends, Charlie. What could be more harmless than a few friends watching the Super Bowl?"

"Those rooms aren't supposed to be open," said Charlie, who was perched on one of the chrome stools drinking a diet cola.

"Hey, Charlie, your mother trusted me enough to make me the off-season manager of the Bentley. That function room up on the third floor has the big screen, forty-eight inches of football magic. Where's the harm? And afterward I'll sweep and polish and nobody'll ever know that I was there." Victor removed the stem of the cherry from his mouth and looked at it critically.

"Okay, okay," said Charlie. He had no wish to disappoint Victor, and as for what happened in the function room Charlie hardly cared, unless, of course, it got into the newspapers. "And you'll help me this evening?"

"Whatever you say. I'll find someone to watch the bar."

Victor tossed another cherry into the air and caught it on his long pink tongue. Then he winked at Charlie. "I could eat these all day," he said.

The bar at the Bentley was strictly Art Deco with lots of shiny chrome and black and white tiles. The long mirror behind the bar was framed with a thick silver tubing and every foot or so were little bulbs like makeup lights. Apart from the kitchen, the bar was the most modern room in the Bentley, the others being pure Victorian, which seemed appropriate for one of the last Victorian hotels in Saratoga Springs.

Charlie's mother, Mabel Bradshaw, owned the Bentley and usually she ran it herself. But this year she had decided she couldn't stand another winter in Saratoga and was spending the cold months in Paris, studying high fashion—an idea that startled Charlie every time he thought of it. Victor was keeping the hotel open just on the weekends, managing the bar, serving a limited menu in the grill, renting a few rooms mostly to the parents of Skidmore students but sometimes to the students themselves for amorous trysts, as Victor called them. As befitted the manager of a big hotel, he no longer wore the ragged sweatshirts that had kept him warm during his years as Charlie's assistant in the Charles F. Bradshaw Detective Agency. Now he wore a dove gray suit, dove gray shirt and dove gray tie, which exactly matched his dove gray hair, expensively styled to surround his head much as an olive surrounds its pimiento stuffing. In the midst of all this gray, his large, elbow-shaped nose stood out like a beacon. Victor was about sixty and appeared to be speeding up, rather than slowing down, with several girlfriends, a severe Nautilus regimen and a red Renault Fuego parked in the manager's slot of the Bentley. He was also Charlie's best friend.

Charlie had left his office and crossed Broadway to the hotel around lunch time that Friday, motivated by what he ever afterward thought of as a bad idea. It had occurred to him that much might be gained by improving on George Whitman's scenario for the coming evening. If, for instance, someone like Victor were watching the spot where Charlie dropped off the money, that person might get a lead on whoever was trying to ransom the painting of Man o' War back to the racing museum. Then, if Charlie actually tracked down the thieves, saw to their arrest and recovered the money, possibly Mr. George Whitman might be pleased enough to send more business in his direction, in which case Charlie would never feel in the least bit tempted by an offer like the one from Blake Moss. But even as he was planning these events Charlie knew he would never have considered ignoring Whitman's instructions if he hadn't made that foolish remark about getting Man o' War into a Ford Pinto. He wanted to do something that would gain him a little credit in Whitman's eyes.

Charlie reached forward and nudged Victor's sleeve with his hand. "But you have to be careful," he said. "If these guys spot you, we're in big trouble."

Victor stirred his finger around the bowl of maraschino cherries, then wiped his hands on the bar towel. "So I'll be invisible, just like Lamont Cranston himself."

"There'll be snow."

"I seen snow before."

"These people will be suspicious."

"I'll disguise myself as a parking meter. Cut the worrying, will you?"

"Okay, okay," Charlie finished his diet cola and sat back. Probably he was wrong to be nervous. "So what's this thing on Sunday?"

"Just a few guys watching the game, a coupla beers, a big bowl of popcorn. Nothing elaborate." Victor grinned, showing his gold molars.

"What about Eason's knees?" asked Charlie.

"Come on, Charlie. Who you been talking to? You don't care squat about football."

"Is the line still the Pats by four and a half?"

Victor squinted at Charlie, uncertain if he was being teased. "It's dropped to three. The knees don't look so good."

"I'll bet you two to five that the Eagles' yardage in the third quarter will be two-tenths of a mile more than the Patriots' in the second quarter and that the referee has a daughter named Agnes."

Victor moved down the bar to the kitchen. "I'll get your sandwich. I don't like these traces of humor, Charlie. Makes me think I'll have to start reading joke books just to keep up."

Charlie chewed some of the ice in his glass and looked around the room, which was empty. The mirrors on three walls threw back his reflection and he winced. The previous April he had turned fifty, and ever since he'd been unable to look in a mirror without a little voice saying in his ear, "You're fifty. Think of that, you're fifty."

His response wasn't regret for life unlived or anxiety over what lay ahead; rather, it was surprise. He didn't feel fifty. He didn't know what he felt like exactly, but he'd felt this way for many years and it didn't feel like fifty, not five-zero, not half a century. He supposed he kept saying it just so he would get used to it, but even now, nine months after his birthday, he was still saying it—"You're fifty"—and each time it came as a surprise.

He looked all right, he thought, rather innocuous, even un-assuming, someone your eyes passed over to look at someone else. A little overweight, but not much, thanks to swimming. Not quite as tall as he would have liked. A private face, round, relatively unlined, with graying hair combed straight back across his head. At the moment several strands were sticking up some-what foolishly and he patted them back down again. He felt that his large blue eyes bore a thoughtful, even intelligent expression. His nose, on the other hand, was much too small, a little blip of a nose, a flesh-colored grape.

Victor returned with two plates each with a roast beef sandwich and potato chips. He put one in front of Charlie, then poured him another glass of diet cola. "But even though this party is just for a few friends, Charlie, I wouldn't want your mother to hear about it. After all, she's a lady, what does she know about a bunch of guys watching the Super Bowl?"

With his mouth full of sandwich, Charlie thought, with some surprise, that his mother really was a lady, despite her forty-five years as a waitress in Saratoga. A half interest in a winning trotter, some good bets, a lucky week in the casinos of Atlantic City had turned her into the owner of a big hotel and now she was studying high fashion in Paris. But gambling was in her blood, as it had been in Charlie's father's, the man who had bet that Lindbergh wouldn't make it, that Lou Gehrig was a flash in the pan, that Hoover would be reelected, and who had welched on his IOUs by committing suicide when Charlie was four years old. As a result, Charlie had ambivalent feelings about gambling, knowing how easily he could let himself be swept away, trying to parlay his pennies into dollars and handing out bad checks on Friday, hoping to redeem them before Monday with a few big wins. He was a romantic. It was his great fault. It was too easy for him to believe in things that would never happen. Consequently, his betting was limited to a few horses at the track each August—horses with every virtue except the ability to win.

Charlie looked at Victor and wondered if he had any reason to be suspicious about his party. "That's okay," he said, "I won't tell her. Just don't make a mess, that's all. How come you didn't invite me as well?"

Victor drank down some Vichy, then coughed. "Charlie, you're my best friend. Whenever I have a party, you're first on my list. Numero uno. It's just that you hate football, that's all. You'd be a wet blanket, sitting around reading a book or something. You really want to come?"

"I've got to work that day." Charlie thought Victor looked relieved. "Somebody's been breaking into cottages out around Lake Cossayuna. I'm supposed to find him."

"Cold work."

"Tell you the truth, I'd prefer it to watching football."

That evening around five Charlie drove back to his small house on Lake Saratoga for supper. It was already dark, and although on this January twenty-third he knew the days were getting longer and that in terms of daylight this day was more or less equal to November nineteenth, the dark was still oppressive and Charlie felt that his whole body had been clenched for several months. Several inches of snow had accumulated on the road and it was still snowing heavily. Charlie stayed in the tracks of the car in front of him, going about twenty-five. Big flakes shone in his low beams, blurring the red taillights up ahead. Charlie's car was a Renault Encore purchased nearly two years earlier when his old Renault 12 had died. He supposed he had bought another Renault simply for sentimental reasons. Although inexpensive, it had not been a wise choice and had developed a hunger for something called C.V. joints, going through two sets in 40,000 miles. Charlie had never heard of C.V. joints before and now he didn't know much more except that C.V. joints were expensive. He felt irritated at the car, that it was made so cheaply, and sometime earlier, when the president of Renault Motors had been assassinated in France, Charlie suspected that it was the owner of a Renault Encore who had done him in.

Coming off the bridge across Fish Creek, Charlie slowed to make the right-hand turn to Pellegrino's Grocery. He needed milk, coffee and maybe a six-pack of Rolling Rock. Joe Pellegrino hardly ever had any customers and by occasionally shopping here Charlie felt he was doing his bit in the battle between the little grocers and the supermarkets. Making the turn, Charlie's headlights swept across the snow-covered expanse of Lake Saratoga, interrupted only by several fishing shacks way out on the ice, snow-covered and gloomy. He parked by the front steps and got out, pulling his blue sailor's watch cap over his ears and forehead.

Perhaps he was paying too much attention to keeping the snow out of his shoes and wasn't watching where he was going. Certainly he wanted to get inside as quickly as possible. Whatever the case, as he began to ascend the steps, he immediately bumped into someone coming down.

"What the fuck, man, why don't you watch where you're going?" A man of about forty in an army fatigue jacket stood at the bottom of the steps rubbing his arm. He was about Charlie's height, maybe an inch shorter.

Charlie would have apologized if it weren't for the man's rudeness. As it was, he ignored him and began climbing the steps. The man reached out and poked Charlie's arm, stopping him.

"I said, why don't you watch where you're going?"

Charlie turned on the third step and looked down at the man, surprised by how angry he seemed. He had a round face, dark eyes and long black hair now speckled with snowflakes. He wasn't carrying a package and Charlie guessed he had stopped to buy cigarettes. "You were pretty much in a hurry yourself," said Charlie. "Let's just forget it."

"Maybe I don't want to forget it, fuckhead." The man took a step toward Charlie who remained where he was.

"You really want to fight?" asked Charlie, hoping he didn't. "Roll around in the snow, get wet, act stupid? Is that what you want?"

"Asshole," said the man, stepping back and walking to his car, a dark-colored Oldsmobile. Charlie watched him start up and then fishtail onto Route 9P back toward Saratoga. His heart was pumping and he took a deep breath to calm himself before he turned and entered Pellegrino's Grocery. In his twenty years as a Saratoga policeman, he had learned a variety of restraining holds but he was just as glad that he hadn't had to use one.

Joe Pellegrino was standing behind the counter, a small balding man in his early seventies with a little halo of white hair. Over his clothes he wore a white butcher's apron. "Mr. Owl,

Mr. Owl, was that you quarreling with one of my customers?"

Whether because he couldn't remember people's names or because he chose not to, Pellegrino gave everyone animal names. After half a dozen years, Charlie hardly noticed it anymore. He supposed he would have preferred to be Mr. Lion. He was just as glad not to be Mr. Pig.

"He was in quite a hurry," said Charlie, going to the cooler for the milk and beer.

"Young people are always in a hurry," said Pellegrino putting a little wad of snuff under his lip, then dusting a few particles from the bib of his apron. Beneath the apron he wore a white shirt. "They're in a terrible hurry and then they're not happy when they get there. That's the trouble, Mr. Owl, not enough happiness."

Charlie took a can of Chock Full o' Nuts from the shelf, then added a box of Freihofer's fruit cookies, just for happiness's sake. "So you ready for the Super Bowl?" asked Charlie, putting the coffee and cookies on the counter.

"It's the knees, Mr. Owl, it all comes down to Eason's knees. But I'll tell you, ten minutes after he comes out of the doctor's tomorrow, I'll know about it."

Charlie took a twenty from his wallet and laid it on the can of coffee, as Pellegrino rang up his purchases. "You follow it that closely?"

"You gotta. Eason's knees, Fryar's wrists, Haley's colitis. Is Grogan depressed? Will Tippett move his bowels before the game? It all adds up. They run that stuff through a computer and they get the spread—Pats by three. Personally, though, I don't think the Pats are gonna do it. There's too much psychology in a Super Bowl. It makes their feet too big and their hearts too little. Who do you favor?"

Charlie picked up his bag of groceries. "The Red Sox. I'm not much of a football fan."

"You wanna make a little bet? One box of fruit cookies to you if you win, one buck to me if you lose."

Charlie laughed. "Sure, I'll take the Eagles." He nodded to Pellegrino, then headed toward the door. The grocery was small, crowded with dusty boxes of soap powder and saltine crackers, cans of soup that Charlie thought had probably been on the shelves for several years. Again, he wondered how Pellegrino managed to stay in business. A box of cookies riding on the Eagles—Charlie hoped he wouldn't forget. But as it turned out, he thought a lot about that small bet over the next few weeks.

3

Shortly before ten o'clock that night Charlie was driving across Saratoga through the snow. The green light on his CB radio seemed to beckon, urging him to call Victor. But he had already told Victor that they couldn't use it. There was no telling who might bc listening. Next to Charlie on the seat was a dark metal attaché case containing $5,000. He felt uncomfortable—uncomfortable with lying to George Whitman, uncomfortable with Victor, who was on another street several blocks away also driving across Saratoga, uncomfortable with himself and his questionable motivations, uncomfortable with the snow which whipped across his windshield in a thin curtain, forcing him to squinch and lean forward over the wheel, uncomfortable with the emptiness of the streets and the fact that there wasn't another car to be seen. Charlie wondered if Jesse James had ever been uncertain about his actions—for instance, that disastrous Minnesota raid. "No, sir, brother Frank, I think we should stay out of Northfield." But Frank and the Younger gang had talked him around and consequently Jesse had lost three men and the Youngers had becn captured. Second thoughts, Charlie was cursed with second thoughts.

At eight-thirty that evening, Whitman had delivered the metal attaché case to Charlie's office. He had not been friendly and for the tenth time that day Charlie told himself that Whitman hadn't become rich by being a nice guy. Once again Whitman had seemed unable to tear his eyes from the photograph of Jesse James, either because he was trying to decide what Jesse's picture was doing in a detective's office, or because he felt a certain kinship with the outlaw.

Giving Charlie the attaché case, Whitman had said, "Just follow directions, Bradshaw. I'll call you when I hear from the thieves."

Charlie had waited with his feet up on the desk reading a book about Doc Holliday—ex-dentist turned tubercular gunslinger and gambler—and the rise of three-card monte in the Old West. Outside, he could see the snow swirling around the street lamps, piling up on the window ledges. At twenty of ten the call had come from Whitman.

"Leave the case at High Rock Spring. You know where that is?" Whitman's voice over the phone was a mellifluous whisper.

"Out on High Rock Avenue," said Charlie.

"Don't make any mistakes, Mr. Bradshaw."

"I won't, Mr. Whitman. You can trust me."

Immediately after hanging up, Charlie had called Victor. He felt guilty, but the thought of Whitman's gratitude when he retrieved the money and captured the thieves made it seem all right. Far back in his mind, however, he kept asking himself: What's five thousand to a guy like Whitman? Absolutely nothing.

"I can stay up on Excelsior Avenue," Victor had said, "then look down the hill with the binoculars. Fuckin' piece of cake, Charlie. Don't sweat it."

Charlie listened to Victor breathing heavily into the phone. "Just be careful, Victor, otherwise they'll destroy the painting."

"Vic, Charlie. Not Victor, Vic."

"Sure, Vic."

Charlie hung up, pulled on his dark blue overcoat, then headed for the door. Just as he was locking it, he decided to go back for his .38. As usual the door to the safe was stuck and it took him five minutes to get it open.

High Rock Spring was on the north side of town, just south of the arterial linking Broadway with Route 87, the Northway. Five roads came together around the spring but there were no houses nearby, just a garage, an oil company and a soft-drink distributor. Charlie parked at the curb, leaving his car running, then hurried up to the spring with the metal attaché case, wading through the snow which in some places was up to his knees. No other cars were in sight. He looked up toward Excelsior Avenue, but could see nothing. The spring had a roof but was open on four sides, and the snow had drifted high against the fountain. Each of the springs specialized in certain cures and High Rock was the spring most effective in curing hangovers. At least this was what Charlie's mother had once told him, and long ago, when Charlie had just gotten out of the army, he had drunk from it often. Charlie set the attaché case on the far side of the fountain, then hurried back to his car, trying to walk in his own footsteps to keep from getting even more wet.

As he drove back across Saratoga he again kept glancing at his CB radio. It would be so simple to give Victor a quick call just to see if he was watching. He resisted the temptation. The moment he entered his office, Charlie hurried to the phone and dialed Whitman.

"Then we should be hearing from them soon. Good work, Bradshaw."

Charlie waited for about ten minutes but then couldn't stand it anymore and hurried up to the hotel. Eddie Gillespie was tending bar. Normally, he worked at the hotel during the summer and was filling in this evening while Victor was skulking around High Rock Spring. Even though Eddie would only be tending bar about two hours he had put on a dark purple uniform for the occasion. The soft light, the Count Basie trios on the stereo, the two young women talking quietly at one of the tables made the bar feel warm and sophisticated.

Eddie gave Charlie a nod, then poured him a glass of diet cola.

"I'd prefer a Scotch," said Charlie. Years before, Charlie had given Eddie a job as a stable guard when Eddie had been on probation for car theft. Eddie had been twenty-two at the time. Between the ages of fifteen and twenty-five he had been what he described as a speed freak, meaning not drugs but that he was only happy at speeds in excess of 120 mph in cars which he had liberated for the occasion. In the past several years Eddie had tamed this passion, or rather it had been tamed by a strong dislike of jail. He was an energetic young man with tousled black hair who seemed morally to disapprove of standing still. Even talking to Charlie he kept shifting his weight from one foot to another. He had a long, narrow jaw and he kept turning his head as if cutting the air with it.

"There are diet cola nights and there are Scotch nights. That's the great pendulum, Charlie." Eddie poured him his drink.

Charlie wanted to ask Eddie if he'd heard from Victor but he knew that was foolish so he asked him about the Super Bowl instead.

"I got fifty riding on the Pats," said Eddie. "But if Eason turns out to have punk knees, I'm gonna hedge my bet. You coming to Victor's bash?"

"Bash?" asked Charlie, somewhat startled. "I thought it was just a couple of guys."

"Sure, sure," said Eddie, "that was just my little joke."

Charlie stared at him a little suspiciously over his glass and would have asked another question, but at that moment he saw Victor coming through the lobby, brushing the snow from his gray overcoat.

"Like falling off a log, Charlie. I don't know why we're not millionaires."

Charlie looked over at the two young women, but they

weren't paying attention. Victor took off his coat and climbed onto the stool next to Charlie. The flecks of snow in his hair were already turning to water. Eddie set a glass of Scotch down in front of him.

"I could see the whole thing, saw you mousing through the snow, putting the case behind the fountain. Fifteen minutes later someone picked it up."

"What was it?" asked Charlie. "What kind of car?"

"A tan Subaru wagon." Victor told him the license-plate number. "Four-wheel drive."

Charlie wrote down the number in his notebook. "That doesn't sound much like a crook's car."

"Modern times, Charlie. Even the crooks have gone Japanese."

"You get a look at the person?"

"Not really, it was a guy in jeans and a jean jacket, wearing a hunting cap or something." Victor looked at the two young women and speculatively sucked his teeth.

"And he didn't see you?"

"No way."

"Could anyone else have seen you?"

"Wasn't anyone else around. Too much snow."

"Positive?"

"Shit, Charlie, will you lay off that stuff?"

Charlie briefly covered his eyes and bowed his head in a gesture indicating intense apology. Climbing down from his stool, he went to the phone in the lobby. It was almost quarter to eleven. Whitman answered on the first ring.

"I thought it was them," he said, with a trace of excitement.

"No," said Charlie. "I'd just wondered if you'd heard anything."

"Not yet."

Charlie gave Whitman his number, then went back to the bar, had another Scotch, then had a roast beef sandwich as well. Eddie took out a deck of cards and dealt out blackjack hands for the three of them. Charlie couldn't make himself pay attention and was down ten dollars in no time.

"Are you sure they couldn't have seen you, Victor?"

"Cut it out, will you?"

At midnight, Charlie couldn't stand it anymore and called Whitman a second time. Again, Whitman answered on the first ring.

"No, I still haven't heard. I said I'd call you."

Charlie went back to the bar. The young women had gone. Eddie was cleaning up as he and Victor talked about Eason's knees and the Eagles' ground game. Charlie went back to drinking diet cola. The clock behind the bar was in the shape of a sunburst and Charlie kept thinking it was broken and kept checking it against his watch. Maybe both were broken.

Around one-twenty, Charlie decided to give it up and go home. He put on his coat and said his various farewells.

"You want a hot date for tomorrow night?" asked Victor. "I know a lady who'll curl your toes."

"I'm seeing Grace," said Charlie.

Victor opened his mouth wide and showed his long tongue. "Rinse and spit," he said.

Charlie walked toward the door. As he passed the phone, he couldn't help himself and called Whitman one last time.

"No, Mr. Bradshaw, I haven't heard anything." Whitman was silent for a moment, breathing shallowly and hissing slightly. Then he asked, "You didn't do anything stupid, did you, Mr. Bradshaw?"

4

In the morning it was still snowing. As he waited for his coffee
to perk, Charlie stood by his picture window looking out at the
lake and he couldn't tell what was earth and what was sky in
the confusion of white flakes and blowing snow across the ice.
Sometimes his own mind felt like that. He had awakened at
daybreak from a dream in which he was being found fault with
by one of his grade-school teachers—Miss Brewster. He hadn't
cleaned the erasers sufficiently and clouds of chalk dust were
blowing through the classroom. His immediate sense on waking
was that he had done something wrong. Then he remembered
Mr. Whitman and the missing painting of Man o' War.

Charlie's house by the lake was quite small, only three rooms
including the kitchen, but it had a big stone fireplace and its
own dock and the houses nearby weren't pressed too close. He
had bought it after he had left his wife and quit his job as a
sergeant in the Community and Youth Relations Bureau. He
had wanted privacy, to be away from Saratoga gossip and his
own family, specifically his three older, successful cousins, men
who meant well but who were constantly bullying him with
advice. As Charlie stared out at the white wall of snow, unable
even to see where the land ended and the lake began, he felt

that buying this house was the one smart thing he had done in fifty years. It made him happy even now and he grinned to think of it. The house was everything that his ex-wife Marge disapproved of: messy, slightly smelly, jammed with bookcases and pictures of disreputable folk on the walls—Dillinger, Cole Younger, the Wild Bunch in a group portrait, the Dalton Gang lying dead.

Charlie walked back to his kitchen to pour himself another glass of orange juice and see if the coffee was ready. He was getting a cold, he knew it. The scratchy feeling in his chest was worse and there was an unpleasant tickling in his nose. Still, he wanted to go swimming and do his required laps at the Saratoga YMCA. He kept brooding about the missing painting and had the premonition that the next week would be very busy. Better to get his swimming done while he could. Cold or no cold.

He had breakfast, washed up and before leaving the house an hour later he again considered calling Whitman. It was only nine-thirty. He'd wait until lunchtime.

Putting on his boots and blue overcoat, Charlie went out and shoveled a narrow path to his car, then shoveled part of the driveway. Fifteen minutes later, sweaty and a little out of breath, he drove the six miles into Saratoga. So much fresh snow reminded him of when he was a boy and lots of new snow meant doing something with it, like building snow forts or snowmen, or having snowball fights, or even sledding. Although Route 9P had been plowed, the snow was still collecting and he passed only one other car. All the trees wore heavy snow hats and many driveways remained unshoveled. Charlie kept brooding about the stolen painting until he wanted to scream at himself to stop. But he kept thinking it must be a local job, even an insider's job. Professionals would have returned the painting. After all, they had to protect their reputation. But perhaps Victor had been seen after all. Was that possible? The thieves had seen him and had destroyed the painting out of spite?

The YMCA pool was nearly empty, with only several over-weight ladies of Charlie's age whom he kept passing, thus sup-porting the illusion that he was fast. His mile of seventy-two lengths took him forty-five minutes. The record, he believed, was under fifteen. But he loved how swimming made him feel outside of the world, even outside of his body, as if his spirit for a short time was being given the chance to rest and re-strengthen itself away from his mortal remains. He felt graceful in the water; he felt unencumbered.

In the locker room two lawyers were discussing tax shelters. They nodded to Charlie and he nodded back. He dried himself before the mirror. As he observed his reflection, he thought, You're really fifty. How can you be fifty when you only recently graduated from high school? He remembered the night of grad-uation, how he and five other boys drank beer out at the lake in somebody's '49 Ford and how a girl named Lucy let herself be kissed and fondled by three other boys in the backseat, but not by Charlie. Fifty, how amazing it all was.

It was eleven by the time he got to his office. The few cases he was working on—a missing husband, bad checks, an insur-ance scam—were all at the stage where he was waiting for phone calls that never came. He called a few numbers, looking for the missing husband. No one had seen him. The man's wife had a high, screamy voice, and Charlie couldn't really blame the man for lighting out to Mexico or wherever. Leaning back, he glanced at his telephone and thought about Mr. Whitman. Then he looked over at Jesse James standing proud and determined. No waiting around for Jesse. His life had had all the hustle-bustle anyone could want. Happening to glance out the window, Charlie saw Grace Washburn waving to him from her window across the street. He got up and walked to the glass. "See you tonight," she mouthed at him, then smiled. He smiled back. His mouth ached and he could feel his gums twitching with anxiety. Why couldn't they just hold hands like other couples?

When the outside door opened minutes later, Charlie at first thought it might be Mr. Whitman. Then he saw two men through the frosted glass. As the dividing door was pushed open, it occurred to Charlie that the only people to enter without warning were crooks or your own family. Even Victor knocked. Seconds later two of Charlie's cousins stood before him.

"Jack, Robert," said Charlie, getting up from his desk, "what a nice surprise." As he reached out his hand, he considered the hypocrisy of his words. But he loved his cousins, he truly did. It was only that he knew they hadn't come to tell him of their affection, but to ask something of him, or give him advice, or to get him to do something.

Both were big men. Jack, who had begun pumping Charlie's hand, was several inches over six feet, with wavy graying hair and a chin as square as a fist. He was a year older than Charlie, and Robert was three years older. Robert was the thinner of the two and looked more distinguished than athletic, with silver-gray hair, tweeds and a pipe. Both men were successful businessmen—Jack as the owner of a hardware store and Robert as the president of an insurance and real estate office—and both were active Elks, Lions, Rotarians, all those organizations that entailed lots of lunches, speeches and handshaking. As Charlie extracted his hand from Robert's grasp, he decided it was in such fraternal organizations that they had perfected their grips.

Charlie leaned back against his desk as his cousins smiled at him affably—professional handshakes, professional smiles. "I don't suppose you two are in the market for a private detective?" he asked.

Jack laughed, a confident, rumbling noise, like the idle of an expensive car. Then he sat down in the visitor's chair, first giving the blue fabric above his knees a slight tug.

"Actually, we're here about James," said Robert, mentioning their oldest brother, who had begun as a carpenter and was now a successful developer. "In two weeks, he and Peggy will be celebrating their silver wedding anniversary. We want to do something for them."

"Like hiring a private detective?" asked Charlie. This time his cousins ignored the joke.

"We were thinking of a party at the country club," said Jack, "and we wondered if you'd like to contribute."

Charlie took out his wallet. It was pretty light. Each time he opened it he expected moths to fly out. "Would ten bucks be okay?" He saw from their faces that it wouldn't. "That's all the cash I have at the moment. Or I could write you a check for fifty."

"Fifty would be fine," said Robert, unbuttoning his overcoat. Around his neck was a thick red, black and blue wool scarf, one of those British scarves showing off the colors of some public school. Robert was married to Charlie's ex-wife's sister Lucy, a woman who had despised Charlie steadily for almost thirty years. Presumably she would be at this party, as would his ex-wife herself. It would be understood that Charlie would have the good taste not to attend.

"And how is your mother doing?" asked Jack, as he put Charlie's check in his pocket. "She's a wonderful old woman, they sure don't make many like her."

"She's still in Paris," said Charlie. "Having the time of her life."

"What about the hotel?" asked Robert, glancing at his brother. "Do you think it's wise to have this fellow keep it open?"

"Why not?" asked Charlie. He disliked how Robert could never address a supposed problem directly but always slid into it from the side.

"Isn't he a rowdy kind of person?" asked Jack. "I know he used to work for you, but can he run a hotel?"

"If he got into trouble," said Robert, "it would be embarrassing for your mother, embarrassing for us all." He took his pipe from the pocket of his tweed jacket. Then he began to fill it from a red leather pouch that smelled of apples.

"What kind of trouble?" asked Charlie, growing irritated.

"It's only open on a limited scale on the weekend. Victor's completely trustworthy."

"But what kind of crowd are you going to get with a fellow like that running it?" asked Robert. Lighting his pipe, he sucked on it tentatively, before blowing a small cloud toward the ceiling. He had remained standing as if his time were too precious to let him sit down.

"He's my friend," said Charlie. "Has he done anything to irritate you?"

"No, nothing," said Robert, "but he's loud and we hadn't thought the Bentley was going to be that sort of place."

Charlie felt like telling them that Victor had hired a couple of strippers. "I'm over there often. Nothing happens I'm not aware of."

Jack stood up, and he and Robert began moving toward the door, not happy but at least reassured.

"What do you think about the Super Bowl?" asked Charlie, hoping to lighten the occasion. "They say it's still the Pats by three if Eason's knees hold."

Jack turned and Charlie was aware of their disapproval. "Gambling ruins a game, Charlie," said Jack. "It takes the sport out of it. I'd hate to think you were involved with that."

"So you're not going to watch it?" asked Charlie, sorry he had spoken.

"I may catch a quarter or two," said Jack.

Charlie glanced at Robert, who looked equally disapproving. He had an impulse to offer them fantastic odds, just to get them to bet—a thousand to one against the Patriots. It was almost with surprise that he recalled he had little interest in the game himself.

"Don't forget to tell me about the time and date of James's party," said Charlie, unable to restrain himself. "I'm sure we'll have a great night."

His cousins glanced back with expressions that gave away nothing as they hurried out into the hall. Moments later he heard their feet on the stairs. Charlie felt angry, then laughed at himself as he shut the door. It amazed him that he still let them get under his skin.

Returning to his desk, Charlie picked up the telephone and dialed Whitman. Although it was only eleven-thirty, he couldn't wait anymore.

This time it took longer to get through. At least Whitman wasn't hovering by the phone. A distinguished male voice requested Charlie to hold. Charlie held for five minutes. Most likely the painting had been recovered. He was worrying for nothing.

Then Whitman came on the line. "No, Mr. Bradshaw, we've had no word from the thieves."

Neither spoke for a moment. It seemed to Charlie that the silence between them was filled with winter wind.

"What was your agreement with them?" Charlie asked. He stood by his desk, feeling too uncomfortable to sit down.

"They were to receive the money and if they were not interfered with in any way, I would get a call within half an hour." Whitman had stressed the word "interfered," and again Charlie felt a cold wind blow.

"Did you have any reason to believe they would actually return the picture?"

"Not necessarily, but that's what they did last time."

Charlie blinked. "You mean this has happened before?"

Whitman was silent for a moment and Charlie could hear him breathing. "About fourteen months ago another picture was stolen," Whitman said. "The thieves wanted five thousand dollars for its safe return. We delivered the money and they delivered the picture."

"Were the two thefts and your dealings with the thieves the same in each case?" asked Charlie.

"Not particularly." There was another pause.

"So you don't necessarily know that the same people were involved."

"Mr. Bradshaw, what else could it be?" Whitman sounded almost angry. "You think this is a common occurrence?"

"And you plan to let it keep happening?" asked Charlie. "You don't mean to call the police?"

Mr. Whitman appeared to be breathing a little more heavily. "After this picture is returned, I intend to contact the Pinkertons."

Cut to the quick, thought Charlie. "Maybe I could find the picture for you."

"I think you've done enough, Mr. Bradshaw. I'd appreciate it if you didn't involve yourself in this affair any further."

Charlie sat back against his desk and made a face at Jesse James—the sort of face a person might make if he'd been shot in the back. "Certainly, Mr. Whitman, whatever you wish. I'll check with you later to see if you've heard from the thieves. Good talking to you." Charlie hung up. The Pinkertons indeed! He put on his overcoat and cap. He had to talk to Victor again, just to make sure.

"You think I'm a liar, Charlie? An incompetent deceiver? Jesus, I'm your old buddy!"

Charlie rubbed his eyes with the heels of his hands, making sunbursts and lightning flashes behind his closed lids. Then he looked back at Victor with what he hoped was an encouraging smile. They were sitting at the bar of the Bentley working their way through a pile of tuna-salad sandwiches. The bread was stale but Charlie decided not to mention it.

"I just wondered if there was any way you might be mistaken?" asked Charlie.

"I was parked up the hill with some other cars. I got there about fifteen minutes before you showed up and left about ten minutes after the Subaru picked up the money. All told, I was there about an hour. No cars passed and my windows were pretty much covered with snow—all except for a little hole for my binoculars. Maybe somebody saw me but it seems pretty much impossible."

"It's just that the picture hasn't been returned," said Charlie.

Victor reached several large fingers into his mouth, grabbed hold of an upper molar and appeared to shake it. "What do you expect? Crooks is crooks. Look, Charlie, you got the license number of that Subaru, you got the expertise. Catch 'em yourself."

"Whitman wants me to stay out of it."

"And you're gonna curl up and forget it, right? Don't give me that crap. You're like a beaver in a three-piece suit. People forget you have sharp teeth."

Charlie felt rather more flattered by the comparison than not. He ate some of his sandwich, which was cut into little triangular sections. "Well, I'm sure the picture will be returned in the next day or so."

They both chewed for several moments as Charlie tried to determine the best way to bring up the next subject. At last he decided to plunge right in. He took a drink of diet cola.

"Victor, two of my cousins showed up this morning. They're concerned you're not being as discreet as a manager of the Bentley should be."

Victor had been poking at some suspicious foreign matter in the tuna salad. He looked up at Charlie through his bushy eyebrows. "I hope you told them to take a flying fuck," he said.

"I've been wondering about this party you're having tomorrow night. Just what do you plan on doing?"

"For Pete's sake, Charlie, just a few guys watching the Super Bowl. . . ."

Taking several chunks of ice, Charlie splintered them with his teeth. It was the sort of thing that Grace Washburn specifically disapproved of. "Who's coming?" he asked.

"Eddie Gillespie, Maximum Tubbs, maybe one or two others. I asked you to come. You know I asked you."

Charlie pushed his stool chair back from the bar. He had a desire for something sweet—maybe a piece of Bavarian chocolate cake from Mrs. London's. It occurred to him that since he'd been dating Grace Washburn, he'd been abusing his teeth and eating more sweets than he had in twenty years.

"I've already told you I'm going to be working," said Charlie. "You already knew that. Is there going to be gambling? I can't believe Tubbs would be coming otherwise."

"A few bets on the game. Charlie, it's the Super Bowl. Maybe we'll play a little cards at halftime."

Charlie stood up. It offended his sensibilities to be taking his cousins' side against Victor. What did it matter what Victor did? "Just don't do anything to get my cousins on my back," he said.

"They're welcome to come over," said Victor, placing a hand over his heart. "Any blood of yours is a pal of mine, even dimwit blood."

"They don't gamble."

Victor came out from behind the bar and walked with Charlie toward the door. "Guys like that, you know what they go in for? Enemas. I'll betcha three to five they love enemas."

But Charlie had a busy day ahead of him and a date with Grace that night. He had no time to discuss the peculiarities of his cousins. "Just don't cause talk," he said.

One of the things that Charlie liked about Grace Washburn was that she was soft—not only her skin but her flesh itself. Sometimes it seemed as if she didn't have any bones. She was soft and pink and reminded Charlie of the raspberry junket he had enjoyed as a child. Once he had seen her naked in her bath and she had looked like a whole tub full of pink junket.

That evening he again allowed her to clean his teeth. He saw it as the payment he had to surrender in order to be with her. He sat in her kitchen half-blinded by the goosenecked lamp while she picked at his teeth and gums, saying only, "Spit," and "Now rinse," and he would spit into an aluminum saucepan or take a drink from a peanut-butter glass with pictures of Daffy Duck. On her kitchen wall was a clock in the shape of a black cat with its tail being the swinging pendulum. Charlie concentrated on that swinging black tail and forced himself to relax, trying to pretend he was far away and that another human being didn't have her fingers in his mouth.

Afterward they watched the original *Three Musketeers* on Grace's VCR and she gave him glass after glass of orange juice for his cold. He told her about the stolen painting of Man o' War and she was very sympathetic. She was always sympathetic even when he didn't think she was listening or understood what he was saying. Later still, they made love and again Charlie took pleasure in her softness. Their lovemaking was very conventional, although once, several months earlier, Grace had asked Charlie if he would like her to tie him up, but Charlie had said he didn't think he would enjoy that.

The next morning Charlie's cold was worse. Leaving Grace around eight, he drove home to put on warmer clothes. The day was clear and the glare of the sun off the new snow was blinding. Snowmobiles were racing out on the lake, and their distant whine sounded vaguely like summer insects. Charlie suspected that all day and part of the night he would have to slog through the snow around Lake Cossayuña as he searched for whoever was breaking into the cabins. The thieves never took much, maybe a radio or some food now and then, and Charlie suspected it was kids. After he changed his clothes, he stopped by Pellegrino's Grocery to fill his thermos with coffee. He was wearing two pairs of Levi's and several flannel shirts over his long underwear, plus a heavy sweater and his blue down jacket. He felt like the Pillsbury Doughboy.

"Mr. Owl," called Pellegrino, wiping his hands on his apron, "you've come to increase your bet to two boxes of cookies."

Charlie had forgotten about the bet. "I'll stick with the one," he said, giving the old man his empty thermos.

"Eason's knees are fine. Everyone's putting their money on the Patriots. You want to change your bet?" Pellegrino finished pouring the coffee into the thermos and handed it back to Charlie.

"No, the Eagles are okay with me."

"You going to see the game?" Pellegrino had a small color TV behind the counter which was always tuned to the cable sports network. Constantly from behind the counter came the murmur of crowds.

"I've got to work. Maybe I'll see the end of it. Give me a box of those fruit cookies, will you please, and some cherry cough drops, and do you have any aspirin?"

Half an hour later Charlie parked his Renault Encore at a closed gas station up in the hills near Lake Cossayuna. Cossayuna was much smaller than Saratoga Lake, being long and narrow. Often during the winter they raced cars on it. This morning there was no one in sight. The sun off the snow was so sharp and painful, so white, that Charlie had to keep his eyes squinched half shut. Near the gas station was a telephone booth. Charlie looked at it, tried to look away, then walked slowly toward it like someone who has no control over his actions.

Mr. Whitman answered after several rings.

"No, Bradshaw, I've heard nothing. . . . Yes, I promise to let you know. . . . No, you don't have to call again. In fact, I particularly wish you wouldn't."

5

Victor liked to see people having a good time—eating, drinking, pleasuring every orifice—he liked to see them having a ball. And indeed the fourteen men attending his Super Bowl Gambling Fete seemed on top of the world, even the losers. It struck him that maybe they didn't need girls after all, although girls could liven up any occasion. But maybe girls would have been out of place at a gambling party, unless they were serious bettors. No, the party was going swimmingly without them and the one sour note was that the Patriots were down by eighteen points at the half. Not that Victor gave a damn. He was a Giants fan, so any bad luck for the Pats made Victor feel good inside.

The function room on the third floor was really intended for meetings, but Victor had moved in some couches and smaller tables so that now it had the appearance of a Victorian smoking lounge done up in purple wallpaper with black stripes, heavy purple drapery and a couple of leather armchairs. The room was about thirty by fifteen feet, and at the south end on a raised dais was the television with its forty-eight-inch screen where a fast-talking commentator was explaining what had happened during the first half, as if the millions of people watching hadn't seen it for themselves. Most of Victor's customers—he thought of them as that—had turned their attention to the two poker games in the middle of the room, but three or four were idly talking and Victor wondered if he should try to interest them in a little dice, since there was no point in letting their money lie fallow.

Each of the fourteen customers had paid a hundred bucks for the pleasure of watching the Super Bowl at the Bentley. In return, Victor supplied food and drink, the television and the chance to place as many bets in a three-hour period as any lively human being could hope to place. And if they grew tired of betting on the game, there was always poker and dice. So far the game had held their interest with a variety of side bets being placed not only on individual plays, but also on how soon the trainer would make another trip onto the field and if the next ad would be for Wang or Nissan.

Only one poker table had been running during the first half, the dealer being Victor's partner in the Super Bowl Fete, Maximum Tubbs, a spry, dapper man in his early seventies who had been gambling in Saratoga for over fifty years. He was about the size of a steeplechase jockey with a narrow face, thick gray hair and wearing a three-piece brown suit. His long, thin fingers were never still, as if they constantly hungered for cards and hard cash. Five men were playing with him now and Tubbs wore the expression of a man with a sweet taste in his mouth.

The other game was being dealt by Eddie Gillespie. Eddie liked everything fast—cars, games, women, talk, even poker, and he dealt the cards so rapidly that his hands were a pink blur. Victor had first met Eddie nearly ten years ago, when Victor had come up from New York City and he and Eddie had worked as stable guards with Charlie as their boss. Eddie liked uniforms and probably would have been a cop if it hadn't been for his various convictions for car theft. As a bartender, he insisted on wearing a dark purple uniform onto which he occasionally pinned a little silver star. Over the winter he was working at the racing museum as a guard, and Victor thought he had taken the job only because it gave him the chance to wear another variety of uniform.

Victor was fond of these people—good-hearted people who liked to laugh, drink and spend money. He poured himself a double shot of Jack Daniel's and wandered over to Tubbs's table. It was going on nine o'clock and outside the streets were deserted. It was bitter cold, maybe five below. Most likely everybody in Saratoga was watching the Super Bowl.

Maximum Tubbs had sent out fifteen invitations but one guy still hadn't shown up. Of the others Victor knew about eight— a local plumber, a baker, a man who sold ladies' lingerie. About half were from Saratoga, the rest came from Albany and Schenectady—guys between twenty-five and sixty, thin guys, fat guys, bald guys, weasely guys, handsome guys, guys whose only point in common was that they liked to gamble and liked the Super Bowl. How could you not feel kindly toward them?

The only important person missing was Charlie himself, and Victor hoped it would stay that way. Even though Charlie was his best friend, Victor knew he wouldn't appreciate the gambling and was afraid that harsh words would pass between them. In fact, Charlie would probably disapprove of the whole party atmosphere. But it wasn't as if Victor was doing this just for fun. After all, he needed the money: $1,400 in entrance fees and five percent of every pot. Of course, he had to split it with Maximum Tubbs and give a chunk to Gillespie, but after that a few bills would get paid and Victor could even have a little fun, take his new sweetie up to Montreal for a weekend and sample the French cuisine. Old Charlie would have no sympathy with this. He'd worry about the hotel getting a bad name or the news getting back to his cousins. What an old maid he could be. Well, Charlie had to be protected against his worst inclinations. It was better he just didn't know.

But moments later when there was a knock on the door, Victor worried that it might be Charlie. That, however, was impossible, unless Charlie had learned their secret knock—one, pause, two-three, four—and who would have told him? It must be Mr. Fifteen, coming late but still welcome. As he walked to the door, Victor wondered if he should let him in for half price since he'd missed half the game, but no, he could still drink and gamble. After all, there was a whole table full of turkey sandwiches and potato salad. Hell, he should even charge him a late tax. Make him pay an extra twenty-five bucks.

Victor fashioned his face into a big welcoming grin and opened the door. Then suddenly everything sped up and got blurry as two men in ski masks rushed at him. One grabbed him and spun him around, shoving something hard against his head. The other ran into the room carrying some kind of pole. No, thought Victor unhappily, it's not a pole. It's a shotgun.

"Nobody moves! Keep your hands on the tables or this man's dead!" shouted the man with the shotgun. Victor was being jostled from behind with an arm around his throat and it was hard to see. The man with the shotgun had hurried to the tables and was making everyone stand up. Several chairs fell over with a clatter. Maximum Tubbs seemed to make some protest, and Victor saw the man with the shotgun club him with the barrel so that he fell to the floor.

"All of you move over toward the TV!" shouted the man. "Lie down on your guts! Don't be brave!"

Tubbs was slowly getting to his knees by the table. The man pushed him down again, then hit another man in the back with the stock of the gun. People were scared and not saying anything as they walked slowly toward the open area near the TV. Three men were already lying down and most of the others were moving. Eddie Gillespie stood by the second table, staring angrily at the intruders. The man with the shotgun ran at him, pointing the barrel straight at Eddie's face. Eddie flinched and raised a hand. The man swung the barrel, hitting Eddie on the side of the head, making a dull thunking noise. Eddie tumbled back holding his face, knocking over two of the chairs.

The man holding Victor pushed him forward. "Lie down with the others!" he said.

Victor moved slowly, trying to get a good look at the two men. Both were fairly average-sized, although maybe the one with the shotgun was a little heavy and a little shorter than the other. The ski masks were dark yellow with black around the mouths and eyes and made the men look like cats. Otherwise the men wore brown coveralls, while the taller one had on workboots and the one with the shotgun was wearing an old pair of brown cowboy boots. Victor could also see that the taller one had a dark mustache. He guessed they were in their late thirties or early forties but had no real way of telling.

"Lie down, fucker!" The man behind Victor gave him another push and he got down on his knees. They were all lying down now, even Eddie, lying with their arms outstretched, like poison gas victims. Turning his head, Victor saw the man with the shotgun scooping the money on the tables into a pillow case, then bending over Maximum Tubbs to search his pockets.

"Nobody makes a move," said the other man. "You boys had a nice party and now it's over."

"Don't talk, asshole," said the man with the shotgun.

"I just want them to know we don't give a fuck if we kill somebody or not."

Victor felt a gun being shoved against the back of his head, then his wallet was taken from his coat pocket. The man checked his other pockets, just patting them as if looking for a weapon, then moved on to another man, a bald guy from Albany who looked depressed. Victor had put the $1,400 which he had received from the fourteen guests in a desk by the door and he didn't plan to say a word about it.

"We really appreciate this, you guys," said the talkative thief. "We're really happy to have the chance to spend your money." He laughed and Victor, with his nose in the carpet, thought of the painful things he wanted to do to him.

It took the thieves ten minutes to rob them. They emptied their billfolds into the pillow case, then tossed the wallets back on the table, leaving the credit cards and identification alone. No one else had a gun, a few had knives—Swiss army knives mostly and a buck knife. The thieves took cash and three ruby rings which they managed to pry off a fat man from Cohoes. The football game had started up again and the Eagles scored a touchdown in the first three minutes. After the thieves collected the money, one of them took a length of rope and began tying their hands and feet.

"You guys can get loose okay," said the talkative one. "We just need a head start, that's all. We'd hate to have to waste someone, get blood over these nice rugs and fuck up the decor."

Victor felt the rope being wrapped around his wrists, then attached to his right ankle and pulled tight as he was hogtied.

"Aren't you afraid someone's going to get you for this?" he asked irritably, his nose still in the rug.

The man with the shotgun walked over to him until Victor could only see him from his old brown cowboy boots to the knees of his brown coveralls. "We don't like that kinda talk," said the man. Then one of the boots disappeared. A second later Victor received a kick in his side, throwing him back and making him gag and hurt.

"You boys just forget this ever happened," said the man.

Charlie was sitting in the tub when the telephone rang. After ten hours in the snow around Lake Cossayuna, he felt he had never been so chilled in his life. Even his teeth were cold, even the fillings. Now after an hour in the tub he was feeling a little better, despite the fact that his sore throat and sniffles had gotten worse and he was having to blow his nose about every thirty seconds.

He was tempted to ignore the phone, but then he thought it might be Mr. Whitman calling to say the painting had been recovered and everything was fine. Climbing from the tub, he wrapped a towel around his waist and hurried into the living room. A fire was burning in the fireplace and the room temperature was about ninety degrees. Warm, thought Charlie as he picked up the phone, but not warm enough.

It was Victor. There was something funny about his voice and Charlie knew something was wrong. The horrible idea struck him that the hotel had burned down.

"Charlie, I wanted to be the first to tell you."

"What is it?"

"I got bad news." Victor spoke slowly, enunciating every word.

"What is it?" Charlie pictured smoking ashes and mounds of debris. At least Victor hadn't been killed in the fire.

"You gonna be angry with me?"

On the other hand, maybe Victor had started the fire. He'd been smoking in bed or hadn't turned off the stove. "What is it?"

"I got held up."

Charlie almost laughed he felt so relieved. "You?"

"Well, not just me. It was me and sixteen other guys."

"You call the police?"

"I can't."

Charlie began to worry again. "Maybe you better explain."

So Victor told Charlie about the gambling party he had organized with Maximum Tubbs and Eddie Gillespie, and how they had had fourteen eager guests up in the third-floor function room of the Bentley. Food, drink, cards, football, a little dice, lots of fun, but no girls.

"It was a wonderful occasion, Charlie. We were all sorry you couldn't make it."

"Don't lie to me, Victor. How much did they get?"

"About ten thousand, plus some ruby rings."

"And the police?" asked Charlie.

"They don't know a thing."

"How'd they get up to the third floor?"

"Old Jimmy Hoblock was downstairs letting people in. They just shoved him aside and tied him up."

The trouble, as Charlie immediately realized, was that the police couldn't be notified. The gambling party was illegal and any police involvement would lead to charges against the hotel. As he stood in his living room with the red towel wrapped around his waist and a growing puddle of water on the floor, Charlie considered how his mother and cousins would respond to the news that Victor was using the hotel as a gambling den. He imagined his mother receiving a telegram at her fancy hotel in Paris. Charlie shook his head. Wherever he turned his mind there were unhappy thoughts.

"You can't say anything about it, Victor. You've got to keep your mouth shut."

"Some of those guys were pretty angry. They even suggested the whole thing was a setup."

"Was anybody hurt?"

"Maximum Tubbs and Eddie got banged up a little and I got kicked in the ribs."

"But you're okay?" Charlie began to worry again. A log popped in the fire and he jumped.

"Just angry, that's all. Tubbs and me, we want to hire you to catch the guys who did it. We got $1,400 that the thieves didn't find."

Charlie took a tissue from the coffee table and blew his nose. "I don't want to get involved. I mean legally I couldn't do it. I could lose my license."

"Charlie, these guys are angry. If we don't get their money back, they could make a lot of noise."

Charlie blew his nose again, then tossed the tissue toward the fireplace and missed. The room was getting cold and he needed to put another log on. "Great," he said, "that's just great."

There was a pause as Charlie realized he was stuck. He'd have to help Victor. "Who won the game?" he asked, unable to think of anything else to say.

"That also pissed everybody off. Pats got their ass kicked, got beat thirty-eight to six." Victor was silent again. Then he asked, "How'd you do out at Lake Cossayuna?"

Charlie blew his nose. "It was two twelve-year-olds. I caught them inside a cabin."

"You turn them over to the police?"

Charlie remembered how frightened they had been—two undersized redheaded boys eating Ritz crackers and frozen Marshmallow Fluff in the kitchen of a camp they had just broken into. "I got their names. I yelled at them, threatened to tell their parents and let them go."

"Jesus, Charlie, how are you ever going to get rich behaving like that?"

Charlie said the word to himself: "rich." Like Mr. Whitman was rich. He couldn't imagine it.

6

Monday morning was so shiny and bright and the sun bouncing off the new snow made such a glare that even with dark glasses Charlie had difficulty seeing as he drove in from the lake around eight-thirty. He was also brooding about Victor and the robbery at the hotel and what he should do about it. And then there was the problem of the missing painting and whether or not Whitman had heard any news. As a result, Charlie had almost passed Pellegrino's Grocery before he noticed all the police cars parked in the small lot. He braked sharply, skidded about twenty feet in the snow, then had to cross the bridge and drive on another hundred yards before finding a plowed driveway where he could turn around. As he turned, he fumbled with the box of Kleenex on the seat beside him and blew his nose.

Seven police cars were parked in front of the grocery, including two from the State Police and one from the Sheriff's Department. The rest were from Saratoga. As he parked, Charlie recognized the dark blue Lincoln Mark VII used by Chief Peterson and purchased for him by a committee of appreciative Saratoga businessmen headed by Charlie's oldest cousin, James. Charlie, of course, had no business stopping, but even though he had quit the police department nine years earlier, deep down he still saw himself as a policeman. Hadn't he spent twenty years on the force? Anyway, he liked Pellegrino and if something was wrong, then Charlie wanted to know.

He blew his nose again before getting out of the car, then hurried across the parking lot and up the front steps to the grocery. It was cold, not much more than zero degrees, and his rubber boots squeaked on the snow. An older Saratoga patrolman by the name of Schmitz, who had once worked with Charlie in the Community and Youth Relations Bureau, stood on the top step stamping his feet to keep warm.

"Bad business, Charlie," said Schmitz.

"What's going on?" As Charlie spoke an ambulance pulled into the parking lot. No siren, no flashing lights, it made Charlie realize that someone was already dead.

"The junkies got Pellegrino," said Schmitz. "Blew 'im away."

Charlie felt a deep chill in his stomach. Even though he knew that Schmitz took all his language from television detective shows, the basic facts of death and murder were probably correct. Again he thought how much he liked Pellegrino. He had known him for years. They were practically neighbors. Where there had been a person, there was now a blank space, a blue hole in the air. With an awful dismay Charlie turned and opened the door to the little grocery.

Inside, half a dozen lab men from the State Police were scouring the room under their portable lights, while two more with a measuring tape were getting the dimensions. Behind the counter, in the usual place of Pellegrino himself, was Chief Harvey L. Peterson, Commissioner of Public Safety, in a dark blue overcoat and three-piece blue suit. Seeing Charlie, he frowned and wrinkled his brow.

"Charlie, you just stick your nose in anywhere, don't you."

"I saw the cars," said Charlie. "What happened to Pellegrino?" To his left by the wall, he saw a plainclothesman talking to Pellegrino's wife, a small, gray-haired woman, who was shaking her head and crying. Charlie wanted to go to her and offer some consolation, but didn't know what to say. He always felt clumsy in such situations and he remained with Peterson.

"Somebody got him," said Peterson, raising himself up so he stood on tiptoe behind the counter. "Came in here last night and shot him. How come you can't read about it in the paper like everyone else?" Peterson had a gravelly voice which Charlie thought he exaggerated in order to sound tough.

"Sorry, Chief, I wasn't thinking. I shouldn't have stopped, but Pellegrino's been a neighbor of mine for years. . . ." Charlie paused to blow his nose. He knew Peterson was only slightly irritated and that this small apology should satisfy him. Peterson enjoyed talking about his discoveries and Charlie was a good listener. Again Peterson raised himself up on his tiptoes. He stood about six feet four and was always trying to make himself look taller. A year or so older than Charlie, he had thick graying hair and bushy eyebrows. Beads of sweat stood out on his round red forehead from the heat of the lights.

"You know, Charlie, if every private citizen came busting in here, how could we ever get anything done?"

"What happened to Pellegrino, Chief?"

"He was shot, shot three times. Must of been watching the Super Bowl when he got it. You want to see him? He's back there." Peterson jabbed a thumb over his shoulder. Charlie looked through the doorway of the small office behind the counter. Against the back wall he saw a mound covered by a white sheet. Where it covered Pellegrino's face, Charlie could make out the bumps of the grocer's nose and chin.

"That's okay. Was his wife here when it happened?"

"She was up in Glens Falls visiting their daughter. He seems to have been here by himself."

"You have any idea who did it or why?"

Peterson looked away toward one of the lab men who was dusting for prints on the far end of the counter next to a display of Hershey bars, then moved his tongue around the back of his mouth as if feeling for a bad tooth. "The cash register was open and empty. Papers were strewn about. As of yet no witnesses have come forward."

"So you think it was a robbery?"

Peterson turned his large blue eyes slowly toward Charlie. "What the hell you think I'm saying?"

Charlie stepped back from the counter. He thought of Victor and hoped that Peterson wouldn't learn about the robbery at the hotel. For years Peterson had disapproved of Charlie, and if he learned about Victor's party he would certainly think Charlie was at fault. After all, the hotel belonged to Charlie's mother and Victor was Charlie's best friend. And why did Peterson disapprove of Charlie? Perhaps for no better reason than Charlie quitting the police department. But Charlie knew it was more than that. Peterson was tall and strong looking and ultraprofessional, while Charlie was smallish and slightly overweight and just poked around. Peterson looked like a hero and Charlie didn't. For Peterson it was a great injustice that Charlie should compete with him and, what's worse, often beat him.

"Schmitz said it was junkies," said Charlie.

"Schmitz is always blowing out hot air," said Peterson. "What would junkies be doing out at Lake Saratoga in a snowstorm on a Sunday night during the Super Bowl? Maybe it was kids. Maybe they stuck him up and got scared. Whatever it was, it was probably something pretty small and we should get it wrapped up in no time."

But Charlie was hardly paying attention. He had just noticed something in the small office behind Peterson and he walked around the counter to look more closely. There was a lot of congealed blood on the floor and scattered within it were dozens of pieces of paper. But it wasn't the paper which had caught Charlie's attention but a scarf, a thick wool British public school scarf with red, black and blue stripes which was folded neatly across the back of a straight chair to the left of Pellegrino's body. At first Charlie couldn't think where he had recently seen it. Then he realized it had been worn by his cousin Robert when he had visited Charlie at his office on Saturday morning. Charlie could think of no good reason why it should be here at Pellegrino's Grocery. He started to mention it to Peterson, then stopped.

"So you want to see the body after all?" said Peterson, following Charlie into the office. "He was hit three times in the chest. Pretty neat shooting, especially for kids."

"No, thanks," said Charlie. Sticking out from the side of the sheet was one of Pellegrino's hands, a gray, old man's hand. Charlie thought of all the times he had touched it in giving him money or receiving change. It was Pellegrino's left hand and a dull brown trickle of dried blood was stuck to the back of it, disappearing between the middle and third fingers by his wedding ring.

"What're all these papers?" asked Charlie, looking away from the hand and back at Peterson, who was scratching his nose.

"Junk, as far as I can see. Sales receipts, bills, little notes to himself. I'll get someone to sort through it after the body's gone."

Charlie looked again at the scarf. What was it doing here? Maybe there were lots of scarves like that, but Charlie didn't think so.

"Did you know Pellegrino?" asked Charlie.

"Not at all," said Peterson. "Sometimes in the summer I might stop in for a Pepsi, but that was it. You liked him?"

"He was a good guy. We'd talk, tell a few jokes." And Charlie remembered the box of cookies he had bet on the Super Bowl, a bet, he realized, he had actually won. "Let me know what happens, okay?"

"Sure thing," said Peterson, already looking away.

Minutes later Charlie was again driving into Saratoga. He passed a deserted and snow-covered campground, then crossed the bridge over the Northway. Looking toward the woods on his left, he saw pine trees weighed down with cloaks of snow.

Then on his right appeared the first buildings belonging to the track—white buildings with several feet of snow on their roofs. Then on his left again came the track itself, first a portion of the stabling area in the backstretch, then the track which appeared as an unbroken expanse of white, then the grandstand and pine trees again, looking like tall ghosts or white soldiers. Charlie's mind kept going round and round. First he'd think about the scarf and Pellegrino's murder, then he'd think about the robbery of Victor's Super Bowl party, then he'd think about the theft of the painting of Man o' War, then he'd think about the scarf again. It seemed he hadn't had so much to think about for months, but none of it was lucrative and nothing seemed to lead anywhere.

But as he passed the Museum of Racing on Union Avenue, Charlie decided to stop. It was almost an unconscious decision. He didn't intend to investigate, of course. After all, as Mr. Whitman had told him, the theft was none of his business, just as Pellegrino's murder was none of his business, and even perhaps the robbery of the Super Bowl party was none of his business. He only wanted to buy a few postcards.

Built in the mid-fifties, the National Museum of Racing was made of red brick and had a front porch like a Greek temple. Charlie parked around the corner and walked back along the road. Jumping the mound of snow at the curb, he went up the walk, climbed the front steps, then stamped his boots on the mat. Taking a tissue from his pocket, he blew his nose and went inside.

A postcard display stood in the lobby and it took only a moment for Charlie to find the card he was seeking: MAN O' WAR AS A TWO-YEAR-OLD, 1919. (*Chestnut colt by Fair Play—Mahubah by Rock Sand. Foaled March 29, 1917—Died November 1, 1947.*) *Oil on canvas 28" × 37 ¼". Painted by Franklin B. Voss.* The picture showed Man o' War and a jockey posed on the track before the stands at Belmont Park. In the background on the left were a crowd of men in dark suits and fedoras and homburgs and on the right was the track with three horses in the distance cantering toward them. Although seen in profile, the jockey and Man o' War were turned slightly to look at the artist. Both horse and man looked somewhat impatient, even bored, as if they had more serious business to attend to elsewhere. The jockey wore the black-and-gold silks of Samuel Riddle's Faraway Farm. Johnny Loftus had ridden Man o' War in ten of his twenty-one starts, but Charlie thought the jockey in the picture looked like someone else. Maybe Clarence Kummer who had ridden Man o' War for nine of his other starts, but Charlie didn't think so. Elsewhere in the museum were the boots and saddle that Loftus had used on Man o' War. The painting wasn't very big, not much more than two by three feet, but presumably there had been a frame. Even so, it could have fit into a Ford Pinto quite comfortably.

Charlie took half a dozen of the cards. Perhaps they would come in handy. As he continued to study the postcard, he became aware of one of the museum guards approaching him.

"You looking for me, Charlie?"

The guard was Eddie Gillespie. It took Charlie half a second to remember that Gillespie had been one of the organizers of Victor's gambling party and that Gillespie must think that Charlie was here to ask him about the robbery. Gillespie wore a dark green uniform which seemed tailor-made, so well did it show off the muscles lovingly tended on a series of Nautilus machines at least a dozen hours a week.

"I thought I'd ask you some questions," said Charlie. "Is that where they hit you?" A large black-and-blue mark partly covered the left side of Eddie's handsome face.

"Smacked a shotgun barrel against me, Charlie. That's why I'm happy to give you the money that's left so you can catch those guys."

They were still standing in the lobby of the museum by the postcard display. The front door opened and two women entered, followed by about twenty little kids walking in pairs and holding hands. The kids were about six or seven, wore brightly colored parkas and all were chattering. Another woman brought up the rear. Charlie and Eddie waited until the group had gone past.

"You have any sense what they looked like?" asked Charlie.

"I couldn't see anything with those damn ski masks. They looked like cats. Believe me, I tried hard. Both had brown eyes but so does most everyone else in the world." Eddie pushed a hand back through his black hair, tousling it a little more. "But there's one thing I keep thinking about. How'd they know the knock?"

"What d'you mean?"

"We had a special knock—one, pause, two-three, four. All the guys used it, then these guys used it as well."

"So you think someone told?" asked Charlie.

"Sure, but who? I mean, these fellows that came to the party have been around. You don't blab about a thing like this. And they all swore they hadn't told a soul. So I keep thinking about the other guy."

"What other guy?" asked Charlie, not following. In the coat-room he could hear the grade-school class all chattering at once. They sounded like birds.

"Tubbs invited fifteen men. They all said they would show up and then one didn't. If I was investigating this, I'd go talk to the one who didn't show."

"Who was it?"

"Either I forgot his name or I never heard it. You'll have to ask Tubbs."

"And there's nothing else you can tell me about the two robbers?"

Gillespie touched his fingers to the bruise on his cheek as though touching it might help him to remember. "They were both about six feet. One seemed a little heavy. The other one kept talking a lot and the heavy one didn't like it. And then these yellow ski masks. You get 'em, Charlie. You get 'em and I'll help you pound 'em."

"I'll go talk to Tubbs," said Charlie as he walked over to pay for his postcards. Eddie followed him to the cash register.

"That Man o' War?" asked Eddie. "How come you're buying those?"

"Just need some postcards, that's all." It occurred to Charlie that Eddie knew about the theft of the painting, but then as guard it was obvious he would. Charlie wanted to talk to him about it, but this wasn't the right time. Anyway, perhaps the painting had been returned. "You like your job here?" asked Charlie.

"It's okay. Pretty slow mostly except for these school field trips. Nice uniform though, don't you think?"

"Makes you look sharp," said Charlie.

Leaving the racing museum, Charlie spent several hours trying unsuccessfully to find Maximum Tubbs, who tended to occupy his days either playing cards or shooting craps in the backrooms of gas stations, barber shops or in apartments scattered around Saratoga. Charlie left lots of messages but no one knew where Tubbs could be found. Giving up around noon, Charlie took an hour off to go swimming, despite his cold, telling himself that the chlorine was good for it. After all, chlorine was supposed to kill germs. As he swam, he thought again of Joe Pellegrino and how much he had liked him, how much he would miss him. It made Charlie angry that someone had killed him or that people felt they could kill one another and that it didn't matter. Then Charlie worried about his cousin's scarf and why it had been neatly folded next to Pellegrino's body. By the time he finished his mile he decided there must be some perfectly reasonable explanation. He might have dropped it while shopping. But why should his cousin shop at Pellegrino's Grocery?

Charlie left the Y about one o'clock and walked the several blocks down Broadway to his office to eat lunch—two bologna sandwiches packed that morning. Congress Park was buried in snow and the red brick Canfield Casino had drifts up to its lower windows. It was only a few degrees above zero and Charlie could feel his wet hair freezing under his watch cap. He hoped it wouldn't make his cold worse. Two figures in red sweaters were cross-country skiing across the park toward the library. They looked graceful and energetic, and Charlie considered buying some cross-country skis. No, he was probably too old. Swimming was exercise enough. The mound of snow pushed by the plows to the sides of the road had narrowed Broadway to two lanes, and the street was crowded with honking cars.

When Charlie climbed the stairs to his second-floor office on Phila Street, he found Maximum Tubbs waiting outside the door working on his nails with a small ivory-handled file.

"I heard you wanted to see me, Charlie."

Charlie unlocked the office door, then stood aside to let Tubbs enter. "You're a hard person to track down."

"You just got to know the right games, that's all. Does this concern that robbery yesterday at the hotel?" Maximum Tubbs had continued through the waiting room into the office. As he walked he removed his rust-colored overcoat, which he hung carefully on the coat tree by the door. He was several inches shorter than Charlie and seemed immaculately groomed with not one strand of his thick gray hair out of place. He even gave off the slight smell of baby powder. Before sitting down in Charlie's visitor's chair, he took a white handkerchief from the breast pocket of his brown suit and dusted it off.

"Did they hurt you at all?" asked Charlie. He had known Tubbs since he was a little boy and later, as a policeman, Charlie had even arrested him several times for gambling, although he had hated to do it. Tubbs had known Charlie's father and often told stories about the older Bradshaw's ferocious gambling. Consequently, besides liking Tubbs, Charlie valued him as a link to his own past.

"They pushed me around, that's all. On the other hand, I

don't like being touched. You never know where their hands have been."

Sitting down behind his desk, Charlie opened the paper bag containing his sandwiches. "You want a sandwich?" he asked, hoping that Tubbs would say no. He also had a can of Diet Pepsi and he popped it open.

"What is it?" asked Tubbs, leaning forward.

"Bologna."

Tubbs wrinkled his nose. "Pig snouts and assholes, Charlie. You're better off with tofu. And that plastic junk you're drinking. . . . Jesus, your stomach must hate you."

Charlie bit into a sandwich. With his nose all stuffed up, he could hardly taste it anyhow. "Anything about those guys who robbed you that you can especially remember?" he asked.

"They wore work clothes and ski masks. We couldn't tell much. One was a little heavy."

"Gillespie said there was a fifteenth guest who didn't show. Could it have been him?"

"Bobo Shaw, he's too short and the voice was wrong."

"Why didn't he show?" asked Charlie, with his mouth full. He'd always liked bologna. It reminded him of the sandwiches he'd had packed for school when he was a kid—bologna and ketchup on soft white bread, plus a little bag of carrot sticks.

"I've no idea. He never called. But I've been thinking about him. Did you hear about our special knock? I'm almost positive that none of the guys at the party told anybody about it. At least they swear they didn't. That leaves Shaw." Maximum Tubbs looked down at his fingernails, then took the nail file from his pocket and gently prodded the cuticle on his left thumb. "Shaw's a fellow who always owes a lot of money," he continued. "Cards, horses, football, basketball—he makes about ten bets a day. He used to have a pretty good garage down in Albany. Specialized in stock cars. The bookies just took it away from him."

"Where can I find him?" asked Charlie.

"He's been working as a mechanic somewhere in town. I don't know where, but I can find out. He lives down in Malta in a trailer park on Route Nine."

Charlie finished his first sandwich and decided to save the second until Tubbs had gone. "If we locate these men who robbed you and Victor, what do you plan to do? You can't get them arrested."

Putting away his nail file, Maximum Tubbs folded his arms across his chest and looked serious. He had thin, delicate features and very few wrinkles despite his seventy-some years. "There are a lot of games—Albany, Troy, Schenectady, Saratoga, even Glens Falls. These are professional games run by professional guys. They can't afford to have bozos knocking them over. Either we get our money back or we turn this business over to them. I think these fellows will see reason."

And if they don't, thought Charlie, they'll be pulled out of the river or found in the trunk of a car. He knew he didn't want to be a party to that.

Maximum Tubbs was staring past Charlie at the picture of Jesse James. "Charlie, don't you think it's odd for a detective to have a picture of Jesse James on his wall?"

"It seems better than those pinups that Victor used to have everywhere."

"Not necessarily. I mean, if I'm in the market for a private detective, I expect him to have pinups on the wall. Detectives like pinups. But Jesse James, that's something else again."

Charlie couldn't see why everyone was always making such a fuss about Jesse James. He had to have something on the wall, didn't he? Then, as he looked away, he had a sudden image of Pellegrino lying on the floor of his office covered with a white sheet and his hand sticking out from under it. "By the way," he said, "did you know that grocer out at the lake? Joe Pellegrino? The police found him this morning. He'd been shot. It looked like a holdup."

Tubbs leaned forward and his whole face became wrinkled.

"Pellegrino? He was a good friend. The bastards. So there's another Super Bowl casualty for you."

"What do you mean?" asked Charlie.

"Joe Pellegrino was one of the biggest bookies in Saratoga County. He didn't have many customers but his yearly handle must have been three-quarters of a million. He was probably holding a lot of Super Bowl money and somebody snatched it."

7

Tuesday morning Charlie again pulled his Renault into the small parking lot in front of Pellegrino's Grocery. This time there were no other cars and the grocery seemed deserted. The sky was gray and it was warmer. More snow was expected that afternoon. Charlie sat staring at the building, a one-story bungalow covered with brown shingles. At least a foot of snow had built up on the sloping roof. In the windows were cigarette and soft-drink ads. Charlie's cold was worse and he had a slight fever, which made it difficult to get moving, as if his whole body was saying, Don't move, don't jiggle a muscle. He found himself thinking that if it snowed very hard, then he might be trapped in his house for days and nobody could blame him for not investigating this or asking questions about that. He wondered if Jesse James had ever had colds, if Dillinger had ever caught the flu, if Pretty Boy Floyd had ever been struck down by bronchitis or strep throat. Bullet wounds—that was all that ever laid them up.

Charlie blew his nose for the thousandth time, then got out of his car and climbed the steps to the door of the grocery. It was locked. He wanted to talk to Pellegrino's wife, and since the back of the grocery connected to their small house, he thought she must be somewhere inside. He knocked, then after about twenty seconds knocked louder. Out on the surface of the lake he noticed people fishing through holes in the ice. It made him colder just to see it.

He again knocked, using the side of his fist, more of a hammer than a knock. He felt he had gotten behind in his work, that his cold and some of his other cases—a chronic shoplifter out at the Mall, an insurance fraud concerning a fellow who had had three cars burn up in two years—were making him move too slowly. Yesterday afternoon, for instance, he had wasted another hour with Blake Moss, the private detective from Albany who wanted to hire Charlie to set up an office for him in Saratoga. Moss had promised health benefits and even vacations. Charlie figured he hadn't had a vacation in five years, unless one counted the time when he simply didn't have any clients, when he was sitting around waiting for someone to walk through his front door and say "Help me." But Charlie didn't want to work for Moss. He didn't want to work for anybody. If Moss wanted to open an office in Saratoga, then okay, but Charlie was going to keep his own office open no matter what, and he had a momentary vision of himself slumped at his desk with cobwebs stretching between himself and the wall.

Charlie had just raised his fist to knock again when he noticed a round gray face pressed to the glass around the level of his chest. Charlie stepped back in surprise. The face—Mrs. Pellegrino's—was angrily mouthing two words over and over. The words appeared to be "Go away!" Charlie tried to smile and then sneezed instead. Mrs. Pellegrino often ran the store and Charlie knew she must recognize him. Probably she thought he wanted to buy something. Taking his wallet from his breast pocket, Charlie held up his private detective's license. Then he looked at Mrs. Pellegrino and nodded encouragingly.

She stopped saying "Go away" and stared back at him. Charlie thought how unhappy she looked. Her gray hair was pulled back from her moon-shaped face in a tight bun and she wore a black dress. Charlie didn't think she was more than five feet tall. Mrs. Pellegrino moved away from the door and Charlie heard the sound of the lock being unbolted. The door slowly swung open.

"No cookies today, mister," said Mrs. Pellegrino in her slight accent. "The store's closed."

Charlie felt embarrassed. Surely he bought other things at the grocery than cookies.

"I'm a private detective, Mrs. Pellegrino, and I'm investigating certain incidents connected to your husband's murder." He hoped that sounded serious enough, although it would have been better if he hadn't stopped in mid-sentence to wipe his nose. But Charlie felt he understood Mrs. Pellegrino's nervousness. The police didn't know that her husband had been a bookie and she didn't want them to.

"You sick?" said the old woman.

"Just a slight cold." Charlie again blew his nose.

"You get in here where it's warm. What's the matter with you? You should be in bed."

That's right, thought Charlie, as he entered the grocery, I should be in bed. "It's okay, Mrs. Pellegrino, I've got a lot to do. . . ."

"Go on back to the living room where there's a fire. I can't stand a man who don't know how to take care of himself," she added crossly.

Charlie walked ahead of her, half expecting her to prod him in the back. He had always known Mrs. Pellegrino to be snappish, but mostly she had been irritated when he had given her too many pennies or big bills, or brought back bottles dirty, or came to the store too close to closing. Behind him her slippers made an angry scuffling sound on the linoleum.

The living room had a wood stove, a color TV, two soft armchairs with light floral prints and on the walls were about twenty pictures of famous scenes from Italy: St. Peter's in Rome, the Pantheon, the Colosseum, the Leaning Tower of

Pisa. On a table by the door to the kitchen was a large framed photograph of Joe Pellegrino surrounded by a black ribbon. The picture showed Pellegrino playing horseshoes in his shirt-sleeves. His arm was pulled back, he was taking a step forward and he looked eager. He also looked about ten years younger. A fire was burning in the wood stove, and the room was hot and dry and smelled of cloves.

"Sit down, sit down!" ordered Mrs. Pellegrino. "I'll get you something hot to drink."

Charlie took off his overcoat and blue watch cap, then sat down in an armchair to the left of the stove. "I'm very sorry about your husband, Mrs. Pellegrino. . . ."

The old woman stuck her head through the kitchen door. "He was the best man in Saratoga County and I won't let anybody say different." She was smiling but Charlie could see tears in her eyes. He nodded vigorously, then sneezed. When he looked back she had disappeared.

A minute later she returned and shoved a glass at him. "Lemon juice, honey and a little whiskey." Then she stepped back to the kitchen door, taking small quick steps that made her look like a mechanical toy.

"Mrs. Pellegrino, I wanted . . ."

"Just drink." She stood with her arms folded. Around her waist was a white apron with pictures of purple flowers.

Charlie drank. It was hot and made his eyes water. He guessed it contained a double shot of whiskey. But it was good and he could feel its warmth soothing his insides.

"You want another?" asked Mrs. Pellegrino, taking the glass as if she didn't trust him with it.

"No, that's okay, thanks." Charlie wiped his nose on a tissue. The wood stove was making pinging noises and he stretched out his hands toward its warmth.

"Now what do you want? Don't dawdle. I have a hundred things I have to get done and poor Joe still needs a new suit."

"Mrs. Pellegrino, I know your husband was a bookie and it

seems likely that his murder was connected to that. I don't care that he was a bookie and I won't make any trouble about it."

The old woman moved from the kitchen door and sat down in the armchair next to Charlie. "If the police find that Joe made book, they'll tell the tax people. Then the tax people will come and make a lotta trouble. But if the police don't know he was a bookie, how'll they ever catch the person who did it? That's an awful circle, mister, and I keep going round it again and again." She had small dark eyes like little marbles and she kept turning them on Charlie, then looking away.

"Did your husband have many customers?"

"I don't think so, but I don't know much about it. Maybe he had six, maybe seven, but they were all men who made a lot of bets and he was always busy."

"Did he keep any records?"

"Why do you want to know this?"

Charlie wondered if he had any good answer to her question. He wanted to prove that the scarf he had seen was not his cousin's, but also he was struck that there had been two crimes, two robberies during the Super Bowl, and he wondered if they were connected. Beyond that, he was a tidy man who disliked loose ends.

"I think it may be connected to another case I'm working on. Besides, I liked Joe, although I didn't know he was a bookie until yesterday."

Mrs. Pellegrino sat straight on the very edge of her chair. She kept rubbing her hands together, then wiping them on her apron as if they were wet. "Could you find the person who did it?" she asked, looking up at Charlie sharply.

"I don't know."

"Mister, the police won't find him and I can't find him, so I need to get somebody who can."

"And what would you do if you knew who killed him?" asked Charlie. "Would you go to the police?"

"Joe had a lot of connections, a lot of friends. Sometimes he had to lay off his bigger bets to a couple of bookies in Albany. All day yesterday and today the phone's been ringing. People calling to say how sorry they are. If I knew who killed Joe, I would tell these men who it was."

Charlie stared over at the small, grandmotherly-looking woman in her black dress and white apron. "I don't like vendettas," he said. "If I found out who killed Joe, I'd turn that person over to the police."

Charlie and Mrs. Pellegrino continued to stare at each other, until Charlie was forced to turn away to blow his nose. The heat in the room had begun to make him sweat. When he looked back, Mrs. Pellegrino was still staring at him.

"You know, Joe liked you," she said. "He said he'd heard good things about you, that you were a good private detective. He said you were smart like an owl but that you were also like a snapping turtle, that you'd bite into something and not let go."

Charlie tried to feel flattered but the image of a creature half owl and half snapping turtle took all his attention.

"Joe had many hiding places," continued the old woman, "but since the police were here I have been searching and I have found many papers. But no names, Joe was always careful not to write down any names."

Charlie felt disappointed. "Are you sure you looked everywhere?" He had hoped to get a list of the men who placed bets with Pellegrino.

"I think so. But I did find something." Mrs. Pellegrino got to her feet. "I will show it to you." She walked to a plain oak desk against the wall, opened a drawer and took out a bound record book, which she carried back to Charlie.

It was an old-fashioned oversized book, maybe fourteen by eight, with a fake leather cover. Charlie opened it. Inside were page after page of numbers and dates and sometimes a little notation like Aqueduct or Georgetown or Syracuse or Boston, but there were no names, at least not proper ones. Instead there were five separate headings under the words Grouper, Lynx, Spaniel, Horse and Gibbon, then numbers and dates below each.

Charlie thought of Pellegrino's fondness for naming people after animals. Then he sat back and considered his cousin's face. Not a grouper or spaniel, unlikely a lynx. Maybe a horse.

"By the way," said Charlie, "when I stopped by yesterday there was a scarf in your husband's office, an English scarf with red, black and blue stripes. It was folded neatly on the chair. I wonder if you could tell me where it came from?"

Mrs. Pellegrino got to her feet and went to a small closet. Opening the door, she carefully removed the scarf which was rolled up. She shook it out so that one end fell to the floor. Then she raised it, partly obscuring herself behind it. The scarf was thick and warm, and Charlie again remembered seeing it around his cousin's neck.

"I had never seen it before," she said. "It was in Joe's office when I came back and found him." At the memory of seeing her husband's body her voice shook a little. Then she recovered herself and began rolling up the scarf. "The police asked about it. I said it was Joe's."

"Are you sure it wasn't in the store when you left on Sunday?" asked Charlie.

"I'm certain."

"And whose do you think it is?"

"I think it belongs to the man who killed my Joe."

"Let me take it," said Charlie, worrying suddenly about his cousin. "It might help us."

8

Charlie's cousin Robert had an office right downtown on Broadway in a three-story renovated red-brick Victorian building across the street from the boutique owned and operated by Robert's wife, Lucy, and her sister, Marge, the woman whom Charlie had divorced nine years earlier. These women were a plague to Charlie and it sometimes seemed that their life outside the boutique consisted of seeking out opportunities to make him experience all the guilt, shame and self-loathing which they felt it appropriate he should feel. Charlie's fault, other than being born, was that he did not deserve to live in a nice place like Saratoga and be related to such respectable people as his cousins. Additionally, he had insulted Marge by marrying her and then insulted her again by asking for a divorce. Even more, he had quit being a policeman, the one respectable thing in his life, and insisted on living out at the lake like a hippie. Well, thought Charlie, as he parked his car by the Adirondack Trust, this list of faults was the reason he spent little time on this particular block in Saratoga. Lucy and Marge aspired to be like that old Greek woman who turned people to stone. They wanted to make Charlie into a statue, a cheap statue that they could stick out in the woods for the birds to make little messes upon.

Hurrying from his car to the office building, Charlie kept his head down, half expecting a shout from across the street. He opened the door, stamped the snow off his feet, then climbed to the second floor. Normally he didn't feel so guilty but he realized he was about to challenge the wall of correctitude and propriety with which his cousins had bullied him for fifty years. In his hand was the red, black and blue wool scarf he had gotten from Mrs. Pellegrino a half hour earlier. "And what about this?" he would say, throwing the scarf at Robert's feet.

Robert's secretary, Mrs. Dawson, was an elderly woman with a wonderfully cultured and honeyed voice who told Charlie that his cousin was busy but would see him shortly. Despite her voice, she had hard little black eyes and it seemed to Charlie that she thought he had come to borrow money, even though he had never borrowed money from Robert in his life. Occasionally she eyed the scarf in Charlie's lap as he leafed through an old *National Geographic* and kept blowing his nose. Maybe she thinks I stole it, thought Charlie.

It was fifteen minutes before Robert appeared. Dressed in dark tweeds, smoking a pipe and with his thick gray hair combed back over his head, he reminded Charlie of an English squire, as if that was the image necessary in order to sell real estate in Saratoga. But then Charlie considered his cousin's long face and his large teeth, the large brown eyes. What kind of animal did he look like?

Charlie got to his feet. "I've brought back your scarf," he said.

"How good of you, Charlie. I've been looking for it all over. But you could have left it with Mrs. Dawson." Robert stretched out his hand for the scarf.

Charlie kept the scarf at his side. "I think we better talk about it."

"I'm terribly busy right now, Charlie, can't we make it next week?" Robert wore a little smile that seemed fixed in place. It was the sort of smile that said, Whatever you know, I know a bit better.

"It has to be now."

"It can't be now, Charlie. Let me have the scarf." Robert still had his hand outstretched.

Charlie felt uncomfortable about saying anything in front of Mrs. Dawson, who was staring as if amazed that anyone could ignore her employer's commands.

"Don't make me threaten you," said Charlie. "It has to be now."

Robert spread his hands apart and gave a little shrug. "Two minutes then." He turned to reenter his office.

"Is everything all right?" Mrs. Dawson asked him.

"Yes, yes, it's just my cousin," said Robert, as he stood aside to let Charlie enter.

The office was designed to comfort and reassure. It had a leather Chesterfield couch and a leather wing-back chair. The desk was large, dark and imposing. On the walls were Currier and Ives prints and on the floor was a deep red Oriental rug. Charlie didn't quite trust himself to sit down so he leaned against the desk instead.

"So where did you find it?" asked Robert, pausing by the chair. His expression was one of amused tolerance.

"It was next to Joe Pellegrino's body."

Robert continued to look at Charlie as there occurred a sort of hiccup in the forward movement of time, evidenced by a slight widening of Robert's eyes. Then he recovered himself. "And who is that?" Robert asked.

"Joe Pellegrino, he had a grocery out at the lake. He was murdered Sunday night."

"And I'm supposed to know him?"

"He was your bookie. He called you Mr. Horse." Is this all true? thought Charlie. But he felt certain it was true.

Robert removed his pipe from his mouth, lowered his head

and pinched the bridge of his nose between his thumb and index finger. When he looked back at Charlie it was with an expression of saddened disappointment. "Charlie, this is the most preposterous thing I've ever heard. What have I done to make you want to attack me in this way?"

Charlie glanced at the scarf in his hand. If Robert was lying, he was doing a good job. On the other hand, thought Charlie, he's a gambler. According to Pellegrino's records, Horse bet several hundred thousand dollars a year. But then another thought struck him—what if I'm really wrong?

"Sunday night you visited Pellegrino and you left your scarf behind. I'm not saying you killed him, but you were there. When Pellegrino was found the next day, your scarf was next to the body. Either you dropped it or somebody put it there. In any case, the police are going to want to know what you were doing out at the grocery. You'll be a suspect. Pellegrino was a bookie with five customers. He gave each one an animal name. And you're one of them, you're Mr. Horse."

"Charlie, this is ridiculous," said Robert, still not moving. "I really think you've gone crazy. Have I done something to upset you, something you want to get even about?"

He really does look like a horse, thought Charlie, that narrow head and long jaw with big teeth, those eyes set wide apart. "Then you're saying this isn't your scarf?" he asked.

"Not necessarily," answered Robert, relighting his pipe, "it's just that I don't know how it got there. By a dead body, you say? How is that possible?"

"And the gambling?" asked Charlie.

"You've known me all my life. Do I go to the track, do I play cards? Charlie, I'm not that sort of person."

Charlie began to search his pockets for a Kleenex. He found himself questioning himself. How could he have ever suspected his own cousin of murder? "What about the scarf?" he asked.

"Somebody must have put it there."

"Who? Do you have enemies?"

"Nobody comes to mind," said Robert, blowing out a cloud of smoke, "but I'm a successful businessman. Anybody who is successful has enemies." The observation seemed to sadden him.

"What if I gave the scarf to Peterson?" asked Charlie. "Aren't you worried about a police investigation?"

"If I'm suspected, then I'd welcome it. But I must say it would be rather mean of you, Charlie." He again drew on his pipe.

I'm sure he looks like a horse, thought Charlie, I'm almost positive. He realized that if he went to Peterson, it would become known that Pellegrino was a bookie, which would mean a lot of trouble for his widow. For the moment Charlie was stuck. He needed to find more evidence that Robert was a gambler. Charlie tossed the scarf to his cousin. "Let's hope you haven't been lying," he said. "In any case, I'm going to keep looking around."

Robert held the scarf in his left hand and stroked it lightly with his right. "The family would be upset if they knew about your accusations, Charlie."

"Then you better keep your mouth shut," said Charlie. He again blew his nose on a Kleenex, then walked around Robert to the door. It had seemed that for the smallest fraction of a second Robert had been nervous, but then Charlie had lost the advantage. It had slipped from his hands like water.

Outside, it had again begun to snow, great fat flakes like little pieces of paper. The sky was the color of old concrete. Charlie drove slowly back to his office. Was it possible he had secret hostile feelings against his cousin that had led him to the wrong conclusions? Wasn't it ridiculous to suppose that his cousin, one of the most respected men in Saratoga, was a gambler who might even have killed somebody? Maybe it's my fever, thought Charlie, maybe I'm just losing control.

He parked his car in the lot across from Mrs. London's Bakery, then climbed the hill to his office. He tried to think when he had last made a serious mistake in judgment. Actually, not asking more questions about Victor's party before it occurred had been a mistake. As was not following Whitman's instructions about dropping off the ransom money. In fact, perhaps I make errors of judgment all the time, thought Charlie. But a horse, didn't his cousin look like a horse? And who were the others? Grouper, Lynx, Spaniel and Gibbon.

The second Charlie entered his office, he called Whitman. He stood by his desk as the phone rang, still wearing his overcoat and brushing the melting snowflakes from his sleeve. It was about eleven o'clock, and through the window across the street he could see Grace Washburn working on a patient. Charlie felt a twinge of sympathy, followed by a little poke of guilt.

It took several minutes for Charlie to get through the secretary, then Whitman came on the line.

"This is Bradshaw," said Charlie. "I was just wondering . . ."

"No, Mr. Bradshaw," said Whitman, cutting him off, "no word, no nothing. Why do you keep bothering me?"

"I just thought you might have heard."

"Well, I haven't and, in any case, it is no longer any concern of yours. How many times do I have to explain this?" There was a long silence as Charlie waited for Mr. Whitman to say something else. Then the dial tone abruptly began to buzz in Charlie's ear.

As he stood holding the handset, Charlie studied the photograph of Jesse James. Would Jesse have put up with this kind of runaround? Fat chance. He was the sort of outlaw you addressed as Sir. Again blowing his nose, Charlie thumbed through the Rolodex card file on his desk until he found the number of a State Police office in Albany. He dialed and as the phone rang he fished out his wallet for the card with the license-plate number of the Subaru driven by whoever had picked up the ransom money.

A man answered and Charlie asked to speak to Rick Mahoney, feeling that the "Rick" would get him through faster than asking for Captain Mahoney. As he waited, he kept snuffling and clearing his throat. Mahoney had been just a trooper when Charlie first met him twenty years ago. Now he was one of Charlie's few friends in high places.

"Bradshaw," said Mahoney, speaking abruptly, "you been bullying that police chief up there again?" He spoke in a mild bellow and Charlie moved the handset away from his ear.

"Not me, Rick, I'm as good as gold."

"I can't believe that, Charlie. What little favor do you want me to do for you today?"

"Can you trace a license plate?" Charlie hated to think he only called his friends to ask for favors.

"Is this a criminal case?"

"No, no, there's some money owed, that's all."

"You're a deceptive son of a bitch, Charlie. What's the number?"

Charlie told him. Was he deceptive? Perhaps he occasionally stretched the truth a little.

"Okay, call me in the morning. You catch the Super Bowl?"

"I had to work."

"Lot of unhappy Patriot fans around here, Charlie. Unhappy and broke. And you know what," added Mahoney, "I'm one of them." He laughed loudly and Charlie again moved the phone a few inches from his ear. "But you, you sly devil, I bet you cleaned up."

"I won a little," said Charlie, thinking of his bet with Pellegrino for a box of Freihofer cookies. "But I haven't collected yet."

After hanging up, Charlie happened to glance out the window. It was still snowing heavily. Across Phila Street, he saw Grace Washburn waving at him. Charlie smiled and waved back. Grace blew him a kiss and Charlie made a little show of pretending to catch it and sticking it to his cheek. He found himself wondering if he should get curtains, then, guiltily, he wondered where such a thought had come from. Putting on his overcoat, he headed for the door. It was time to visit the racing museum again.

Ten minutes later Charlie located Eddie Gillespie in a far corner of the museum seemingly studying a painting of the famous trainer Sunny Fitz. Eddie was leaning forward like a serious student of the turf and Charlie almost felt proud of him. James Fitzsimmons had trained nearly one hundred and fifty winners in his eighty-year career and for Eddie to take this interest proved that Saratoga history was at last seeping through his hedonistic skin. When Charlie got closer, however, he saw that Eddie was actually polishing the gold buttons of his uniform with a small travel toothbrush. No one else was in the room, and when Eddie Gillespie turned and saw Charlie, he put the toothbrush back in his pocket and looked embarrassed.

"These buttons are a real chore, Charlie. I hate to clean them on my own time."

"You got toothpaste in the other pocket?" asked Charlie, joining him by the painting.

"I find baking soda works best." Eddie tugged down the jacket of his green uniform, then lifted his chin and stretched his neck. "You got a line on those guys that robbed Victor?"

"Not yet. I've some other stuff to clear up first. I want you to tell me what you know about the painting of Man o' War that was stolen last week."

Eddie looked suddenly nervous and took several steps away from Charlie, then he glanced back over his shoulder. "Jesus, Charlie, nobody's supposed to know about that. I could get in real trouble."

"Were you working then?" asked Charlie, ignoring Eddie's concern. Eddie kept looking toward the open door leading to the main hall. Around the room running from the floor to waist level were glass display cases filled with dozens of racing silks. They were bright, colorful and made the room seem full of flowers.

"I came on Monday morning and it was gone. I didn't discover it, though. Old Hacker, the cashier, noticed it. He figured someone had taken it off to be cleaned or something. Then after an hour or so, he decided to ask the director just to make sure. They really yelled at him for not reporting it right away." Eddie kept backing up, retreating from Charlie, who paced slowly after him.

"So they broke in on Sunday night?"

Eddie winced and again looked past Charlie toward the door. "It looks that way," he said.

"Aren't there alarms?"

"They were turned off."

Eddie had been lowering his voice until Charlie could hardly hear him. "What about the theft last year?" asked Charlie. "Were the alarms turned off then as well?"

"No, that was a different kind of robbery. The museum was open but nobody was around. Whoever took the painting grabbed it right off the wall, snuck into the back, then passed it through a window to someone waiting outside. These guys last week knew the museum, or at least they knew about the alarms." Eddie bumped up against one of the glass display cases. Charlie stopped in front of him.

"Was the door forced?"

"A back door was. But it occurred to me that somebody could have opened it with a key, then done some damage with a crowbar afterward, just to make it look forced."

"So you think it was an inside job?" asked Charlie.

"Maybe." Eddie looked again toward the lobby.

"Anybody working here now?"

"I can't believe that. I mean, apart from me and the guy who cleans up, everyone's pretty old or they're broads, you know?"

"Perhaps it was somebody's husband."

"I doubt it. I mean, the guy really had to know the museum."

"Can you get me a list of people who have quit working for the museum in the past year, or at least since that other painting was stolen?"

"Jesus, Charlie, I shouldn't even be talking to you."

Charlie patted the younger man on the shoulder. He remembered all the times he had bailed Eddie out of jail or gotten him out of trouble. It was good to see him trying to go straight. "That's okay, just try to have that list by tomorrow morning. How come you're so nervous about this?"

"The director, you know, he said he'd fire anybody who opened their mouths."

"You like this job?"

"I like the uniform."

"I'll stop by around ten," said Charlie. "Names and addresses, don't forget."

9

About eleven that night Charlie was lying in bed reading a biography of Lucky Luciano, who, among other things, had once managed some gambling property in Saratoga. He had just finished his second hot toddy and could hardly keep his eyes open, which was the reason, he later thought, that he didn't hear the car. Or perhaps the snow had muffled the sound. Whatever the case, Charlie was just reading about Luciano's control of the Chicago Club when a tap-tapping on the window a few feet from his head drove him from beneath the covers with a speed that sent his book skipping across the room. Charlie stared at the window and saw a dark figure staring back. He tried to keep his face blank and to calm his breathing, then went into the living room to the front door and opened it.

"Who's out there?" he called. With his stuffed-up nose, it sounded like "Who'd oud dere?" It occurred to Charlie, perhaps a trifle late, that he should have gotten his spare .38 from the kitchen where he kept it with the dish towels. His feet were bare, and as he held open the door he could feel a cold wind blowing across them. "Who is it?" he said again.

"Me," came a voice. Charlie saw a vague shape moving toward him through the snow. "Doesn't your doorbell work?"

"It's broken."

"Well, in any case, I rang." It was Charlie's cousin, Robert, and around his neck was the red, black and blue scarf that Charlie had returned to him earlier that day.

"I want to talk to you," said Robert, wiping the snow from his boots. "I'm in pretty serious trouble."

As Charlie watched him enter he was struck by how Robert was trying to avoid his eyes. "You lied to me, didn't you," said Charlie.

"I couldn't help it," said Robert. "My whole life is about to explode. I don't know what to do." He stood on the mat, his dark overcoat buttoned up to his neck and a reddish brown Irish tweed hat pulled down to his ears.

"You can close the door for starters," said Charlie, "then you can come in and tell me about it. Let me get a bathrobe." He walked toward the bedroom, unsure whether to feel vindicated or irritated. Then he stopped in the doorway and looked back. "Just tell me one thing. Did you kill Pellegrino?"

"No, Charlie." Robert was half out of his overcoat and his body seemed to turn rigid. His long face looked frightened. "I would never do anything like that."

"Do you know who killed him?"

"He was dead when I got there. That's why I panicked." Robert finished taking off his coat and hung it on a hook behind the door. Then he put his hat on the hook beside it. Charlie had always thought that such hats looked somewhat effete.

"How much did you lose on the Super Bowl?" asked Charlie. He was cold and his nose was running but he couldn't help asking these questions. He kept telling himself that this was the cousin he had known for his entire life and now it appeared that he hadn't known him at all.

"Thirty thousand."

"And now you don't have to pay?"

"I guess not."

Charlie started into the bedroom again, then stopped as he thought of something else. "And you're Mr. Horse?"

"That's what he called me." Robert seemed embarrassed. "Do I really look like a horse?"

"Maybe a little," said Charlie, "but it's nothing I would have thought of myself."

A few minutes later Charlie and Robert were seated by the fieldstone fireplace in which several birch logs were burning. Robert was nursing a cup of tea on the couch, while Charlie in his blue terry-cloth robe sat in the armchair with another hot toddy. He had offered to make one for Robert but his cousin explained that he didn't drink. Of course Charlie had known he didn't drink, but then Robert had claimed not to gamble as well. As far as Charlie was concerned, Robert's whole personality was now suspect.

"What I don't see," said Charlie, "is why you changed your mind and came out here." And for a moment he wondered if Robert had felt so guilty about lying to his own flesh and blood that he had come out in the middle of the night to try and fix things between them. Charlie felt touched.

Robert leaned forward, putting his cup on the coffee table. "Someone called me this afternoon, Charlie. The man knew about the scarf and that I had dropped thirty thousand on the Patriots. I've had to take some loans and the man knew about those as well. I've had a streak of bad luck lately. I was betting horses again. They always mess you up. Too many variables."

Charlie could hardly believe these words were coming from his cousin's mouth. "What did the man want?" he asked.

"Five thousand to keep his mouth shut. He said if I didn't give him the money he'd call Chief Peterson and the newspaper. I can't afford that, Charlie. I've always been careful about my gambling."

"You're a hypocrite," said Charlie, unable to help himself.

Robert sat back on the couch. His brow was creased and the

lines around his large brown eyes and oversized mouth were all turning down. Charlie thought it made him look even more like a horse.

"It's never done anyone any harm," said Robert. "Mostly I do pretty well, or at least break even. And when I lose, it's never that much. It's just this past year that I've hit a streak of bad luck. This Super Bowl seemed like a sure thing and I was hoping the money would bail me out. I mean, I'm part of the community, Charlie. The Chamber of Commerce, the Rotary Club—I can't let people know I'm a gambler."

"Could you have paid the thirty thousand?" asked Charlie. He kept thinking how sanctimonious Robert had always been about gambling and drinking, any activity slightly outside of proper society.

"I don't know, there's already a mortgage on my house."

"So you had a motive for killing Pellegrino."

"But I'm not a killer, Charlie." Robert leaned forward again with his elbows on his knees. He wore a brown tweed jacket, a tan oxford shirt and a brown tie with pictures of little Model T Fords.

"That's what a lot of killers say," said Charlie. "Why should I believe you about this when you've turned out to be a liar about the gambling and God knows what else?"

"I've got a family, Charlie. You've known me all your life. You really think I could kill somebody?"

Robert tried to smile, indicating the outlandishness of the suggestion and showing off his large horse teeth. But it had often occurred to Charlie that almost anybody could kill with enough provocation. If Robert were the murderer, then Charlie would find it out and in due time he would turn his cousin over to Chief Peterson. Yet the fact of Robert being a gambler kept striking Charlie, and each time it was a surprise. He didn't condemn his cousin—indeed, he felt sorry for him—but he was angry about all those occasions when Robert had gone out of his way to point out one of Charlie's faults: that Charlie seemed shiftless or lacked ambition or occasionally drank and went to the track or had been divorced.

"So what do you expect me to do?" asked Charlie.

Robert leaned back on the couch. "I want you to give this fellow the five thousand and try to make sure he keeps his mouth shut."

"You could have him arrested."

"No, no, Charlie, I just want to keep him quiet. I can't afford to have anyone learn about my connection with Pellegrino."

"So you want me to be your errand boy?" Just like Mr. Whitman, thought Charlie. He blew his nose, then tossed the tissue into the fireplace where it flared and disappeared.

"I need someone to help me," said Robert, leaning forward again. "You've had dealings with crooks and people like that. You know what to do. I've never had any experience with that sort of thing."

Charlie felt a kind of insult, as if his life outside of polite society had given him some expertise, as if his experience with the mire had made him good at slogging through the mud.

"You make bets every day?" asked Charlie.

"Just about."

"More than one?"

"Two or three, sometimes more, sometimes less."

"So you do about two hundred thousand a year?"

"Maybe. I don't keep track. Actually, it's probably more than that."

"Three hundred thousand?"

"Maybe. But those aren't losses. That's just what I bet." Robert spoke with some degree of pride as if admitting a secret that showed him off as better than he normally appeared to be.

"And how much does Pellegrino get?"

"Between three and five percent."

"How long you been using him?"

"About fifteen years. He was a friend, Charlie, I really respected the man."

Even so, there was a note of condescension in his voice. "Do your brothers know about this?"

Robert looked frightened. "No, nobody."

"What about your wife?"

"Of course not. Lucy would never understand."

"So tell me what happened Sunday night," said Charlie, finishing his hot toddy. "But let me warn you, if you hold anything back or if I find you've been lying, I'll go straight to Peterson. It won't matter that we're cousins."

Robert had taken his pipe out of the side pocket of his tweed coat and was fiddling with it. "Charlie, I only want you to pay this fellow his five thousand."

Standing up, Charlie walked to the mantle until he could feel the heat of the fire on his legs. He took a tissue from the pocket of his bathrobe, blew his nose, then threw the tissue into the flames. How quickly it disappeared, a little explosion of light. "Then you better get out of here, Robert. I'm not going to do anything unless I know the whole story."

Robert appeared ready to protest. A little of his old supercilious manner showed itself in the tilt of his jaw, the slight raising of an eyebrow. Then he took a deep breath and leaned heavily back on the couch. "It was clear by halftime that I'd lost the bet," he began. "I even stopped thinking about the game. I belong to this betting service, two of them actually. I don't use them as a rule but sometimes it's useful to have the additional input. Anyway, before the game was over, I'd worked out seven or eight safe bets on some basketball games over the next week, bets that could put me in the clear. So I drove out to see Pellegrino. On the car radio, I heard the final score, but by then it hardly mattered because with these other bets I could wipe the slate clean. All I had to do was to convince Pellegrino to let me hold off paying the thirty thousand until I got the money from these other games."

"And did you have any reason to suppose he would do that?" asked Charlie. It occurred to him that his cousin was crazy, not really crazy but crazy in the way gamblers can be crazy—to have complete certainty about the outcome of a future event, despite all the evidence of their past losses.

"He didn't like to but he'd done it in the past. After all, I was a good customer."

"Do you know who his other customers were?"

"Not by name, but I knew there were some others. He had animal names for all of us. It was very private. Nobody knew anything about anybody."

"So what happened?"

"Nothing. He was dead."

"But what did you see?"

Robert shifted his position on the couch. "Do you mind if I smoke my pipe?"

"I'd rather you didn't, I've got a cold."

Robert gave a little shrug, then put his pipe back in his pocket. It was a disdainful gesture and Charlie didn't like it. "I got there around ten," said Robert. "The door was unlocked. I went in and found Pellegrino in his little office behind the counter. Then I left."

"How'd you happen to lose your scarf?"

"I looked around a little. I was afraid he might have some papers with my name on them. There was blood over a lot of papers and I couldn't touch them. Joe was lying on the floor. His eyes were open. You've probably seen a lot of corpses but this was the first I've seen, except for my father, of course. I was nervous and in a hurry. I must have dropped the scarf without even noticing."

Charlie went back to his armchair and sat down. "Did you touch anything?"

"You mean fingerprints? I was wearing my gloves."

"Did you see anyone else at all?"

"Not really."

"What's that supposed to mean?"

"When I'd almost reached Pellegrino's a car passed me going

toward Saratoga driving fast with its brights on. It was one of those Ford Broncos with oversized tires. When I got to the grocery a minute or so later, the only tracks in the snow of the parking lot were great big tire tracks, like that Bronco would have made. When I saw that car, I thought it might have pulled out from the grocery but I wasn't sure."

"Were there other tracks in the parking lot?"

"No, I mean they'd been covered over by the snow. It was coming down pretty hard. When I left, those big tire tracks were almost gone."

"What about this guy who's blackmailing you, could he have seen you?"

"I don't see how, unless he passed me on the road and knew my car." Robert had again taken out his pipe and was chewing on the stem.

"Obviously he knew your scarf," said Charlie.

"Obviously."

"And obviously he knew more about Pellegrino's other customers than you seem to."

"Charlie, I'm telling you the truth."

Again, Charlie was tempted to make a crack about the gambling and all the lies it entailed, but he said nothing. He reached over for another tissue and blew his nose. Maybe he should have let Robert smoke his pipe. It wouldn't have bothered him that much.

"So you'll help me?" asked Robert, leaning forward. There was a desperateness in his voice that Charlie found almost touching. It made his cousin seem vulnerable and childlike.

"What did this guy tell you to do?"

"To get the five thousand and he'd call me in a day or so."

"What if the guy calls in a couple of weeks and wants another five thousand?"

"He said he wouldn't. He said it was a onetime deal."

"Most likely this guy is one of Pellegrino's other customers," said Charlie, "and most likely he showed up at the grocery shortly after you'd left. He's a gambler and sometimes he needs money badly. When he does, he'll call you again. I'll deliver your money but I think you're making a mistake. I'm also looking into Pellegrino's death. The police don't know Pellegrino was a bookie and if they find out, then Mrs. Pellegrino could be in trouble with the IRS. I'll try to keep your name out of it, but I can't promise anything."

Robert's long face again took on a supercilious expression. It made him look as if he intended to buy something. "Why can't you just forget about Pellegrino?"

"Because I don't want to." He considered adding that Mrs. Pellegrino had asked for his help, but he didn't feel it would carry any weight. Robert seemed to have no grief for Pellegrino. His death was merely a nuisance. Again Charlie was struck by how different his cousin was from the person whom he had always imagined him to be.

"The family is as much yours as mine, Charlie," said Robert, getting to his feet. "And there's your mother's hotel to consider. If there's a scandal, it will look bad for all of us."

"Scandals don't bother me," said Charlie, standing up. "Murder does." Charlie considered how Robert and Lucy had been saying bad things about him for years and he'd put up with it. How would another scandal be any different? "Let me know when you hear from the guy," added Charlie, walking his cousin to the door. "Did you bet on those basketball games?"

"Four of them so far."

"How'd you make out?"

"I won on the Syracuse game and lost the others."

"So you're down?"

"Broke even, but there're still four more games. I'll be flush by the end of the week." Robert began putting on his coat.

"You have another bookie?"

"Sure, a guy in Albany. He's not as good as Joe but at least he's there."

"Have you ever thought of giving it up?" asked Charlie, opening the door.

"I'm still learning, Charlie, and I've almost got the basketball figured out. And in football I came out way ahead."

"Except for the Super Bowl," said Charlie.

"Sure, but I'm off the hook on that."

"Too bad for Pellegrino," said Charlie, feeling angry.

His cousin looked at him, surprised. His collar was turned up and the red, black and blue scarf was wrapped around his neck. He stood in the open doorway with his hat in his hand as snow blew into his thick gray hair. His surprise changed to confusion and perhaps embarrassment. He put on his Irish tweed hat and pulled it down to his eyes.

"Of course," said Robert. "Too bad for Pellegrino."

10

Victor slapped his hand down hard on the bar. "Charlie, I know you're busy and I'm tickled pink that the old detective racket has gotten so hot, but you're supposed to be working for me and Tubbs and not messing around with this other shit. Who stuck up my party? That's the number-one question."

Charlie looked up at Victor. The floor behind the bar of the Bentley was raised, making Victor seem about six and a half feet tall. He wore his three-piece dove gray suit and looked disapproving. It was nine-thirty Wednesday morning and Charlie was sipping a large glass of orange juice. He felt somewhat better but his nose was still running and he had developed a nasty cough. "The painting . . . ," said Charlie, then broke off to clear his throat.

"Forget it, Charlie. Whitman's not even paying you. Where's Bobo Shaw, the missing guest at my party? Charlie, I'd hate to think you were dragging your feet."

"Look, Victor . . ."

"Vic."

"Okay, okay, but Whitman's not even talking to me. He thinks I messed up on Saturday night. And I did, you know, I had you out there watching. . . ."

"But nobody saw anything."

"If you say so, then all right, but I still have to find that painting."

"What about Shaw?" asked Victor.

Charlie finished his juice. He figured he'd drunk at least four gallons of orange juice in the past three days. He wondered how long it would take before his skin developed an orange tint.

"I found out where he lived this morning," said Charlie, "a trailer park on Route Nine in Malta near the drive-in. I drove down there but no one was home. He's probably at work."

"And where's that?"

"I don't know yet."

Shaw's mobile home had been packed together with a lot of others and Charlie had considered talking to some of his neighbors, but there had seemed nothing, as yet, to warrant it. After all, Shaw might have had a perfectly good reason for missing the Super Bowl party. But even as he made that excuse, Charlie knew it was foolish. He felt rushed and Shaw wasn't at the top of his list of priorities. Beyond that, he was still angry with Victor for having had his party, and sometimes he found himself thinking that Victor should just solve his problems by himself.

"So when are you going to find out?"

"Tubbs was going to ask around. I'll be seeing him later. I've got to see Gillespie in about fifteen minutes and I'll find Tubbs after that." But he also had to call his friend in the State Police and he wanted to talk to Mrs. Pellegrino again and then there were his other cases. "Look," said Charlie, "you can try to find out a little about Shaw yourself, you know. It might help."

"I got stuff to do, too," said Victor, stepping away from the bar.

The large Art Deco mirror behind him reflected the back of Victor's balding head as well as Charlie leaning forward and looking determined, with two little up-and-down creases in the middle of his brow. Charlie saw that he had spilled orange juice on the lapel of his brown corduroy jacket and he wiped it off with a paper napkin.

"I guess it depends on how much you want to find your crooks," said Charlie, getting off the barstool and reaching for his overcoat. "If you got a line on Shaw and learned who his friends were . . ."

"Okay, okay," said Victor. "I'll check around. But then you better start looking for him."

"I promise I'll talk to him today," said Charlie, moving toward the door. "Thanks for the juice."

"Anything to keep Dick Tracy healthy," said Victor.

There were seven names on Eddie Gillespie's list of people who had left the museum since the time the first painting was stolen, but four could be disqualified right away—two elderly women had retired, a shipping clerk had moved to California and a secretary had left to have a baby. Charlie and Eddie Gillespie stood in a far corner of the museum under a painting of Gallant Fox, and Eddie was as nervous as if he were doing a drug deal. Gallant Fox stared out at Charlie from a pasture of brown grass—a big lazy horse that had been the second Triple Crown winner, but then had lost the Travers in Saratoga in 1930 to a hundred-to-one shot, Jim Dandy. "Who's Jim Dandy?" Gallant Fox seemed to be saying. "He's nowhere."

"Just take the list and go, Charlie," said Eddie Gillespie. "I don't want anybody to see you."

"But who are these people?"

"Tony Schwartz was a janitor. He'd been here about five years. He left in August to take a custodial job at the high school. Bob Franklin worked in the office. I don't know what he did. He's over at the harness track now. Andy Clamper was a guard, just like me. They fired him."

"How come?"

Eddie pushed one hand back through his black hair. "He kept coming in late or missing work altogether. I don't know, I never met the guy. Now clear out, will you?"

"Have you seen any of these three around the museum recently?"

"Not a trace."

"Ask the people at the desk, will you?"

"Jesus, Charlie, you're going to get me canned."

"Just ask. You can call me at my office around three and tell me what you've learned."

Leaving the museum, Charlie drove over to the high school to talk to Tony Schwartz. It was a sunny day but extremely cold, with the temperature hovering around zero. Charlie's heater in the Renault hardly worked and he drove with a thick wool blanket across his lap. He kept thinking of his cousin as he had seen him the previous night with a whole new personality suddenly revealed. It was as if Robert had had a sex-change operation or had become a religious fanatic. He thought how obsessed and callous his cousin had seemed and again he had to remind himself that compulsive gambling was a disease, that Robert couldn't help himself. Charlie found himself disliking his cousin but he didn't suppose that he loved him any less. After all, he had known him fifty years. Fifty, thought Charlie, can I really be fifty?

Charlie found Tony Schwartz kicking the door of a furnace in the basement of the high school. Great pipes covered the ceiling and stacked around the room were dozens of cases of empty Coke bottles.

"You think the damn thing ever breaks down in September? No way. It waits for the coldest day of the year. These things, they hate you, you know that? They got no souls. They wait till they figure they can really fuck you up, then they let you have it. Never put your trust in a machine. They're out to get you. It's what they were born for."

Schwartz was a short, burly man of forty-five with a bald head and thick rimless glasses perched on the tip of his stubby nose. He had left the museum because he could make more money at the high school and because the vacations were better. He knew nothing of the first painting being stolen and hadn't been to the museum for months. The Sunday night that the painting had disappeared he'd been down at a topless bar in Albany. Charlie could check with the place if he wanted. The star dancer was a girl named Boom Boom Roberta and Schwartz had slipped thirty bucks' worth of singles into her G-string. Schwartz went there every Sunday night. It was what he did instead of going to church. He'd even missed the Super Bowl. Why watch guys killing each other when he could see Boom Boom Roberta? He'd proposed to her last fall, but she'd just laughed. Tony Schwartz laughed as well. Who could blame her turning down a short little bald guy like him?

By quarter of eleven Charlie had left the high school and driven over to the administrative offices of Saratoga Raceway, which were in a sprawling Tudor mansion just past the harness track. Bob Franklin worked in the public relations office. He was young, superior, impeccably dressed and suspicious.

"I don't quite see what you're investigating, Mr. Bradshaw."

"It's not really an investigation," said Charlie. "I'm just asking a few questions."

They stood in the downstairs hall next to a huge desk. The walls were paneled with dark wood. A stairway to Charlie's right led up to a second-floor balcony which surrounded the hall on three sides. Twenty feet above, the ceiling was dark and ornate with painted beams. Bob Franklin looked at Charlie impatiently. He was tall with a thin, pink face and a narrow jaw. As he did with everyone lately, Charlie tried to compare his face with a gibbon, lynx, spaniel and a grouper. Nothing seemed to fit, or maybe they all did, Charlie couldn't be sure. Franklin wore a dark green suit, a white shirt and a purple bow tie.

"But who is employing you, Mr. Bradshaw?" asked Franklin.

"I'm afraid that's confidential information," said Charlie. "So you knew about the first painting being stolen?"

"Has there been another theft?"

Charlie felt depressed. It seemed he was giving out more

information than he was getting back. "Yes, but the way it was done was quite different and the thieves appear to have had some knowledge of the museum."

"And that's why you're here? You think I stole the painting?" Franklin seemed more amused than angry, although it wasn't a friendly sort of amusement.

"It's part of the routine to question former employees," said Charlie, snuffling and clearing his throat. He could have kicked himself for not handling Franklin differently. Most certainly Franklin would be on the phone to the museum or perhaps even Mr. Whitman within the hour.

"I left the museum because I thought I could see a better future with the Racing Commission. Why else does anyone change his job, Mr. Bradshaw? Really, I had no idea that a second painting was stolen. Which one was it?"

"Gallant Fox," said Charlie.

Franklin didn't blink. "And when did this happen?"

"Sunday before last."

"And I suppose you want my alibi for that time?"

"Not necessarily. Primarily I'm interested in knowing if you have any ideas about who could have stolen the painting."

"Was it ransomed back to the museum as before?" Franklin spoke quickly, pressing Charlie with his questions before Charlie felt ready to answer.

"Not really. The ransom money was paid but the painting wasn't returned."

"When was the ransom paid?"

"Friday night."

"Were you employed to deliver the ransom money?"

"That's right," said Charlie. He disliked how clever Franklin seemed to be, as if he understood Charlie's motives without Charlie having to mention them. If Franklin were indeed the thief, his eventual arrest would require a careful, not to say subtle, investigation and at the moment Charlie felt he was only muddying the water.

"I'm afraid I have no ideas about the theft, Mr. Bradshaw, especially since I just learned about it this moment. I don't even know how the painting was stolen."

"Everything is useful, Mr. Franklin," said Charlie, moving toward the door. "You've been a big help. I'll be in touch if I need anything else."

"One thing, Bradshaw."

"What's that?"

"Call first." Franklin gave a little smile, then turned and walked back down the hall, his shoes making an abrupt clicking noise on the hardwood floor.

The third and last name on the list was Andy Clamper, the museum guard who had been fired the previous September. His address was a house on the west side of Saratoga near the train station. Charlie was half tempted to put off his visit until after he had been swimming, but he still felt behind in his investigation and that if he could only move a bit faster he might actually solve something. Yet he hated to miss swimming, cold or no cold, and he imagined his waistline swelling another inch just because of this missed Wednesday in January.

The house was a run-down three-story Victorian with flaking white paint. Some of the windows had a pair of black shutters, some had one shutter and some had none. The walk hadn't been shoveled and at one point Charlie slipped and sank his right leg up to the knee in the snow, about a pound of which went down inside his rubber boot. He climbed the steps of the front porch and rang the bell. As he waited, he took off his boot and shook out the snow. This entailed hopping on one foot since his shoe had remained inside the boot. When he replaced the boot and looked up, Charlie saw a thin, dark-haired woman about forty staring at him through the storm door. She was saying something that he couldn't hear.

"What's that?" asked Charlie.

The woman pushed open the door. She was wearing a quilted pink housecoat open at the top to reveal a triangle of pink flesh.

Her black hair was cut short and lay across her head every which way, as if she never bothered brushing it. "I asked if you were doing a little dance," she said.

"It's called the slip and shuffle," said Charlie. "Why don't you shovel your walk?"

"My husband took off last week and there's been no one to do it."

"I'm sorry," said Charlie, regretting he had spoken.

"That's okay, he was one real son of a bitch and I'm glad to be done with him." The woman scratched under her arm, then gave Charlie a little grin. "Come into the hall before we both freeze to death. You selling vacuum cleaners or something?"

Charlie stepped inside the door, then closed it behind him. The hall was cluttered by about four or five bicycles and a bunch of empty cardboard boxes. "No, I'm looking for Andy Clamper. Does he live here?"

The woman frowned. She had dark brown eyes and a narrow triangular face with a long straight nose. "He rents a room from me but he's at work now, most likely. You got yourself a cold, don't you? Practically everyone does. It's this freezing weather. It gets right inside your lungs and messes you up."

"My cold's almost gone," said Charlie, snuffling a little. "You know where Clamper works?"

"He pumps gas down at that big Sinclair station on Broadway near the Spa City Diner. I had a cold about two weeks ago. My no-good husband gave it to me. First he gives me his cold, then he leaves. That's our marriage in a nutshell."

"I'm sorry," said Charlie. "Couldn't you get Andy Clamper to shovel your walk?"

"That lazy good-for-nothing? Clamper's the sort of person that if he saw a car hit you, he'd cross the street so he wouldn't have to get involved." The woman looked up at Charlie. She had a friendly face that always seemed on the verge of grinning. "Would you like a little drink for that cold? I was just going to have one myself."

"I wouldn't mind," said Charlie.

The woman led the way to the kitchen. Even in her quilted housecoat, she looked trim, as if she'd once been a dancer or a gymnast. He thought of Victor's stories about hot divorcees. Not that Charlie was the kind to start anything.

"What's Clamper like?" asked Charlie, sitting down at a table with a white enamel top. The kitchen smelled of garlic. About thirty chartreuse tennis balls were scattered across the floor and it was impossible to walk without kicking them.

"My littlest kid," said the woman, "she loves tennis balls." She took a bottle of Jim Beam from the counter. "Ice?"

"No thanks."

"Just the way I like it myself," said the woman. She took two jelly glasses from the cupboard, poured a double shot in each, then set one down hard in front of Charlie so a little whiskey sloshed out of the glass. "I don't suppose you smoke," said the woman. "I'd just about kill for a cigarette." And when Charlie shook his head, she sat down across the table, tugged her housecoat closed at the neck, then took a sip of whiskey. "So you don't know Clamper?"

"Never laid eyes on him," said Charlie. He found himself liking this woman and disliking her husband.

"You serving papers or something?"

"Nothing like that, I just want to talk to him."

"You a cop?"

"Private detective. My name's Charlie Bradshaw. Are you going to tell me what Clamper's like?"

The woman looked at him seriously as if trying to make up her mind about something, then she stuck her hand across the table and Charlie shook it. Her hand felt cool and dry. "My name's Janey Dumkowski, or it used to be Dumkowski, maybe it's just Janey Burris again now." She took another sip of whiskey, then coughed and wiped her lips on the back of her hand. "Andy Clamper," she continued more vigorously. "Well, if you ask me, he's one dumb son of a bitch. He spends his life at the track except when he makes little trips to Bridgeport to see the jai alai. He used to cost me a fortune in phone bills until I told him he couldn't make any more calls. He said he had a sick aunt but I didn't believe him. He's a tall, dark-haired guy with hands that seem too big for him. You remember those whoopee cushions you used to be able to buy from joke catalogs? His hands look like whoopee cushions. He's always behind on his rent, keeps his room like a pigsty and I'll bet you five bucks he's the one that stole my toaster oven."

Charlie drank some whiskey. It felt good trickling down his throat, like a benevolent flame. "Why don't you kick him out?" he asked.

"I don't know, I'm used to him, I guess, and he doesn't mind my kids." Janey leaned back in her chair and looked up at the ceiling. Then she straightened up and took another drink. All her movements were quick and abrupt, as if she moved or reached for things at the very last moment of the impulse. Despite this, she still had a kind of grace, and Charlie again wondered if she'd ever been a dancer.

"The nice thing about whiskey," said Janey, "is that it gets you going again."

"For a while," said Charlie. "Then you start slowing up real fast. You think Andy Clampor could be a crook?"

"I don't see why not. The only problem is that Andy's not too bright. If somebody else had him on a leash, then he might be okay, but by himself he'd just make a mess of things. You think he's a crook?"

"He might have swiped a painting of a horse."

"That's just like the guy," said Janey, giving Charlie a wink. "He can't handle the real horses, so he tries the fake ones. Next thing you know, he'll steal a merry-go-round."

Charlie stayed with Janey Burris for another half hour, drinking whiskey, talking about the snow and how she could break her five-year-old daughter of collecting tennis balls or if it really mattered. Apparently, there were more tennis balls in the living room and even more upstairs. Charlie kept telling himself that he was in a hurry. He had to see people, ask questions, solve crimes. Instead he was drinking whiskey in the middle of the day with a woman he hardly knew. He'd even missed swimming. As for Andy Clamper, Charlie didn't learn much more, except to realize that it was extremely unlikely that Clamper could have initiated and carried out the theft of the painting by himself.

"All thumbs," said Janey. "How can you steal a painting with whoopee-cushion hands?"

11

"Roger Phelps," said Captain Mahoney. "I'm telling you, Charlie, that Subaru station wagon was registered to Roger Phelps. Don't keep saying it can't be."

"But it can't be," said Charlie. He was sitting in his office talking to Mahoney on the phone. It was early afternoon on Wednesday and Mahoney had just given him the name and address of the man who owned the car that had picked up the ransom money, but it was all wrong. It couldn't be Roger Phelps.

"Anyway, that's my information," said Mahoney somewhat gruffly. "At least you could thank me for getting it."

"I'm sorry, Rick. I was just surprised, that's all. You know I'm grateful."

"Okay, Charlie, but don't forget, you got to invite me out for ice fishing sometime soon."

"Sure, Rick, as soon as it gets a little warmer." Charlie hung up the phone. The very thought of ice fishing made him reach for another tissue.

But it couldn't be Roger Phelps. Charlie had had no idea who the car might be registered to, but he assumed it would belong to some petty crook down on his luck, someone who could have encouraged Andy Clamper to help him steal the painting. Most likely they were both small-time gamblers and the five thousand for the ransom would take care of some debts, although probably they had gambled it and lost it and bemoaned it before any of those debts had been paid.

But Roger Phelps was a high school science teacher active in a number of liberal causes, well liked, and a superb squash player. The previous fall, he had married Doris Bailes, a woman whom Charlie had been dating for several years. For just a moment Charlie imagined Phelps being arrested and going to jail. What would Doris do? Divorce him? A minuscule spark, not unlike hope, kindled itself deep within Charlie's heart. He had spent many months trying to strip all trace of Doris from his memory until she had at best become no more than a shadow somewhere in a corner of his brain, but now Charlie began to experience a small spiteful pleasure at the thought that Roger Phelps might have stolen the painting: it would certainly show Doris that she had made a mistake.

If Charlie's eminently respectable cousin could have a secret life, then why couldn't Roger Phelps have one, too? And perhaps he had been wrong about Andy Clamper. After all, Phelps was at the high school, and so was that janitor, Tony Schwartz. They could have stolen the painting together. Charlie got up from his desk and put on his overcoat. He'd talk to Phelps; he'd confront him with the evidence.

It took Charlie five minutes to drive to the high school, and he felt confident enough about his suspicions that he went straight to the school office, showed his identification and said it was necessary to see Phelps right away. He was taken down to the teachers' lounge and then stood by the coffee machine, looking stern as Phelps was summoned from class. Actually, Charlie hated being in the high school and he again experienced that trapped and imprisoned sensation which he had felt for most of his school years. As a teenager Charlie had had the misfortune of being both shy and rebellious, which meant he was often the focus of unwanted attention. Many times he had been kicked out of class for talking back or simply talking. His dream had been to slip through without ever being noticed but he just couldn't keep his mouth shut. Even now, as he waited in the teachers' lounge for Phelps to appear, he felt that at any moment someone would start yelling at him.

The door to the hall opened and Roger Phelps hurriedly entered the room. He had a face that was always on the verge of looking sympathetic—moist brown eyes and large, almost rubbery features ready to mold themselves to the needs of whomever he was talking to. Yet there was nothing of the hypocrite about Phelps. His every gesture was laden with sincerity. At the moment he looked concerned and expectant. Phelps was a tall, thin man in his mid-forties who took a day off each April to run in the Boston Marathon. He wore a blue tweed jacket with leather patches on the elbows.

"Charlie, how good to see you. Is something the matter?" Phelps reached out his hand and took Charlie's in both of his. As they shook hands, it struck Charlie that he had nothing against Phelps except that Phelps had married the woman whom Charlie had sometimes imagined marrying himself. But Phelps personally had always treated him well, had been friendly, even respectful. If he had a fault it was that he had absolutely no doubt of Doris's affections. He'd never been jealous of Charlie because it was clear that Charlie had posed no threat. And Charlie, wishing to pose a threat, had been unforgiving.

"It's a case I'm working on," said Charlie. "I have a question for you and it couldn't wait."

Phelps bent toward Charlie so their foreheads were on the same level. He was the sort of tall man who often tried to shrink himself when talking to men shorter than himself, bending his back and his knees, as if not wanting the shorter person to feel uncomfortable. Unfortunately, seeing Phelps hunch toward him tended to make Charlie feel shorter than he actually was.

"That's okay, Charlie," said Phelps. "What's your question?"

"You have a Subaru wagon, is that right? Could you tell me where it was last Friday evening?"

Phelps seemed surprised but the look of concern, plus an eagerness to help, never left his face. Certainly he didn't appear guilty. "It was in the shop, Charlie. I took it in on Thursday for a tune-up and some other work and they couldn't finish it until yesterday."

"Where'd you take it?" asked Charlie, feeling disappointed and then angry with himself. How could he ever have suspected Roger Phelps?

"That big Sinclair station on Broadway just up from the Spa City Diner. Was there some trouble about my car?"

"No, Roger. I mean, it may have been used in a robbery. But don't mention this to anyone, will you?"

Phelps seemed astonished. He still bent over Charlie as if afraid to miss anything he might say. "My car in a robbery?"

"A small robbery. I just wanted to make sure you weren't suspected yourself." To himself, Charlie said, You hypocrite! You awful liar! It depressed him how willing he had been to suspect Phelps and the high school janitor. Maybe it was the whiskey he had drunk with Janey Burris or maybe his cold. Clearly he wasn't thinking straight. As for that Sinclair station, it was the same place where Andy Clamper worked pumping gas.

"Everything will be fine now," Charlie added, again shaking hands with Roger Phelps and standing up as tall as he could. "Give my best to Doris, okay?"

From the high school Charlie drove directly to the gas station on Broadway. He had the sense of slipping farther behind, as if he were wading through deep snow while the crooks, whoever they were, sped forward on plowed roads. It worried him that he had suspected Roger Phelps. If he couldn't see the dividing line between the honest and dishonest, then at least he should be able to distinguish between the probable and improbable. He kept coming back to his cousin and his surprise at Robert's secret life. He had also been surprised that Pellegrino had been a bookie and that Victor had had a gambling party after swearing it would be no more than a couple of friends watching the Super Bowl. These surprises were leading him to doubt everybody, himself most of all. But he had to stop that. He had to get back to the place where he could trust his hunches. It didn't do any good to doubt himself. Maybe it's my cold, he thought again, all this nose-blowing is weakening my brain.

Charlie parked his Renault on the restroom side of the gas station in front of a small mountain of dirty snow. Taking a tissue from the box on the seat, he wiped his nose and tossed the tissue onto the pile accumulating on the floor. Then he got out. It was a large gas station with four bays and a sign saying that foreign cars were their specialty. Charlie entered the office where a pear-shaped woman in blue coveralls was fiddling with the pulley wheel on a greasy alternator. Her brown hair hung in a long braid down her back. Charlie said he was looking for Andy Clamper.

"I haven't seen him all day," said the woman. "Sometimes he's here, sometimes he ain't. He's lucky to be still working."

"Any idea where he might be?"

"Not the faintest. Maybe somebody in there knows." She pointed toward the door to the garage.

Charlie walked to the doorway. Four Japanese cars were being worked on. It pleased him to see that the things could actually break down. A Toyota sedan was up on the nearest rack and a small man also in blue coveralls was working on the front brakes. Charlie went over to him.

"You know where I can find Andy Clamper?" asked Charlie.

The man turned away from the car and wiped his hands on a rag. "I haven't laid eyes on him," he said. "What d'you want him for?"

It occurred to Charlie that he had seen this fellow before. He was a little under Charlie's height, thin and wiry, with a round face and small brown eyes that looked like a pair of buttons. Charlie guessed he was about forty. He had long black greasy hair that he kept brushing away from his eyes with greasy hands. It seemed to Charlie that this fellow recognized him as well but was trying not to show it.

"I had some questions about his car insurance," said Charlie. "There might be some problems with it. You know when he'll be back?"

"Tomorrow morning, most likely." The man kept looking at Charlie, almost suspiciously, yet at the same time trying not to look suspicious. He'd picked up a socket wrench and held it loosely in his right hand. As he spoke, he steadily turned the ratchet so that his words were accompanied by a faint clicking noise. Across the garage another mechanic threw a tire and its rim to the concrete floor where it clanged and bounced.

Charlie kept staring at the man, trying to think where he had seen him before. In a store, in a restaurant? On the street? Then he remembered. This was the fellow he had bumped into at Pellegrino's Grocery the previous week, the man who had wanted to fight him. Maybe he's embarrassed about it, thought Charlie.

"You know where I could find him tonight?" asked Charlie.

"Do I look like his mother?" asked the other man, getting angry. Then he shrugged and tried to look relaxed.

"Maybe somebody else here would know where to find him," suggested Charlie. A Datsun on the end was started up and its motor was revved higher and higher. Charlie had to raise his voice over the noise.

"Feel free to ask," said the man. He turned back to the Toyota, fitting the socket wrench onto a nut holding the caliper of the disk brakes.

Charlie watched the man for a moment, then went off to talk to the other three mechanics. None of them had seen Clamper that day, nor had they any idea where he was. It was clear that Clamper was somebody they hardly knew and didn't care about. He'd only worked at the garage for a few months and many days he never showed up. Charlie asked one man if he might find Clamper at the harness track and was told that if the horses were running, then he was sure to be there. After a few more questions Charlie gave up. He could think of nothing more to ask. Later he'd look for Clamper at the roominghouse and, if he wasn't there, he'd try the gas station again in the morning. As Charlie left, he thought that the first mechanic, the fellow who had wanted to fight him at Pellegrino's Grocery, was being careful to avoid his eye. Charlie wondered if the man didn't feel bad about their encounter. Certainly he himself had sometimes snapped at people and then felt guilty about it for days afterward.

It was two-thirty when Charlie left the garage and he still hadn't eaten lunch. Often he ate with Victor but he knew that if he went to the hotel, Victor would blame him for not having located Bobo Shaw. He hadn't even tried finding Maximum Tubbs to see if Tubbs had learned where Shaw worked. The trouble was that even though Victor and Maximum Tubbs were paying him, Charlie didn't feel happy about the job. The thought of what his mother would say about the robbery at the hotel kept haunting those minutes before Charlie went to sleep each night and was the first thing he thought about in the morning. But Charlie knew he was being foolish. It only made sense to help Victor. It would be terrible if one of the guests at Victor's party got angry and started blabbing all over town. So the best Charlie could do was to grab a sandwich at the Executive, then head down to the trailer park in Malta where Bobo Shaw lived, start talking to his neighbors and see where he could be found.

The trailer park was on Route 9 about ten miles south of Saratoga Springs. Earlier that day Charlie had done no more than knock on Shaw's door, wait for a couple of minutes and leave. He'd even been happy not to find Shaw at home. Let

Victor solve his own problems, he'd said to himself. Shaw's particular trailer or mobile home was mustard yellow and rusting at the bottom. The green curtains in the windows were ragged, and under a plywood shelter to the side was a rusty car engine sitting on cinder blocks. The trailer looked like the sort of place that had changed hands every six months for fifteen years. The park itself was sprawling and shabby, and now in late January it bore a huddled look. A stiff wind was drifting the snow against the trailers and filling the air with a white cloud. Charlie again knocked on Shaw's door but there was no answer. After a moment, he went to the next trailer and knocked. From inside he could hear a television and a familiar jingle advertising toothpaste.

The door opened and a big broad-shouldered man in a brown turtleneck looked down at Charlie. He didn't speak but stared at Charlie as if expecting him to do something.

"I'm looking for Bobo Shaw," said Charlie.

"Next door," said the man. He had a yellowish face and slicked-back black hair. With his wide shoulders and narrow hips, he reminded Charlie of a chubby torpedo.

"He's not home," said Charlie.

"Well, he ain't here either," said the man, beginning to shut the door.

"Wait," said Charlie. "I'm from Credit International and it's my job to ask people sensitive and personal questions. Mr. Shaw has applied for a loan. If Mr. Shaw wanted to borrow one hundred dollars from you, would you lend it to him?" Charlie attempted a forthright and honest smile.

"No," said the man, "I wouldn't."

"Why not?" asked Charlie.

"He already owes me a hundred bucks. He borrows from me, he borrows from everybody. That hundred bucks, you think I'll ever see it again? I would have done better giving it to my old mother." The man looked depressed, then he rubbed his stomach. A tiger-colored cat pushed through Charlie's legs and began scratching at the door. The man let it in.

"What's Shaw do for a living?" asked Charlie. It was cold and Charlie had begun to shiver, but he wanted to keep the man talking.

"He's a mechanic, a good mechanic. He used to have a garage down in Albany. And he did a lot of work on stock cars. But he pissed it all away. He's a gambler. He'll fuckin' bet on anything. So he went bankrupt, although I guess he still works at the track now and then, you know, stock-car racing. If I was you, I wouldn't lend him the money. I mean, I don't want to do him a bad turn, but if you give him the money he'll lose it in no time. Then he'll just be back for more."

"You know where I can find him?" asked Charlie.

Was it just coincidence or a lucky guess that made Charlie realize what the man was going to say before he said it? But Charlie already knew that Shaw was a mechanic. And at how many places in Saratoga could he work? And hadn't he been brooding about seeing that guy at Pellegrino's Grocery?

"He works in a garage on Broadway. You know that Sinclair place down from the Spa City Diner? That's the one."

"What's he look like?" asked Charlie. He began to feel chilled again, but this time it wasn't from the cold.

"He's a little monkey-looking guy with longish black hair. You can't miss him."

All the way back to Saratoga Charlie yelled at himself. How could he have been so stupid? If he had looked for Shaw more carefully that morning, then he would have been able to surprise him at the gas station. But now Shaw knew about his interest in Clamper and would guess Charlie's eventual interest in himself. It was clear there was a connection between Clamper and Shaw just as it was clear there was a connection between Shaw and the robbery at the hotel. Possibly there was even a connection between Shaw and Pellegrino. Charlie had bumped into him coming out of the store. And what kind of animal did Bobo Shaw look like? A monkey, a gibbon. How could Charlie have been so stupid? There was even a chance that Shaw was the one who was blackmailing Charlie's cousin. He might even have killed Pellegrino. Charlie hammered on the steering wheel with both fists. What an idiot!

It was four o'clock and getting dark by the time Charlie made it back to the Sinclair station. Shaw was gone. The woman in the office said he had left in a rush, claiming that something important had come up. "Probably off to see his bookie," she said. Charlie asked what kind of car Shaw was driving. A black Chevrolet Impala, souped up with a lot of chrome. For a moment, Charlie considered going back down to the trailer park to wait for him, but he couldn't just chase him, he had to intercept him and that meant learning more about him.

Still displeased with himself, Charlie drove back to his office. When he entered, the phone was ringing. It stopped when he ran to it, but then it started again about a minute later. The caller was Eddie Gillespie.

"Charlie, I been trying to get you all afternoon. Where you been?"

"Just lounging around," said Charlie. "Just taking it easy and putting my feet up." Jesse James was looking at him as if he were a real dope. I am, thought Charlie, I'm a real dope.

Gillespie was silent for a moment, then continued as if Charlie hadn't spoken. "I been asking people about Andy Clamper. It turns out he was in the museum a couple of weeks ago. He showed up with another guy. They were just looking around. And you know what? He wasn't just fired for being late. There'd been stuff missing. A radio, a typewriter. Nobody could prove anything but they were sure it was him. How d'you like that? The guy's a crook."

12

Janey Dumkowski née Burris bent forward and stared at the amber fluid in the jelly glass. Then she swirled it around, drank a little and coughed. "You think this stuff could really rot your brain?" she asked.

"I doubt it," said Charlie. "Most likely it would just pickle it, like those snakes and frogs you see pickled in alcohol in science exhibits."

"Probably wouldn't be any good for thinking anymore," said Janey. She sipped a little more, then wiped her mouth with the back of her hand. "Sure is good though."

It was five-thirty Wednesday afternoon and Charlie was again back at Andy Clamper's roominghouse drinking whiskey with his landlady. Her three girls were home from school and watching "Sesame Street" on the TV in the living room—that is, when they weren't throwing chartreuse tennis balls at one another. Every now and then there would be a scream and Janey would go into the living room to console whoever had gotten banged on the head. A kettle was simmering on the stove. Charlie didn't know what it was but it smelled of garlic and lemons. Some kind of soup, he thought. Charlie was waiting for Andy Clamper, although he didn't expect him to show up. What he wanted was to get a look at Clamper's room but he hadn't as yet mentioned this to Janey Burris.

"You drink a lot of whiskey?" asked Charlie.

"Only when my husband leaves me," said Janey. She was wearing jeans and a thick blue sweater. Her short black hair clung to her head as if it had been painted on. When Charlie had arrived, she had been drinking whiskey and doing her nails—each nail a different color: red, blue, silver, peach, green.

"Then you keep drinking until he comes back?"

"I don't know, he's never left before. Anyway, even if he came crawling back, I wouldn't let him in. We are over and done. Fred Dumkowski and Janey Burris Dumkowski are history. He said he wanted to travel and see the world. I hope his plane gets hijacked."

Charlie took a sip of whiskey and let it roll around in his mouth. Janey kept smiling when she spoke so he couldn't tell how serious she was. Although he had found her drinking whiskey, she had seemed perfectly sober except for a kind of wild talk.

"Maybe you should eat something," suggested Charlie.

"Now don't start trying to be helpful," said Janey. "I don't need it."

"Okay, then don't eat anything." A chartreuse tennis ball came bouncing through the doorway. Charlie grabbed it and threw it back. Then he gathered up a couple more and threw those back as well. It felt good throwing things. He didn't know why he didn't do it more often. "By the way," said Charlie, "I want to take a look at Clamper's room. Will you open it for me?"

Janey had her elbows on the white enamel surface of the kitchen table, supporting her chin in her hands. She grinned at Charlie. "Isn't that against the law?"

"Sure."

"What if he showed up?"

"You could say I was the exterminator."

"You think he's a crook?" asked Janey. Her grin was lop-sided, going up half an inch higher on the right than on the left.

"Earlier I suspected he was a crook and now I know he's a crook. He and a friend swiped a painting from the racing museum, then tried to ransom it. They got the ransom money but didn't return the painting."

"That's why you're looking for him? Because you think he stole that painting?"

"That's right."

"And you think the painting is in his room?"

"No, but there might be something that'll give me an idea where I can find him."

"Well, shit," said Janey, "if we keep sitting down here we'll just get soused. Let's go take a peek." She jumped up and took a ring full of keys from a hook by the door, then led the way through the hallway, pausing only at the living room to speak to her children. "If you kids want macaroni and cheese tonight, you'd better quiet down."

Janey's three daughters looked like miniature versions of herself—dark brown eyes, short black hair and straight noses. Fred Dumkowski had probably felt badly outnumbered. As Charlie looked in at them, a tennis ball came flying toward him. He caught it and sneezed. Then he tossed it back.

"Haven't you gotten rid of that cold yet?" asked Janey, climbing the stairs. "You need more whiskey."

"I think I've had enough whiskey," said Charlie.

"I bet you just think I'm a fast woman, don't you?" asked Janey, pausing on the stairs and looking back.

Charlie stopped abruptly to keep from bumping into her. "Not necessarily," he said.

"What do you mean, 'necessarily'?"

"You might just be lonely," said Charlie. "I mean, it must

be confusing to have your husband leave, even if you didn't like him."

"You feel like some macaroni and cheese later?" asked Janey.

Charlie again began to follow her up the stairs. "I guess I could manage that," he said. "What's that soup cooking on the stove? It smells good."

"That's not soup. I'm dyeing some socks."

"Oh," said Charlie.

Andy Clamper had a room on the second floor toward the back, right next to the bathroom. It was a large room with an unmade single bed, a green armchair and a table supporting a small color TV. There were no pictures on the walls and no books. The room smelled of sour laundry and beer cans.

Charlie began searching the room. In the closet, beneath the sour laundry, he found a stack of car radios, at least fifty of them, mostly Blaupunkts, but also a few Pioneers and Sonys. There was also a toolkit with a slim jim and several other thin strips of metal which would be useful for breaking into cars. The radios indicated at least one thing that Clamper was pretty good at despite his whoopee-cushion hands: breaking into cars. Charlie again concealed the radios with the laundry, then continued looking around the room. He could find no pieces of paper, nothing with a name on it, nothing to suggest where Clamper might be found except for a stack of old parimutuel tickets on the table by the TV.

"What do you think of this?" asked Janey. She had been looking under the bed and was now holding up a short metal leash with a chrome-plated choke chain and a muzzle.

Charlie went over to look at it. The muzzle was dark leather, partly chewed and seemed to be meant for a smallish dog.

"He ever had a dog up here?" asked Charlie.

"Not that I've seen. My cats wouldn't like it."

Charlie was struck by how thick the chains were. "Then I don't know," he said.

* * *

Charlie left Janey Burris's around eight-thirty. He was tired and wanted to go home but he had several more stops to make. First he drove down to the trailer park in Malta to see if Bobo Shaw had shown up. He hadn't, and the neighbor who looked like a plump torpedo hadn't seen him. Then Charlie drove out to Pellegrino's Grocery. He wanted to talk to Mrs. Pellegrino and half an hour earlier he had called her to say he would be there around nine.

Charlie had stayed at Janey's for macaroni and cheese but Clamper had never arrived. After dinner Charlie had read her daughters weird stories out of the Brothers Grimm. At least a dozen times he told himself that he must leave but he couldn't bring himself to do it. It was comfortable at her house and the whiskey was soothing. At last he decided he was being self-indulgent and foolish. He called Mrs. Pellegrino, said good-night to the kids and left.

"Come back when you want more whiskey," Janey had said.

Mrs. Pellegrino was waiting at the door of the grocery when Charlie pulled into the parking lot. As he got out of the Renault, she began calling to him.

"Come in, come in! It's freezing. How is your cold?"

"Better," snuffled Charlie as he climbed the steps.

"You lie," said Mrs. Pellegrino, pushing him into the grocery and shutting the door. "You should be in bed."

"That's what I keep telling myself," said Charlie. He continued across the dark grocery toward Mrs. Pellegrino's small living room.

"I'll make you something hot," said Mrs. Pellegrino.

"No whiskey," said Charlie. "I'm at my limit."

"Just a touch," said Mrs. Pellegrino, "for your chest." She paused at the kitchen door and looked back—a tiny woman in a black dress. "Have you found the person who killed my Joe?"

"Not yet, but I think I'm getting closer. I have some questions for you."

"You wait till I make your drink." Mrs. Pellegrino disappeared into the kitchen.

Charlie took off his overcoat and sat down in one of the armchairs by the wood stove, stretching out his legs until he could feel the heat on his ankles. Apart from the sounds of Mrs. Pellegrino rustling about in the kitchen, the only other noise was the ticking of the pendulum clock. Charlie knew if he closed his eyes he'd fall asleep, so he rubbed them and propped them open with his fingers. Was he really getting closer? Maybe. At least he was almost positive that Andy Clamper and Bobo Shaw had stolen the painting from the museum and that Shaw had had some connection with the robbery at the hotel. It also seemed possible that Shaw was Gibbon, which was one of the things Charlie had come to find out about.

"Are you falling asleep?" asked Mrs. Pellegrino, returning with a steaming glass that smelled of whiskey and lemon.

"Just resting my eyes," said Charlie.

"You're just like my Joe. You work too hard."

Charlie accepted the glass and sat up. He had to stay alert. He took a sip and burned his lips. Rubbing them vigorously on the back of his hand, he set the glass on the floor by his chair. Then he extracted a tissue from his jacket pocket and blew his nose. All this time Mrs. Pellegrino watched him expectantly from the other armchair.

"I realize you don't know the names of your husband's gambling customers," began Charlie, "but I wondered if you knew anything else about them. For instance, the man he called Gibbon was a garage mechanic and it occurred to me that he might have worked on Joe's car. He might have done that instead of paying some money he owed."

"Joe always took his car to the same place," said Mrs. Pellegrino, wrinkling her brow.

"And where was that?"

"There's a Sinclair station on Broadway. He took it there."

"And did he ever mention Gibbon working on his car?"

"I don't know, he might have."

"What about the others?" asked Charlie. "Spaniel, Grouper, Lynx, Horse. Did he ever mention them in connection with anything?"

Mrs. Pellegrino looked up at Charlie and pointed over his shoulder. "That clock," she said. "Joe got that from the Spaniel and he got an antique bureau from him as well and also our dining room table, a big round oak table." Mrs. Pellegrino looked pleased with herself.

Charlie got up to inspect the clock—a pendulum clock with a cherry wood case. It was clearly an antique and he hoped there would be some stamp with the dealer's name. But there was nothing. Nor was there any name on the bureau or dining room table. Even so, as he returned to the small living room, Charlie decided that Spaniel was possibly an antiques dealer who had given Joe the clock, table and bureau in lieu of money he owed him. Either that or he was just a man who owned a lot of antiques. Perhaps he hadn't advanced very far after all.

"Did you ever see Spaniel?" asked Charlie, sitting down.

"I don't think so, but there were many people who came into the grocery."

"Did you ever see any of the others?"

"I think I saw the Grouper," said Mrs. Pellegrino. "He drives a little truck with great big tires and when it rained it would leave great ruts in the parking lot. I said something to Joe and he just said, 'That's Grouper. He can't help himself.' "

"Was it a Bronco with big tires?" asked Charlie.

"I don't know what kind of car it was. I only cared about the tires. They made a mess of everything."

"Did he say anything else about Grouper?"

Mrs. Pellegrino sat quietly for a moment and looked down at her small black shoes. Charlie drank his hot whiskey. It was good but he felt a little drunk. "I know," said the old woman, "one time Joe said it would be better if Grouper looked like Horse and Horse looked like Grouper since Grouper owned horses. Does that make sense?"

"I guess so," said Charlie. "Did Grouper own racehorses?"

"I don't know."

"What about Lynx and Horse? Did he ever say anything about them? For instance, he might have bought insurance from Horse."

"No, we get our insurance from my son-in-law in Glens Falls." Mrs. Pellegrino thought a moment, then she said, "I don't think he ever mentioned Lynx at all."

Charlie continued asking Mrs. Pellegrino questions for another ten minutes, but she could remember nothing else. Still, Charlie had learned something. He was now positive that Shaw was Gibbon, which made it possible that he was the one attempting to blackmail Robert. After all, Shaw was a petty crook and constantly in debt. And he knew that Spaniel possibly sold antiques and that Grouper owned horses and drove a little truck with oversized wheels, which was likely the same Ford Bronco that Robert had seen on the night of the murder. Thanking Mrs. Pellegrino, Charlie walked with her to the door.

"You'll see," she said, "by tomorrow your cold will be gone."

"I certainly hope so," said Charlie.

By eleven Charlie had his teeth brushed and was climbing into bed. He felt groggy from all the whiskey and too tired to read. But just as he was reaching to turn out the bedside lamp, the telephone rang. Groaning, Charlie climbed from bed and made his way into the living room. It was Eddie Gillespie.

"Charlie, I picked up a little more information about Andy Clamper. You interested?"

"Sure," said Charlie, yawning. He could hear music and people talking in the background, and he assumed Eddie was in a bar.

"Just how interested, Charlie?" shouted Eddie over the bar noise. "I want you to be really interested."

Not only was Eddie in a bar, he sounded drunk. "I'm really interested," said Charlie, wiping his nose on the sleeve of his pajamas.

"Clamper's into dogfights, a real fanatic. There's one down in Albany tomorrow night. You want to go?"

"Dogfights?" asked Charlie. He had never been to a dogfight and for a moment he imagined beagles in boxing gloves.

"Pit bulls. They'll have about eight fights. Guys bet on them. It's in a warehouse. You interested or not?"

"And Clamper will be there?"

"That's what I hear. Give me an answer, my beer's getting warm."

"How d'you know about this?"

"My buddy. You want to talk to him? He says you arrested him once. Larry Corn, he says you got him for drunk and disorderly. You want to say hello?"

"That's okay," said Charlie. He had no memory of the man.

"You sure? He's right here."

There was a banging sound as if the phone had been dropped and then a strange voice came on the line. "Sergeant Bradshaw, you remember me, Sergeant Bradshaw? I tried to smack you with a bottle right outside the Tin and Lint."

"Sure," said Charlie, still not remembering. Larry Corn sounded even drunker that Gillespie. "How've you been doing?"

"Can't complain. How 'bout yourself?"

"Fine. Got a little cold, that's all. Let me talk to Eddie again."

There was another banging noise as if the phone had again been dropped. "Larry says you nearly broke his arm that night," said Eddie. "You want to go to those dogfights?"

"Sure, sure, let's go. What time is this anyway?"

"Around eleven. The very shank of the evening. I'll pick you up at the Bentley."

Charlie hung up, then stood thinking. In his memory was an image of Janey Burris holding up the leash, choke chain and muzzle that she had found under Andy Clamper's bed.

The phone rang again. Charlie almost ignored it, thinking it was again Larry Corn, then picked it up after the fifth ring. It was Grace Washburn. Charlie had meant to call her earlier but had forgotten.

"I've been calling you all evening," she said.

"I've been out," said Charlie. He thought of Janey Burris and felt guilty.

"You've been working?"

"I've had to talk to a lot of people."

"Boy, it seems your job's easy. Just talking to people. I wish I could just talk to people. Do you still like me?" Grace had a high soprano voice. She spoke softly, making her voice sound childlike.

"Sure I like you," said Charlie.

"Do you like me a lot?"

Charlie listened to Grace's breathing. "Sure I like you a lot," he said.

"Have you brushed your teeth?"

"You bet."

"Both up and down?"

"Sure."

"You get all the cracks?"

"I tried."

"I'll see on Saturday. Are we still going out?"

"Sure," said Charlie.

"And you really like me?"

"Of course I do," said Charlie.

"I miss you," said Grace.

"I miss you, too," said Charlie.

They talked like this for another fifteen minutes as Charlie stood with his feet getting colder and colder. But he thought how the cold was good for him. It was a kind of punishment. Consequently it was midnight by the time he got to bed.

13

George Whitman stood in front of Charlie's desk looking down at him.

"Mr. Bradshaw, although I can't go so far as to call your tomfoolery illegal, it's certainly unethical. I asked you to drop this matter, and now I find you are pursuing it on your own. Clearly, if the theft were not so sensitive, I would report your behavior to Chief Peterson and the licensing board. As it is, I will make certain you never again receive employment from anybody of my acquaintance. And Mr. Bradshaw," said Whitman, with a little smile, "I have a wide acquaintance."

"I'm sure you do," said Charlie, who had an image of a great telephone book with a black X across the cover. He remembered how pleased he was when Whitman had hired him. Now he wished he'd never seen the man. Whitman had brought him nothing but trouble. Although perhaps, thought Charlie, I brought the trouble on myself. It was around ten Thursday morning and again it was snowing, a fine blowing snow that was already building up on the ledge outside Charlie's window.

Whitman wore a London Fog overcoat with a thick blue wool scarf. In his right hand he held a tan sheepskin hat of the sort, Charlie thought, that people like Robin Hood used to wear.

Charlie suspected that Whitman had lots of warm coats and warm hats for every gradation of the weather. Whitman's narrow face was red, and he stared at Charlie as if he were a practical joke of which Whitman was the victim.

"Really, Mr. Bradshaw, when I ask that something be done I'm accustomed to being obeyed. You should never have talked to Bob Franklin over at Saratoga Raceway. We can't allow this to become public knowledge. God knows who else you've told. I can't see why you've continued your meddling."

"I've been trying to find your painting," said Charlie stubbornly. Right from the beginning, he and Whitman had had their troubles, just like cats and dogs. He started to reach for a tissue from the box on the desk, then decided to wait.

"The painting will turn up," said Whitman. "They always do. But I promise you, if the thieves learn you're searching for them, they'll destroy it. That would be a terrible loss, Mr. Bradshaw, and you would be responsible. Can't you leave well enough alone?"

"But I think I can really . . . ," Charlie began, but it was too late. Whitman turned and left the room, slamming the door so that the glass rattled, then slamming the outside door as well.

Was Whitman right? Charlie asked himself. Have I done nothing but cause trouble? Perhaps he should forget about Andy Clamper. But even if he forgot Clamper, he still had to find Bobo Shaw—neither of them had been at the Sinclair station that morning. Nor had they been in their respective homes—Shaw in the trailer park and Clamper at Janey Burris's. Charlie had checked both places. Beyond that, Charlie still had to decide what to do about those stolen radios in Clamper's closet. No, he couldn't forget Clamper. And he'd find the painting as well. He'd bring it back and Mr. Whitman would see that he'd been mistaken to doubt him. He might even apologize.

Charlie heard the outside door open again and for a second he imagined it was Mr. Whitman returning to say he was sorry. But then there was a quick tap, the office door was briskly pushed open and Artemis entered—one of the few human

beings whom Charlie could see without wishing to be someplace else. He jumped up and walked around the desk to welcome her.

"When did you get back?" he asked, reaching out his hand.

Artemis was a professional equestrienne and had been per-
forming in Vienna since October. When she wasn't on tour she
was often found at her horse farm near Cambridge, about
twenty miles from Saratoga. She was a small woman, several
inches shorter than Charlie, and her trim figure was at the
moment obscured by an ankle-length raccoon-skin coat. Artemis was probably about forty, although there was no gray in
her dark hair, which fell in a wave over her forehead and nearly
covered her left eye. She had a narrow, beautiful face with what
Charlie thought of as finely chiseled features.

Artemis took Charlie's hand and patted it. "A week. Now I
have to decompress for another week or so before flying to
Buenos Aires. It's summer there and the Argentines want to
see me flit from horse to horse."

"Decompress?" asked Charlie.

"You know those decompression chambers which divers must
brood in before being exposed to real life? Vienna is so rare-
fied." Artemis had left Charlie to investigate the picture of Jesse
James. She moved quickly, swirling her great coat around her.

"They get the bends," said Charlie.

"Exactly," said Artemis. "The same thing would happen to
me if I went directly to Buenos Aires from Vienna. I had to
come home and see dear Phillip."

Phillip was her favorite horse and once Charlie had stood on
his back in his stocking feet. He hadn't liked it much, but neither
had he forgotten it.

"Do any of your customers ever remark on your fondness
for the outlaw life?" asked Artemis, sitting down on the edge
of Charlie's desk.

"Why should they?" How odd that Maximum Tubbs had
recently asked a similar question.

"Some might think it a conflict of interest." Artemis unbuttoned her coat and glanced around Charlie's small office. "I see no improvements since I was here last."

"Things stay pretty much the same."

"You have a cold? Your voice sounds all froggy."

"It's almost gone."

"And you're working?"

"I've got several cases."

"That's too bad," said Artemis, crossing her leg and kicking her foot up and down. "I was hoping to interest you in Buenos Aires. You could be my general factotum."

"Would I have to ride a horse?" asked Charlie, who didn't like to ride horses.

"No, you'd just have to make sure the show was running smoothly. I would amaze the cheering crowds and you would be the secret power behind the throne, like grease on ball bearings."

"I couldn't get away right now," said Charlie. But to himself he was saying, Go, drop everything, get out of here! Where was Buenos Aires anyway? South. Far, far south.

"I was afraid of that," said Artemis, looking disappointed, "but I had to ask."

"What makes you think I'd be any good as a general factotum?" asked Charlie.

Artemis glanced up at Charlie under her wave of dark hair. "You're methodical, you never skip any steps and you're modest. Also, you're amusing. What else can anybody ask in a factotum?"

"Well, I wish I could do it. . . ."

"I know, I know, crime is your first love." Artemis hopped off the desk and made for the door, pausing briefly by Charlie to give him a swift peck on the cheek. "But don't refuse right away. Think about it in the still watches of the night. And even if it's no, you must come out to tea. Phillip misses you. I'll be here through the first week in February."

Charlie began to say good-bye, but Artemis was already out

the door. He imagined calling Mr. Whitman to say he was going to Buenos Aires to be the general factotum of a famous equestrienne. Charlie sighed. There was still that nuisance of a painting. And he had to find the men who had robbed Victor's Super Sunday Gambling Fete. And Mrs. Pellegrino, she was counting on him, too.

Around noon Charlie wandered up to the Bentley where he had agreed to meet Maximum Tubbs. The hotel was closed but Victor had said he'd make them lunch. It was still snowing, a fine, almost dry snow which the wind blew in horizontal planes down Broadway. Charlie was the only pedestrian on the street. Deep within him a sharp voice was urging him to go directly to the Y and swim his mile, but his nose was still running and the very thought of swimming left him chilled to the bone. Besides that, he was depressed, and he never swam well when he was depressed. He thumped on the front door of the hotel and Victor opened it.

"You look like that reindeer with the red nose," said Victor, standing aside to let Charlie enter. "Randolph or Buster or whatever his name was."

Charlie stamped his feet on the mat. "Is Tubbs here?"

"Nope. Come into the bar where it's warm. You want hot alcohol or hot nonalcohol?" Victor led the way. He wore a gray suit and a pair of bright red slippers with curled toes that made him look like a genie.

"Nonalcohol, I guess." There was a fire in the lounge and the logs made crackling noises. Charlie went over to stand beside it, rubbing his hands together. He found himself thinking of Buenos Aires and how warm it must be there.

"So you caught my crooks yet?" asked Victor, bringing Charlie a cup of coffee.

"Not yet, but I got some leads. You feel like going to a dogfight tonight?"

"Jesus, Charlie, I didn't know you were into that stuff."

"I'm not but I might be able to get a line on one of

your crooks. It's in Albany. I'm going down with Eddie Gillespie."

"Sure, sure, I've always been a dog lover. They won't bite me, will they?"

"Not if you don't wear those slippers."

Maximum Tubbs showed up five minutes later, and shortly the three men were gathered around the table eating a thick vegetable soup which Victor claimed to have made himself. Maximum Tubbs was skeptical. He ate it with a spoon which he had brought with him, drawing it out of a little case that he carried in the inside pocket of his brown suit.

"At least I'll know the germs are my germs," he'd said.

"Shit, you could of lapped it up like a dog and saved the bother," Victor answered.

With the soup was a long loaf of French bread that Victor wanted to tear with his hands. Maximum Tubbs insisted he use a knife. As they ate, Charlie told them about Andy Clamper and Bobo Shaw, and how they were the ones who had probably stolen the painting. He didn't mention that he'd talked to Shaw without knowing who he was and apparently had frightened him away. Tubbs had also learned that Shaw worked at the Sinclair station and if Charlie had talked to Tubbs earlier, as he had originally intended, then most likely he could have confronted Shaw by now. Instead, they would have to chase down to Albany.

"And you think they'll be at these dogfights?" asked Victor.

"I don't know about Shaw, but Clamper is supposed to be there."

"Maybe they're also the two guys that robbed our party," said Victor.

Maximum Tubbs dabbed his mouth with his large white cotton handkerchief. "That's not Bobo Shaw's style," he said. "He's not a crook, he's a gambler. Unfortunately, he's also a loser so sometimes he has to sell things like information or sometimes he passes bad checks."

"Could he kill someone?" asked Charlie, thinking of Pellegrino.

"It seems unlikely, but I suppose he might. Who'd you have in mind?"

Charlie explained that Shaw was one of Joe Pellegrino's five customers. He had not told Tubbs or Victor about his cousin Robert, although he expected he would have to eventually. He found himself embarrassed even thinking about him. "If Shaw lost big on the Super Bowl," said Charlie, "he might be tempted to kill Pellegrino."

"Plus he could make a lot besides," said Tubbs. "Pellegrino must have been holding a wad of money to pay off the winning bets." Tubbs patted his hair, which was the color of polished pewter.

"That's the other thing I wanted to talk about," said Charlie. "I've got a little information on two of Pellegrino's other customers. Maybe you have some ideas about them."

"You know their names?" asked Tubbs.

"Just their animal names—Spaniel and Grouper. Spaniel may be in the antiques business and Grouper drives a big Ford Bronco with oversized tires and raises horses. I figured if they were gamblers, you might know something about them."

"So one guy looks like a spaniel," said Victor, "and the other looks like a grouper, is that right?"

Charlie started to answer, but began coughing instead. It seemed his cold was settling firmly in his chest. Victor clapped him on the back while Maximum Tubbs covered his mouth with his handkerchief and looked disapproving.

"Isn't a grouper one of those sexy girls who chases rock stars?" asked Victor when Charlie had recovered.

"Groupie," said Charlie, taking a drink of water.

"Fish face," said Tubbs. "It means the guy looks like a fish." Tubbs pushed back his chair. He had eaten half his soup and was sipping a glass of Saratoga Vichy. "The guy in the antiques business doesn't ring any bells, but the Ford Bronco, I don't know. I've seen one of those around. And that fish business rings a bell. You say he's a serious gambler?"

"He helped support Pellegrino. Maybe you've played cards with him," said Charlie.

"This town's full of gamblers," said Victor. "And what's to say that Pellegrino's customers were from around here anyway?"

But Maximum Tubbs looked skeptical. "I don't know," he said again. "I've seen one of those Broncos somewhere." He got to his feet. "Can I use your phone?"

"You got a quarter?" asked Victor.

"I'll write you a check."

"Okay, okay, use the one in the office."

Tubbs went off across the bar to the lobby. Charlie glanced at Victor, who was trying to pluck one of the hairs from his nose. "Anyone ever tell you you were difficult?" asked Charlie.

Victor made an abrupt yanking movement away from his face, then winced. "Only my friends," he said. He looked at the hair caught between his thumb and index finger, then dropped it in the ashtray. "So how's old Grace Washburn," he continued, "still polishing your choppers?"

Charlie felt a guilty pang which he was at a loss to explain. "She's fine," he said.

"I bit my last dentist," said Victor. "I don't know what came over me. Like I fainted and suddenly I woke up and this guy was howling his lungs out. Nearly took his finger off. He couldn't even finish the job. Had to call in his assistant. I never went back after that, thought he might jab me with his drill just to get even. You ever bite that Washburn girl?"

"Not yet," said Charlie, feeling guilty again.

"I used to date a woman who was into biting," said Victor. "Never got used to it. You know how some horses are gun-shy? I got mouth-shy. What the fuck, we were spending whole evenings shaking hands. I didn't dare turn my back on her."

Maximum Tubbs came back a few minutes later. "I think I

got a line on this fish guy, Charlie. Let's get your car and go find him."

Charlie tossed down his napkin and got to his feet. "Is he in town?"

"He may be at the track."

"Now? It's covered with two feet of snow."

"That's nothing to bother anybody," said Tubbs, heading for the door.

14

The clubhouse at Saratoga Raceway was three-quarters full, and on the TV monitors a race had just begun. Charlie and Maximum Tubbs paused at the top of the stairs, unbuttoning their coats. The murmur of voices grew louder as the race progressed and people began to shout. With the increasing roar, Charlie instinctively looked out through the great windows at the track where the snowstorm continued unabated and an unbroken field of white spread as far as the row of pine trees bordering Nelson Avenue half a mile away. There was no horse anywhere in sight. A waitress asked if they wanted a table. The crescendo of voices peaked and the race came to an end with the usual moans mixed with the few happy voices of the winners.

"We're looking for someone," said Tubbs, turning his head to glance around the room.

Charlie guessed the race was being piped in from Aqueduct. The crowd looked so much like a typical racing crowd that Charlie again glanced out at the snow-covered track just to make sure he wasn't missing something. There were a lot of middle-aged men in shirtsleeves reading the *Racing Form* as they chewed on pencils or cigars. There were men in three-piece suits, men in work clothes, women in flowered dresses with quick laughs. Waiters passed to and fro with drinks and plates of food. It was approaching one forty-five and they had probably caught the end of the first race. Tubbs had gone over to talk to someone, a balding man of his own age who began turning his head and scanning the crowd. Charlie looked more carefully at the men and women with papers and tip sheets, trying to make up their minds about the next race. He had no doubt that Grouper was here. They had already seen the Ford Bronco in the parking lot.

Charlie glanced back at Tubbs in time to see the man with him pointing up at one of the higher levels. Looking in the same direction, Charlie noticed a man in a brown western-cut jacket seated at a small table by himself. He was a mouth breather with a small mouth, large lips and an undershot jaw. His dark eyes were set wide apart. He had a thin face with puffy cheeks and a short turned-up nose. Grouper, said Charlie to himself.

Maximum Tubbs reappeared at Charlie's elbow. "His name is Leonard Graham," said Tubbs. "I've heard of him dropping fifty thousand without batting an eye."

"Thanks," said Charlie, moving off toward the stairs. Graham was studying a *Racing Form*. In one hand he held a yellow pencil and he kept chewing the eraser thoughtfully. Many people were making their way to and from the betting windows and Charlie had to push around them as he climbed, using his elbows to get through the crowd. As he neared Graham, the man apparently reached some decision. He jumped up and headed toward Charlie, not looking at him.

Charlie blocked his path. He was shorter than Graham by at least six inches. "Mr. Graham? I'd like to talk to you."

Graham looked down at him with a mixture of surprise and irritation. "Not now, man, I got to place a bet."

"Would you rather I talked to the police, Mr. Grouper?"

Graham suddenly seemed wary, but the irritation and impatience remained. He kept opening and closing his small mouth. Just like a fish, thought Charlie.

"Let me make my bet, that's all. I'll talk to you after."

Charlie followed him to the hundred-dollar window, then waited while he got his ticket. Graham turned back to Charlie. "You better not have blown my luck, mister. Who are you anyway?"

Charlie showed Graham his identification. They kept being jostled by others hurrying toward the betting windows. The next race was only a few minutes off.

"So what do you want with me?" asked Graham.

It seemed to Charlie that Graham knew perfectly well what he wanted. Charlie leaned toward Graham's ear, standing on his toes and raising his voice. "I'm investigating Joe Pellegrino's death. You were seen driving away from there on the night of his murder. Is there someplace more private where we can talk?"

Along with the wariness Graham began to look frightened. His eyes opened a little wider and two pale marks appeared under his nostrils. He glanced up at one of the TV monitors, then jabbed his thumb toward the stairs. "We can go up there. There's not so many people."

Charlie followed Graham. With his western jacket, he wore brown jeans and heavy work boots. At the top of the stairs he led Charlie back toward a TV monitor by the men's room. Two heavyset men were watching it with their arms folded, waiting for the next race. Graham stopped about ten feet behind them.

Glancing at a clock, he turned toward Charlie. "I didn't kill him," he whispered angrily.

"What were you doing there?" It struck Charlie that Graham was more interested in the next race than in the chance of being arrested for murder.

"I wanted to talk to him about the game."

"Had you lost?"

"Yeah, the fuckin' Patriots. They screwed me. So I wanted to see Joe and try to restructure my loan."

"And what happened?" They were both whispering, even

though the two men watching the monitor showed no interest. They stood at the very top of the clubhouse, and over a shoulder-high barrier Charlie could look down at the crowd of men and women and out the great windows at the track, where the snow and wind continued to whip and swirl without letup.

"He was dead. Fuck, you know, I felt bad about it, but I also felt that somebody had just saved me twenty-five K." Graham grinned; somehow it made him look even more like a fish.

"So what'd you do?" asked Charlie.

"Got outta there as fast as I could."

"Why didn't you call the police?"

"You kiddin' me?"

"You see anyone else around?"

"Not a soul."

Several more people had joined the two under the monitor. It was one minute to post time.

"Anyone else on the road, any cars you recognized?" asked Charlie.

"Nothing."

"You sure?"

"What d'you want, me to write it in blood?" Graham suddenly seemed angry. He glared at Charlie, then looked away.

Charlie felt that Graham was lying. He was lying and he was frightened. His face seemed too quiet, as if he were listening to something far away. He again glanced at the clock, then up at the TV monitor where horses were being urged into the gate.

"So you went there," said Charlie, "saw that Pellegrino had been murdered and left right away. Were there any other tracks in the snow?"

"No."

"You didn't see Gibbon?"

"Who?" asked Graham, still with that quiet expression.

"Don't fool with me," said Charlie sharply. "Bobo Shaw, you didn't see Shaw?"

"Not at all."

"You know Shaw?"

"I see him here now and them. And I used to see more of him in Albany when he had a garage."

"He worked on stock cars?" asked Charlie.

"That's right." All of Graham's attention was now on the screen. About ten other people were watching it as well.

"You bet stock cars?" asked Charlie.

"Sure. Sometimes I even race them."

"Did Bobo Shaw kill Pellegrino?" asked Charlie.

Graham turned toward him, surprised. "How the fuck should I know?"

"What about Spaniel, the antiques collector, did he kill him?"

"Oates wouldn't hurt a fly," said Graham, looking at the TV again. All but one horse was in the gate.

"Where can I find Oates?" asked Charlie.

But then came the bell and the horses were off. Graham moved toward the TV as if Charlie weren't even there. "Where the fuck's Good Luck Lady?" said Graham.

The monitor was bolted to the wall about eight feet off the floor, and the crowd of about fifteen people stood in a semicircle around it.

"Come on, Big Foot," shouted a woman in a red dress.

"Where the fuck's Good Luck Lady?" said Graham, raising his voice.

The announcer rattled off the positions of the horses. Good Luck Lady was bringing up the rear. Graham turned angrily back to Charlie. "Jesus, you really screwed my luck!"

"Where can I find Oates?" said Charlie.

"Glens Falls, he's got a store in Glens Falls."

"What about Horse, you know him?" asked Charlie.

Graham had moved closer to the TV monitor and Charlie followed him. The horses were rounding the far turn.

"Good Luck Lady!" shouted Graham.

"Fearsome Dream!" shouted a small man with a cigar next to Charlie's elbow.

Charlie grabbed Graham's arm. "What about Horse?" he asked.

"Don't know him," said Graham, trying to shake him loose.

"And Lynx?" Charlie was getting jostled by the people behind him. He pushed back a little to give himself more room.

"Big Foot, Big Foot!" shouted the woman.

The front runner, a big chestnut with blinkers, was rounding the home turn by the three-sixteenths pole. He was ahead by a length but two other horses were closing fast. About five other horses were strung out along the rail. Good Luck Lady had moved up to the fourth position.

"Lynx!" shouted Charlie. "Who's Lynx?" He was still holding on to Graham's arm.

"Fearsome Dream!" shouted the man next to Charlie.

The horses were entering the home stretch. Good Luck Lady had moved up to third.

"I don't know him, I don't know him!" said Graham. "Look at that fuckin' horse sit there. Good Luck Lady!"

"Lonely Boy!" yelled a man in a wheelchair.

And Lonely Boy it was. Good Luck Lady came in second. People moved away from the monitor. Graham was disgusted. "You really fixed me," he told Charlie. "That horse was a shoo-in." He started to move away and Charlie again took hold of his arm.

"We're talking about a murder, Mr. Graham. Pellegrino was killed and you know something about it. Can you give me any reason why I shouldn't go to the police?"

Graham looked down at Charlie. His mouth kept opening and closing, and Charlie again felt he was afraid. "Go to them," said Graham, "but I'm telling you I don't know a fucking thing."

"When did you last see Bobo Shaw?"

"Last week sometime."

"Who's Lynx?"

"I swear I have no idea. Oates and Shaw were the only two I knew."

"Who'd you see at Pellegrino's that night?"

Again Graham became still. "No one, I saw no one."

Charlie felt exasperated. "We're not done talking," he said. "I'll see you again soon." Pushing through the crowd, he went downstairs to rejoin Maximum Tubbs. He found him sitting at a small table by himself, drinking a Saratoga Vichy and staring out at the track. Following his gaze, Charlie saw two boys in red parkas throwing snowballs at each other down by the winner's circle, just looping them up through the air, then laughing.

John Oates had floppy brown hair parted in the middle, a long nose, thin face and a small mouth with thin lips. His eyes were brown and droopy, and his hair appeared dyed. He was about fifty-five and wore a rust-colored jacket and khaki pants. He and Charlie were seated in a pair of Victorian wing chairs in the office of his large antiques shop in Glens Falls. He had offered Charlie a cup of tea which Charlie had accepted and now a kettle was hissing on a hot plate.

"Yes, he did call me Mr. Spaniel," said Oates, "but I could never think why."

Oates was slightly effeminate and waved his hands a little when he spoke so they looked like seaweed moving under water. Charlie had driven the twenty miles to Glens Falls through the snow after leaving the harness track. It was now four o'clock and he had reached the store ten minutes earlier. Oates had been very upset about Pellegrino's death, not because he cared about the old man but because he had picked Philadelphia to win by at least twenty points in the Super Bowl and would have made fifty thousand had Pellegrino lived. He said he had heard about the murder on the radio and hadn't been down to Saratoga since.

"My heart was broken, Mr. Bradshaw. Fifty thousand would have put me ahead for the month."

"And you hadn't seen Pellegrino since last week?"

"Several weeks, maybe three, maybe four. We did most of our business over the phone."

"Do you have any idea who might have killed him?"

Oates got up and poured the hot water into two brown mugs. "Your guess is as good as mine, Mr. Bradshaw."

"Could Leonard Graham have done it?"

"Who's to say. Leonard is certainly a man of daring. I have sugar, cream and lemon, Mr. Bradshaw. Which would you prefer?"

"Sugar and lemon," said Charlie. He began to cough and for a moment couldn't stop. The loud hacking noise seemed to break across the expensive antiques like waves upon a shore. "Why do you say he's a man of daring?" asked Charlie when he had recovered.

Oates handed him one of the brown mugs, then sat down again. "He races stock cars, which is certainly something I would never do. Much too dangerous. Besides that, he raises horses and breaks them himself."

"Does he race them?"

"Some of them are trotters, yes. He even drives them."

"What do you know about Bobo Shaw?"

"I've never had the pleasure," said Oates. He leaned over and took a cigarette from a white porcelain box, offering one first to Charlie, who refused.

"And the others, Horse and Lynx, do you know them?"

"I'm afraid not."

"Do you know anything about them?"

Oates lit the cigarette, then blew a small smoke ring in Charlie's direction. He seemed bored by Charlie's questions but perfectly willing to talk. "Joe mentioned Lynx about a month ago. He was his most recent customer. I gather he's not from Saratoga. Joe said I was from the north and Lynx was from the south."

"What did he mean by that?" asked Charlie. He began coughing again. His chest felt full of sharp stones.

"I assumed he meant I was from Glens Falls and this other fellow was from Albany or Schenectady, some place like that."

"Do you know anything about dogfights?" asked Charlie.

"No, and I don't plan to. Nasty, messy things."

Charlie drank a little of his tea. It felt good on his throat. He thought how in Pellegrino's other life, his life as a bookie, there was no feeling. None of his customers seemed to care about his death apart from the money lost or won. Yet Pellegrino's wife had loved him, and others, too, for all Charlie was aware of. And Charlie had liked him. In fact, he still missed Pellegrino and kept startling himself with the fact of Pellegrino's death. He had been a grocer. He had been a nice man. But perhaps, thought Charlie, if he had been my bookie, I wouldn't care much about his death either, except for the money he might have cost me. It was strange, and Charlie felt he couldn't understand it.

15

At first Charlie was struck most by the barking of the dogs. He had always liked dogs and imagined he knew something about them—their affability and canine embarrassment, their ready hunger. He thought back on the barking of dogs he had known and it seemed that their barks could be categorized as angry or cheerful, frightened or anxious. But the barking of the pit bulls struck Charlie as different. They were short, businesslike barks, designed to give specific information, like men exchanging business cards.

The fights were taking place in a warehouse in a rather run-down area near the river in Albany. Eddie Gillespie had said they wouldn't begin until eleven and when he, Victor and Charlie arrived at eleven-fifteen, they still hadn't started, although they seemed about to. The warehouse had a great open floor, perhaps about eighty by a hundred feet, and was crowded with men and a few women surrounding a portable fence set up in the middle. The men were shouting to one another, making bets, laughing. Generally the people seemed all types, ranging from construction workers to men in suits, bikers to bankers. Just like at the track, Charlie thought. Maybe there were eighty people around the fence and another thirty scattered over by the dog cages against the far wall or near the bar (two long tables side by side with bottles of whiskey, plastic cups and bowls of ice) or just milling around.

Since the dogfights were illegal, Charlie was surprised by how relaxed everything was, but Eddie had said the fights were held in a different location each time and were rarely raided.

"Sometimes they have them once a month, sometimes twice a week and sometimes four or five months will go by before there's a fight. They just unroll that fence and they're ready to go."

"But how do you get in?" Charlie had asked as they drove down the Northway toward Albany.

"My buddy, Larry, says you just walk in. I mean, I'll have to give them his name. He should even be there. He said you could have really stuck him in jail for taking a swing at you with a bottle but you didn't seem to mind. He's always been grateful."

Charlie still had been unable to remember Larry Corn. "It'll be great seeing him," he had said. "Is he a drinker?"

"Not so you'd notice," said Eddie.

Charlie had parked a block away and they hurried back through the snow. Although the area seemed deserted, there were a few men on the street who Charlie felt were lookouts, and as they neared the warehouse two men stopped them. Gillespie had spoken to them, mentioning Larry Corn, and they had been passed on, but once inside the warehouse they were stopped a second time by three large young men in dark suits whom Victor later described as "definitely nonjoking types." They seemed to be bouncers or guards, men whose duty it was to keep the proceedings moving smoothly. Again Gillespie gave the name of his friend, but instead of being admitted they were told to wait as one of the men went to fetch a fourth man standing by the dog cages.

As he stood by the door, Charlie listened to the dogs and tried to look around the large shoulders of the two men who were ostensibly guarding them. He had never witnessed a dogfight and didn't know what to expect, although "brutal" was the word that came to mind. Eddie said that pit bulls liked to fight in the way that birds liked to fly, but Charlie found that hard to believe. Primarily, he was interested in finding Andy Clamper and getting a lead on Bobo Shaw, who seemed to be at the center of all these crimes—the theft of the painting, the robbery at the hotel, Pellegrino's murder and even the black-mailing of Charlie's cousin. In fact, Charlie hoped that Shaw might even be at the dogfights and he began glancing around for him. If he caught Shaw, then Charlie thought his labors might be over. He could take some time off. He could go to Buenos Aires with Artemis. How warm it would be. How different.

Charlie's thoughts were interrupted by the return of one of the bouncers with another man who Charlie guessed was the person in charge. There was something of the impresario about him—quick and attentive and a little flashy. He was a man of Charlie's age, a little taller, with wavy blond hair and dressed in jeans and a white cowboy shirt and a black string tie. On his hands were at least seven rings with bright red and yellow stones and a diamond in a large gold setting. He introduced himself as Ralph Bagley.

"I like to know who's here and why they've come," said Bagley, who was friendly without being particularly welcoming.

"Dogs and money," said Victor, sticking out his hand and forcing Bagley to take it. "We're sick of horses, sick of the greyhounds and jai alai. We're sick of cards and craps and roulette. Why, if I could find a cow fight, I'd bet on that just as happily." Victor kept pumping Bagley's hand as he looked at each of the three bouncers and grinned.

"As long as you're here to bet," said Bagley evenly, "then okay, but I don't want trouble."

Victor released Bagley's hand and stuck his hands in the pockets of his overcoat. "What sort of trouble could we cause?" he asked, opening his eyes extra wide.

Bagley stepped toward Victor and took hold of one of his

lapels. He did it so smoothly that Charlie almost had to think twice before realizing the aggressiveness of the action. "Don't fool with me," said Bagley. Then he nodded toward Charlie. "This man's a private detective and he's probably on a case. As I say, you're welcome to bet, but I don't want trouble." Bagley then turned and walked back toward the dog cages.

"Fifty bucks to get in," said the biggest of the three bouncers.

"All together?" asked Victor.

"Each," said the bouncer.

Charlie winced and reached for his wallet. Victor had a lot of singles and doled them out one by one. One of the bouncers took their money and counted it, then he stood aside and motioned toward the bar. "Drinks are five bucks," he said. "Help yourself."

As they walked into the warehouse, Eddie Gillespie nudged Charlie in the ribs. "See how famous you're getting."

Charlie kept looking around, trying to spot people he recognized, anyone who might have mentioned to Bagley that he was a detective. There were several faces he knew—a bartender from Saratoga, a used-car salesman from Ballston Spa. He expected there were others as well, such as Larry Corn. And there was that Albany detective who'd been hounding him—Charlie searched for his name—Blake Moss, who wanted Charlie to work for him. He was shouting to another man and pointing to a dog that was being led on a chain toward the fence, a brown-and-white-spotted pit bull with a thick leather muzzle. Charlie guessed there were at least ten people here who could have told Bagley that he was a detective. He wasn't sure how he felt about that, but it meant they had to find Andy Clamper pretty quick. Charlie kept looking around, hoping to spot Bobo Shaw. Then, beyond the fence, he saw somebody else he knew: Leonard Graham, the man with the big Ford Bronco, edging his way through the crowd toward the far side of the room. Had Graham seen him? Charlie felt certain he had.

Charlie touched Eddie Gillespie's shoulder. "Start looking for Clamper. We have to find him before he learns that we're here." As Gillespie moved off through the crowd, Charlie pointed out Leonard Graham to Victor. "He's the one that Pellegrino called Grouper," said Charlie. "Keep an eye on him and see who he talks to."

"Fish face," said Victor. "He really looks like a fish. I wonder what Pellegrino would have called me?"

"Trouble," said Charlie.

"Heh, heh," said Victor.

Charlie left Victor and walked over to the bar. Seven or eight people were standing by the table and Charlie had to edge his way between them. He ordered a Jim Beam, putting a five-dollar bill on the table. The whiskey made him think of Jancy Burris. The bartender was an average-sized man of about forty with a thick brown mustache and a black shirt with pearl snaps and several gold chains around his neck. His chin, nose, cheeks all seemed oversized, even roughly shaped, as if his face had been carved from a block of wood with a butter knife. He looked angry for some reason and as he handed Charlie the small plastic glass, he bumped Charlie's hand, spilling about half of the whiskey onto the table. Instead of refilling the glass, the bartender turned to another customer.

"Excuse me," said Charlie, "would you mind filling my glass again?"

The bartender ignored him and continued to occupy himself with the other customers standing nearby. Charlie put the plastic glass back on the table, then reached for his five-dollar bill. Just as he had it in his hand, the bartender grabbed his wrist.

"Drop it," he said.

"You spilled half my whiskey," said Charlie. "Either replace it or return my five dollars."

"Drop the fuckin' money," said the bartender, squeezing Charlie's wrist.

Charlie reached forward with his left hand, grabbed the bartender's elbow and dug his thumb into the joint. "Yow!" said the man, letting go of Charlie's wrist.

As Charlie was putting his money back in his pocket, Ralph

Bagley appeared beside him. "Is something the matter?" he asked.

"Your bartender intentionally spilled my whiskey," said Charlie, "then objected to my retrieving my money. Other than that, everything's fine." Charlie nodded at the bartender, who was staring at him furiously.

"Give him another whiskey, Frankie," said Ralph Bagley. He was smiling but again Charlie thought that his smile had nothing to do with his feelings, as if his facial expressions were entirely separate from his emotions. As Charlie accepted the whiskey, he wondered why the bartender had spilled the first glass and what the man had against him.

"So what do you know about dogfights?" asked Bagley as he and Charlie walked back toward the ring.

"Not a thing," said Charlie, drinking his whiskey.

"And pit bulls," said Bagley, "what about them?"

"Wasn't Petey a pit bull in *The Little Rascals?*" asked Charlie.

"The very same."

"And do they really love to fight?"

"It's what they were born to do," said Bagley. When he spoke, he touched his fingers to the metal slide of his black string tie as if adjusting the volume of his voice. Embossed on the slide was a miniature pit bull.

By now they had reached the fence. Although the area was crowded, people got out of Bagley's way without his needing to speak to them. All of Bagley's movements seemed casual and relaxed, but again Charlie had the sense that the appearance was false. Glancing at Bagley's hands, Charlie saw they were perfectly groomed with a shiny transparent polish on the nails. They were square hands with short chunky fingers which Bagley kept flexing, making his rings flash in the light.

"Do the dogs get killed?" asked Charlie. The fence circled an area about fifteen feet in diameter. The floor within it was covered with a gray tarpaulin sprinkled with sawdust. Two dogs were in the ring with their handlers. The dogs were across from each other and each was hooked to a post. Their muzzles had been removed. They stood straining against their choke chains and looking very alert and ready—one brindle or tiger-striped and the other dark brown. They were both male dogs weighing about forty pounds and standing about sixteen inches at the shoulders. People were crowded against the fence three and four deep. Some were still making bets but mostly it was quiet. Charlie saw no sign of Eddie Gillespie or Victor.

"Occasionally they get killed," said Bagley. "We play with very few rules. The dogs fight until one backs down or is clearly beaten or starts pumping." Bagley was watching the two dogs and spoke without looking at Charlie.

"Pumping?" asked Charlie.

"Gets an artery punctured."

"How many fights do you have?"

"Eight."

"And people bet with each other?"

"That's right," said Bagley. "That tiger-stripe's the favorite by two to one. His name's Teeth. The other dog's name is Henry J. I'll bet you two fifty to your one hundred that Teeth takes Henry J. in under six minutes."

"I'd like to see a couple of fights first," said Charlie.

"I thought you were here to bet." Bagley turned toward him for the first time. He had light blue eyes, so light as to be almost colorless.

"Sure, but I'm still learning about it." It wasn't that Charlie minded losing the hundred dollars so much as he minded betting on the dog's death.

"So who're you here looking for?" asked Bagley.

"Who says I'm looking for anyone?"

"I'll give you four to one odds against Teeth," said Bagley.

Charlie glanced around the ring. There was still no sign of Victor or Gillespie. On the other side he saw Blake Moss lighting a cigarette. "Done," said Charlie. He looked again at Henry J., a sleek muscular little dog with a thick chest and slightly bowed front legs. There was a long white scar across his left shoulder and his left ear was half gone. Having committed a hundred dollars to Henry J., Charlie felt oddly paternal toward him.

Bagley put two fingers to his lips and whistled loudly. All talk stopped. Even the dogs grew more alert. "Are the dogs ready?" called Bagley. The two handlers nodded. Each was standing astride his dog, pressing his knees against it, bending over and apparently talking, pinching the dog's ribs with his fingers. "Then free them on the count of three. One, two . . ."

What followed was so fast that Charlie barely saw it happen. The two dogs shot forward, hardly touching their feet to the floor, and met in midair with a crash, digging into each other. Teeth had Henry J.'s flank, Henry J. had Teeth's shoulder. They hit the tarpaulin and rolled in a jumble of sawdust and blood, each chewing deeper, shaking and pawing at each other, seemingly silent, for nothing could be heard over the shouting of the crowd. People were yelling the dogs' names and yelling at each other, making new bets or side bets or just being enthusiastic. Charlie was struck by how eager they seemed. Teeth had Henry J. on the bottom and was into his belly now, chewing and pushing deeper, digging into the tarpaulin with his rear feet. Charlie felt sick to his stomach. Henry J. broke his hold and tried to scramble away, while the other dog went still deeper, working his big jaws. There was a lot of blood and Henry J.'s intestines were showing. He was squealing and trying to escape as he dragged Teeth across the ring.

"Stop the fight," said Charlie. "It's over, he's won."

Henry J. was knocked over onto his back. He was kicking his feet and still trying to scramble away as Teeth held on and kept digging into his stomach. People were whistling and shouting louder than ever. More blood started spurting, a small fountain shooting into the air. "He's pumping," yelled a man next to Charlie.

"Teeth is my dog," said Bagley. "I like to see him finish what he's started." He waited another half minute as Teeth continued to dig into the other dog's belly. A small cloud of dust hung over the two struggling dogs. Then Bagley again put his fingers to his lips and whistled. The handlers ran to pull the dogs apart. Teeth's handler had to prize his jaws apart with a wedged stick.

"Teeth in five minutes," called Bagley. He turned to Charlie. "You owe me a hundred dollars, Mr. Bradshaw. Perhaps you'll do better on the next fight."

Charlie gave him the money. The handlers had separated the dogs. Teeth was being walked around the ring as the crowd cheered. He kept pulling on his choke chain and gagging. Henry J. was still lying on the floor. The people around the fence began exchanging money or moving away toward the bar. There was a lot of excited talk and several people were laughing.

"What's going to happen to the other dog?" asked Charlie.

"He'll be dead within the minute."

"Can't you save him?"

"Why bother? He's a bad dog." Bagley seemed surprised by Charlie's question.

Still feeling sick, Charlie drank off the rest of his whiskey, then turned to look for Victor or Eddie Gillespie. There was no sign of them, nor had he seen any trace of Bobo Shaw. He felt bad about Henry J. and was not convinced that the dog had ever been having a good time.

Charlie circled the fence, trying to appear innocuous. He looked for someplace to throw his plastic cup and at last dropped it on the floor. A man went by carrying Henry J. in a large blue towel. People were talking about the fight and the fights to come. They were excited and Charlie was aware of what he considered a hysterical edge. He didn't judge it, but it reminded him of a wheel spinning too fast. A fat man with a beard and a leather motorcycle cap raised his head toward the high ceiling and began barking. Charlie gave him a pleasant smile. A young woman with bright red lips kept saying over and over, "Dumb dog, dumb dog." Charlie wondered if she was talking about the man with the beard. He walked toward the cages where Teeth's handler was giving him water and tending to his injuries. Although the dog must have been in pain, he gave no sign of it.

Victor appeared behind Charlie and dropped his arm over Charlie's shoulder. "I just won fifty bucks on that little sucker," he said. "How'd you do?"

"I dropped a hundred."

"Henry J. all the way?"

"I guess so. Were you watching Graham?"

Charlie and Victor had moved away from the dog cages and were standing near the wall. It was hot and Victor was carrying his overcoat over his arm. Charlie was still looking around for Eddie Gillespie.

"Yep, he's still over there. He kept looking at you and when you moved toward him, he'd move away. Like he's nervous. What did you do to him, Charlie?"

"Just talked to him, that's all." Charlie couldn't see why Graham should be scared, but the news was encouraging. "Have you seen Eddie?"

"Not a trace of him."

But as Victor spoke, Charlie saw Eddie hurrying in his direction through the crowd. Charlie moved toward him, trying not to push people out of his way, trying to appear relaxed.

"Clamper was here, but he just left," said Eddie. "Larry pointed him out to me. If we hurry, we can get him." He began zipping up his blue jacket and putting on his gloves.

Charlie led the way toward the door, walking quickly but trying not to run. The crowd was so dense that it was hard not to shove people.

"Hey, watch out!" a young man told Charlie.

"Sorry, sorry," said Charlie. "I have to catch a train."

Victor hurried along behind them, pulling on his overcoat.

"Was Clamper frightened?" asked Charlie. He kept looking around, hoping to catch a glimpse of Bobo Shaw.

"Yeah, I was watching," said Eddie. "One of those bouncers went up and pointed you out to him." Eddie grinned and looked happy. "I hope you feel like running."

As they made their way through the crowd, Charlie noticed two of the bouncers hurrying to stop them at the door, which was still about fifteen feet away. "Let's be quick," said Charlie, pushing around several people and breaking into a run.

Eddie reached the door first and opened it for the others. One of the bouncers aimed a kick at Victor and missed. By the time Charlie got outside, Eddie was twenty yards down the street. It was snowing again. Eddie pointed up toward the corner. "There he goes!" he shouted.

16

The best that Charlie could say about his own running was that he was faster than Victor. Otherwise, even the word "fast" was inappropriate. It would be better to say he was less slow than Victor, less poky. Besides that there was the snow and it was dark and basically he was a swimmer, not a runner. He kept slipping on the ice and twice he fell down. But even if the pavement had been dry, he would have been slow. As Charlie hurried down the deserted streets after Eddie Gillespie, he wondered if he should start jogging and lifting weights at the YMCA. Perhaps he just wasn't physically equipped to be a private detective. And then there was the problem with his age. Fifty, he was actually fifty. It felt as if he were running through mud, as if elastic bands were attached to his trousers holding him back. His only consolation was Victor puffing somewhere behind him. Slim consolation.

By now he had lost sight of Eddie, who had turned a corner by another warehouse. There was nothing slow about Eddie and presumably Andy Clamper was somewhere ahead of him. The area was dark and few streetlights worked. They passed lots where tow trucks and wrecked cars were parked, snow-covered and deserted. They passed a junkyard where a dog barked at them frantically. Charlie had a pain in his stomach and there was snow in his shoes. Somewhere he had lost his blue watch cap. Deserted storefronts with "for rent" signs were on either side of him, then a liquor store and a small grocery. He had no idea where he was and had little knowledge of Albany in general. Sometimes he'd drive down to Macy's in Colonie or go to the movies but that was it.

Looking ahead, Charlie saw a figure running toward him. At first he thought it was Eddie coming back, but then he saw another figure chasing the first one. There was little light and it was hard to see. Charlie slowed. Why should Clamper be chasing Eddie Gillespie? Then Charlie realized that the first figure wasn't Eddie Gillespie after all.

"Get him!" shouted Gillespie. "He doubled back."

Charlie stopped in the middle of the street. Glancing behind him he saw no sign of Victor. What a time for him to disappear. He looked forward again at Andy Clamper, who was about ten yards away. The young man showed no sign of nervousness or hesitation and ran toward Charlie as if he were no more than a dark smudge in the air.

"Stop!" said Charlie, getting ready.

Andy Clamper ignored Charlie and Charlie dove at him, slipping a little in the snow. Without slowing, Clamper straight-armed him, hitting him in the face and knocking him to the pavement. Charlie felt his jaw had been dislocated. Rolling over, he quickly scrambled to his feet but Clamper was already ten yards in the other direction. Although tired and out of breath, Charlie ran after him. Now there was snow down his neck as well.

Clamper was running beside some parked cars about twenty yards ahead. Suddenly a gray shape leaped from behind one of the cars, flung itself on Clamper and sent him sprawling to the ground. It took Charlie a moment to realize that Victor had been hiding there. Clamper was trying to hit him but Victor had him wrapped in a bear hug and refused to let go. By the time Clamper fought himself free, Charlie had almost reached them. Clamper shoved Victor away and jumped to his feet. Immediately, Charlie flung himself onto his back and they both tumbled back into the snow. Charlie had his arms wrapped around Clamper's neck and his legs around Clamper's waist and was squeezing as hard as he could. Even so, it took the younger man only a few seconds to disengage himself, hitting Charlie several times in the stomach as he did so. Again Clamper jumped to his feet. But by then Eddie Gillespie had arrived. Eddie hauled off and hit Andy Clamper in the jaw, knocking him onto his back. How simple it looked. Clamper lay in the street with Victor standing by his head and Gillespie by his feet. Charlie stood up. His stomach felt bruised. He walked over to Andy Clamper and nudged him in the ribs with his shoe.

"I have some questions for you," he said. "Why don't you stand up?"

"I got nothing to say," answered Clamper, still lying on his back near the curb. He wore jeans and a jean jacket. He was tall and dark-haired, and his face was pink from the cold. Snowflakes fell on his face and he wiped them away. Charlie glanced at his hands to see if they really looked like whoopee cushions. They were large pink hands, with big palms and stubby fingers. Maybe they looked a little like whoopee cushions.

"Then we'll drive you straight to jail," said Charlie, bending over and taking his arm.

"You ain't cops," said Clamper.

Victor nudged Clamper's shoulder with his shoe. "We're the friends of cops," he said. "We're their buddies."

"I haven't done anything anyway," said Clamper, more concerned. He lay on the pavement with his legs together and his arms at his sides. He was still breathing heavily. Charlie guessed he was in his late twenties.

"You helped Bobo Shaw murder the bookie, Joe Pellegrino," said Charlie.

Clamper's eyes seemed to get bigger. "That's a lie. I had nothing to do with it."

"That's not what we hear," said Charlie.

"Then you and Shaw stuck up that party at the hotel," said Victor.

"I don't know what you're talking about," said Clamper. He spoke in a high voice, almost a falsetto.

"During the Super Bowl game," said Gillespie, squatting down by his feet. "You and Bobo Shaw robbed a bunch of guys at the Bentley Hotel. You could get yourself killed for that."

Clamper tried to sit up and Eddie pushed him back down. "I wasn't even in Saratoga that night," said Clamper. "I was down here in Albany."

"What'd you do with the painting you took from the museum?" asked Charlie.

Clamper didn't answer but looked from Charlie to Victor to Eddie Gillespie, bending back his head, then again wiping the snow from his face. He had a long face with high cheekbones and a small chin—a chin that looked like the heel of a woman's shoe.

"And the five thousand bucks," said Victor. "What'd you do with that?"

"You'd been a guard at the museum," said Gillespie, still squatting by Clamper's feet. "You knew how to get in and out and how to turn off the alarm. That's a valuable painting. You could get ten years for stealing it. Where is it now?"

"Shaw took it," said Clamper.

Charlie knelt down beside Clamper's head. "And the money?" he asked quietly. From far off he could hear a snow plow, the sound of the great metal blade banging across the pavement.

"Shaw took that, too. I owed it to him. I owed him five thousand. So I told him about the painting being stolen last year and he said we could do the same thing. The whole business was his idea."

"Why didn't you give the painting back?" asked Charlie.

"Shaw had already gotten rid of it. He said he gave it to some other guys for insurance. I didn't know what he was talking about."

"Let's take him to jail right now," said Victor, making his voice sound gruff. "Let's let the cops work on him."

"But it wasn't his fault," said Charlie. "Shaw made him do this stuff."

"So what," said Eddie. "I think we should let the cops pound on his head awhile."

Charlie was still kneeling next to Clamper. "Who'd Shaw give the painting to?"

"He didn't say."

"Was it to the guys who robbed the party at the Bentley?"

"I don't know. Maybe. Shaw knew something about that. I mean he knew about it before it took place, but he didn't want to talk about it." Clamper kept his arms at his sides and stared at Charlie. He seemed more relaxed, almost if he were resting there by the curb in the snow-covered street. Although Charlie was freezing, Clamper didn't seem to mind the cold.

"Did he say who robbed the party?" asked Gillespie.

"No, he didn't mention any names."

"What did he do with the five thousand?" asked Charlie.

"He owed it."

"To Pellegrino?"

"No, to someone else."

"Where is Shaw?" asked Charlie.

"He was at the dogfights. Then he left when he saw you guys come in."

Clamper started to sit up and Charlie pushed him back down. A car passed on the next street, its headlights sweeping across the buildings. "But where's he been staying? Where can we find him?"

"I don't know."

"Sure you do," said Charlie.

Clamper looked up him with a worried expression. There was

a streetlight on the corner twenty yards away, and it made the freckles on Clamper's face look like dark spots.

"He's got a cousin over off Fuller Road," said Clamper. "He's been staying there. It's near the university, an apartment over a bar, a place called the Lincoln Grill. It was Shaw's idea, the painting and the rest of it. I knew we'd get in trouble if we didn't give it back."

"Get up," said Charlie.

Andy Clamper got to his feet. He was taller than any of them.

"We're going to look for Shaw," said Charlie, "and you're coming with us."

The four men walked back through the snow to Charlie's car. Clamper seemed ready to bolt but Eddie Gillespie held onto his arm. As they neared the warehouse where the dogfights were going on, they took a little detour around the block. Charlie's car was covered with snow and they passed it twice without recognizing it. When at last they found it, Victor wiped the snow from the windows as the others got in.

"Turn on the heat, Charlie," said Eddie Gillespie. "I'm freezing."

"The heater's broken."

Victor got in front with Charlie. "We could sing dirty songs," he said. "Just to warm us up, I mean."

No one answered. Andy Clamper gave Charlie directions, then added, "Just don't tell Shaw I said anything. He'd kill me."

Charlie turned the corner, heading south to Route 90, then heading west near Memorial Hospital. It was past midnight and there was little traffic other than the bright orange snowplows. The street lights reflecting from the new snow made the buildings shimmer, as if their very stones were shining.

When Charlie turned off Fuller Road onto Green Street and saw the flashing lights of the police cars parked outside the Lincoln Grill, he had an immediate presentiment of what had happened. Maybe it was a lucky guess, maybe it was because he had been involved in police work for nearly thirty years. In any case, it depressed him. He pulled to the curb half a block away and shut off the engine.

The effect of the police cars on Andy Clamper was sudden and violent. Hitting the door with his shoulder, he struck Eddie Gillespie with his fist and rolled out onto the street. Eddie was after him in a second, but Charlie called to him just as he was scrambling out of the car.

"Let him go. We don't need him."

"He hit me, Charlie. I want to hit him back."

"Some other time."

Eddie stood on the sidewalk and Charlie and Victor were turned in their seats, staring through the back window. About thirty yards away, Andy Clamper was just turning a corner, arms held out for balance, feet churning their way through the snow. He looked as if he were trying to fly. Charlie thought how far it was across town to where Clamper's car was probably parked near the dogfights and he felt sorry for him.

"He sure is an eager runner," said Victor.

Charlie turned back toward the police cars, then he got out of his Renault. He wondered about the odds of Bobo Shaw being perfectly healthy.

"You fellows stay here," said Charlie, closing the door. "I'm going to ask some questions."

"Charlie, there's no heat," said Victor.

"Then I guess it's time to sing your dirty songs."

The Lincoln Grill was a two-story yellow brick building on a street of one-story houses and small apartment buildings. It was a dull-looking neighborhood, but the blanket of fresh snow gave it a sort of beauty. The bar was still open and Charlie could see the faces of a few middle-aged men staring out the picture window beneath the flashing Schlitz and Budweiser signs. The stairs to the second floor had a corrugated metal roof and were attached to the left side of the building. A young policeman stood at the bottom flapping his arms to his sides.

Charlie approached him and showed his ID. "I'm looking for Bobo Shaw," he said.

The policeman had a freckled red face and a red mustache from which he was licking the snow. He glanced at Charlie's ID, then at Charlie without much interest. Turning, he called up the stairs. "Tell the lieutenant there's a guy here looking for Shaw." There was a pause and someone called something back that Charlie couldn't hear. "Go on up," said the policeman.

Charlie climbed the covered stairs. The only light came from a door above him. There was no railing and he had to feel his way forward. Halting at the top, he looked through the doorway. Here there was a lot of light, the big lights the police put up when they are dusting for fingerprints. About eight men were in the room, a small living room with shabby green furniture. Over by the couch was Bobo Shaw, lying on the rug with his back to the door. He lay curled up with his knees to his chest. His stringy black hair was spread out around his head like a fan. The blood on the floor looked like it was still wet. More blood was on the wall and a green armchair. Again Charlie had a sense of his own lateness, that if he had been quicker or cleverer he might have gotten to Bobo Shaw while he was still alive. Only three of the men in the room were in uniform. Charlie looked at the others, trying to determine who was in charge. A tall, middle-aged man with a large beer belly approached Charlie.

"You're Bradshaw, aren't you? From Saratoga? We met about five years ago. I'm Bob Boland. You knew Shaw?"

Charlie liked to think he had a good memory for faces but he could have sworn he'd never seen this man before. He stuck out his hand and Boland shook it. "Where'd we meet?" he asked.

"Chief Peterson's office in Saratoga. A local guy had been shot near the track. I was sent up there. I was only a sergeant then."

Charlie still couldn't remember the occasion but he nodded

anyway. "Is that Shaw?" he asked, gesturing toward the body. Shaw was wearing a heavy brown corduroy jacket and must have been shot just after he had come in or just as he was preparing to leave.

"That's what his driver's license says. You want a closer look?"

Charlie nodded, although he didn't want to. He hated seeing dead bodies. They always looked so lonely and far away, and he kept thinking what the people must have been like as children. The two men walked across the room, avoiding the lights and the lab crew. Charlie tried to keep from stepping in the blood but couldn't entirely manage it. They walked around the body so they could see it from the front. Charlie tried not to look at it and kept his eyes on the walls. Then he looked down. He took a breath and held it and felt glad he hadn't eaten recently. Bobo Shaw lay on his side, looking up at the ceiling with an expression balanced between concern and a wince. His dark eyes were scrunched up and his mouth was open as if to say something like "Stop" or "Don't." Beneath his corduroy jacket he was wearing what had once been a white shirt. Where his chest should have been was a red mess.

"Gibbon," said Charlie to himself, then added, "That's Shaw all right."

"Whoever killed him got him with a shotgun," said Boland. "Probably a sawed-off shotgun under his coat."

"Any ideas who did it?" asked Charlie.

Boland looked at him speculatively, then took out a Lucky Strike and lit it. He wore a dark overcoat over a dark suit. He was prematurely bald and it occurred to Charlie that he might have had hair when they had met before.

"What's your interest in this?" asked Boland, shaking out the match.

"Insurance company," said Charlie. "There've been a lot of car radio thefts in Saratoga and they seem connected to a kid named Andy Clamper. Shaw worked with Clamper at a Sinclair station on Broadway. The moment I started looking for Clamper both of these guys disappeared. Tonight I heard that Shaw was staying with his cousin down here."

"You're workin' this late over car radios?" asked Boland.

"It was a lot of radios," said Charlie. "I thought I could catch him at home." Charlie didn't think that Boland believed him. Shaw had been wearing a Yankees cap and it now lay in a pool of blood.

"Shaw showed up about eleven-thirty," said Boland. "About a half hour later the people downstairs in the bar heard a shot. The bartender came out and saw a guy getting into a car and driving away."

"What did he look like?" asked Charlie.

"Average height, maybe a little under, and heavyset. He was wearing brown coveralls. The bartender said he looked like a brick. Does that sound like someone you're looking for?"

"Nope," said Charlie, thinking that it matched the description of one of the men who had robbed Victor's Super Bowl party. "Clamper's a tall, thin guy. What kind of car was it?"

"A late-model Pontiac, dark blue, nobody got the plate."

"Too bad."

Charlie stared down at Shaw's monkey face. A strand of long black hair had fallen across his mouth and Charlie wanted to reach down and brush it away. It seemed that just when he had the case wrapped up, he had to start all over again. Who could have killed Shaw? Most likely it was the men who had robbed Victor. But who were they? Charlie imagined Shaw seeing him at the dogfights and then leaving. He imagined him calling one or both of the men who had robbed Victor and demanding money or help. And then what had happened? Presumably the men had decided that Shaw was a poor risk. But perhaps the murder had nothing to do with Charlie's investigation. And the painting, where was it now? Charlie wanted to think it was in the hands of the heavyset man who had shot Shaw, but he wasn't sure he had a good reason for believing that.

"You know," said Charlie, "Shaw was a pretty serious gambler. He used to have a garage and he lost it to the bookies. Maybe his murder was connected to gambling."

Boland stretched out a foot and nudged Shaw's boot as if trying to wake him up. "Gamblers don't usually kill each other," he said. "They might beat each other up and squeeze each other real hard but as long as there's hope of making another nickel they don't like to pull the trigger. Whoever killed Shaw just didn't want to fuck with him. He wanted to make him disappear. Bam! Like that."

17

At noon Friday Charlie was sitting in George Whitman's office waiting for the secretary to tell him that he might go in now. In the half hour he had been waiting he had grown to dislike the secretary, an otherwise innocent-looking young woman reading a Dick Francis novel. Then it had occurred to Charlie that he generally disliked secretaries, especially the ones who kept him sitting. But was that their fault? Weren't they only doing their job? And he began to worry he was being unfair.

Fifteen minutes later, when the young woman said that Whitman could see him, Charlie had convinced himself of his own unreasonableness and gave her a big smile, despite her refusal to look him in the eye. "Thanks," he said, warmly.

The woman glanced up from her book, twisted her face into an expression between a smile and a yelp of pain, then yawned and looked away.

Maybe she's had a recent loss, thought Charlie. On the other hand, maybe she was born rude and when she dies she will be punished for it.

Charlie pushed open the door and entered Whitman's office. That it was a large office didn't surprise him. Nor was he surprised by the Oriental carpet or the soft furniture. But he would have expected the paintings on the walls to be of horses or big houses since those were the things that Whitman was known for. Instead, the paintings were what Charlie imagined to be modern art, colorful squiggles and zigzagging lines. Charlie couldn't make sense of them, didn't even like them, although he kept those feelings to himself.

"What can I do for you, Mr. Bradshaw?" said Whitman. His manner was decidedly chilly and he didn't look up from the papers on his desk.

"I thought I'd bring you up to date about that stolen painting," said Charlie, walking into the room. For a moment he considered sitting down, then he decided he'd rather stand. After all, it would be a short visit.

Whitman leaned back in his swivel chair, tilted his head slightly and stared at Charlie. "And what can you possibly tell me?"

Charlie wiped his nose with a tissue and tried to appear relaxed. "The painting was stolen by two men by the names of Andy Clamper and Bobo Shaw," Charlie said. "Clamper had been a guard at the museum who was fired some months ago, ostensibly for continued tardiness, but actually because he was suspected in several small thefts. Clamper and Shaw worked at that Sinclair station near the Spa City Diner. Both men gambled a lot and Clamper owed Shaw about five thousand dollars. Clamper had told Shaw about the theft of the painting last year and Shaw convinced him they could do the same thing and that the ransom money would wipe out Clamper's debt. Because of Clamper's knowledge of the museum, they were able to steal the painting quite easily. I don't know if they ever intended to return it, but even before the ransom was paid Shaw gave the painting to another man. I don't have this man's name but I expect to learn it soon."

Whitman was staring at Charlie with a modicum of interest. "What does Shaw say?" he asked.

"Nothing. He was murdered last night. Maybe by the same

person he gave the painting to. As for Andy Clamper, he's in jail. The police went to his apartment this morning with a search warrant and along with Clamper they found about fifty stolen car radios."

Whitman's interest seemed to be increasing. "I had a radio stolen from my car about a month ago."

Charlie nodded as if to say, Well, there you are.

"And now you expect me to hire you to find the painting?" asked Whitman, the chill returning to his voice.

"That's unnecessary," said Charlie. "I'm looking for these men because of their connection to another case."

Whitman lit a cigarette, then pushed his chair back from his desk. "Do the police know about the theft of the painting?"

"I haven't mentioned it to them."

Staring at Charlie for a moment, Whitman tapped some cigarette ash into a glass ashtray. "I don't know whether you are aware of it, Mr. Bradshaw, but there is a reward of five thousand dollars for the return of that painting."

"I didn't know that," said Charlie. Then he gave another big smile and turned and left the office before Whitman could speak again. Maybe I don't smile enough, thought Charlie. Maybe I'm just not a good smiler.

Whitman's office was on Broadway, a block north of the post office and two blocks north of the real estate and insurance office of Charlie's cousin Robert. Charlie wanted to talk to Robert and tell him that he thought his problems with the blackmailer were over. Although he wasn't one hundred percent positive, he was almost sure it had been Shaw. Most likely the blackmailer was one of Pellegrino's other customers and Shaw, or Gibbon, seemed the obvious choice. It had to be someone who had shown up at the grocery after Robert, which left out Graham, while Oates didn't seem the type. Shaw also appeared the most desperate for money, wasn't averse to minor criminal activity, and seemed clever at collecting information and turning it to his own profit. The only flaw in this logic was that Charlie still didn't know the identity of Lynx. But not only was Lynx a new customer, he also wasn't from Saratoga. It seemed unlikely he would know about Robert or Robert's social pretensions, which made him such an easy target for blackmail. On the other hand, if Charlie turned out to be wrong and Robert was still being blackmailed, then it might be possible to catch the person, which might mean learning something new about Pellegrino's murder.

Charlie walked down Broadway, keeping his hands in the pockets of his overcoat and his nose buried in his scarf. It was a cold day and very clear. There was still about a foot of snow on the streets and many of the cars that passed had chains. Charlie liked the muffled *clink-clink*ing sound they made, which seemed to remind him of fifty winters. Then he paused a moment on the number fifty and shook his head.

As he stopped at the light with the post office on his right and city hall with the police station on his left, Charlie thought of Andy Clamper, whom he had turned over to Chief Peterson that morning. Actually, he had only gone to Peterson with the information about the radios but the result was the same. He felt a little guilty about sending Clamper to jail, but he knew he would have to talk to him again and he didn't want him to disappear. Nor did he want him shot, like Shaw. Chief Peterson had been very grateful for the tip and Charlie knew it would be good for several favors in the future.

"You know the guy actually ripped off the radio from my wife's car?" Peterson had said. "My own wife!"

"The nerve," Charlie had said.

Mrs. Dawson, the secretary in his cousin's office, was even less friendly than Whitman's secretary, but she apparently had been told that Charlie was a person of some importance because she called Robert right away. Her voice was so smooth and cultured that Charlie thought she must gargle with honey or had started life as a disk jockey with a classical radio station. Even so she had those mean little black eyes, and Charlie felt she would gladly push him down the stairs if given the chance.

"Your cousin would be happy to see you now, Mr. Bradshaw."

"Thanks," said Charlie, "thanks very much."

Charlie entered his cousin's office and found him staring out the window in his shirtsleeves with his hair all mussed. This was clearly a bad sign and Charlie hurried to give him the good news about the blackmailer.

"I'm pretty sure you're off the hook," explained Charlie. "The fellow who called you is out of circulation."

Robert had turned away from the window and was staring at him in what Charlie thought of as an unhappy and resentful manner. "A fat lot you know," said Robert. "I got a call this morning. The money's been doubled to ten thousand and I have to have it by tomorrow night."

"Ah," said Charlie, not knowing what else to say.

"I thought you were going to help me with this, Charlie, but you've only made it worse."

"Ah," said Charlie again.

"The man said he'd tell Chief Peterson and the newspapers about my involvement with Pellegrino if I said a word to anybody." Robert pushed his hands through his gray hair, making it stand up in little peaks. His horse face looked longer than ever.

"Was it the same man you talked to before?" asked Charlie.

Robert paused with his hands still in his hair. "Now that's the odd part. I really don't think it was."

"Are you sure?"

"Almost positive."

Charlie experienced a moment of hope. If the original black-mailer had been Shaw, then this new blackmailer might be Shaw's murderer. Or perhaps it was one of the men who had robbed Victor. "Where are you supposed to meet him?" asked Charlie.

"He's going to call me tomorrow."

"I'll meet him," said Charlie. "Me and Victor. We'll get this damn thing straightened out once and for all."

"But what if he tells the police?" said Robert, beginning to push his hands through his hair again.

"He won't. If he is who I think he is, he's got too much stuff to hide."

"Charlie, I can't afford for this business to get out. I've even decided to give up gambling. I haven't made a bet since Tuesday."

"No wonder you seem nervous," said Charlie, going to the door. "You call me when you hear from this guy. The fact that he called is really better news than you suppose."

Leaving his cousin's office, Charlie went down the stairs to the street. The reflected sun off the snow made him blink as he buttoned his blue overcoat and turned down Broadway toward his office. It was about one o'clock. The YMCA pool was open until two and Charlie's swimming stuff was in his office. Although his cold was still bothering him, he couldn't stand another day without swimming and he imagined that he'd done nothing but gain weight all week. As a child, Charlie's favorite radio program had been a detective show called "The Fat Man." That'll be me, thought Charlie, I'll be the fat man.

As he crossed Broadway, Charlie tried to forget about his weight and think seriously about Shaw. It seemed that if Shaw had been the original blackmailer, then this new blackmailer had to be someone whom Shaw had told about Robert. Additionally, he had to know that Shaw was dead and saw this as a good chance to make some money. He didn't necessarily have to be Shaw's murderer, but most likely he was. Most likely Shaw had been killed either by the person who killed Pellegrino or by the men who had robbed Victor. As for who had killed Pellegrino, Charlie had no idea unless it was the mysterious Lynx. As for the men who had robbed Victor, one had been described as stocky and perhaps that was the same stocky man who had been seen fleeing the apartment above the Lincoln Grill the previous evening. The other man had been thin, average height, and had a mustache. Well, that could be anybody.

But it seemed to Charlie that the two stocky men were the same, and he imagined a scenario in which Shaw had gone to this stocky fellow and told him about Charlie and how he had shown up at the dogfights. Perhaps Shaw had even tried blackmailing him, saying he had to pay up or Shaw would tell Charlie that he was the stocky fellow who had robbed Victor and maybe had the painting of Man o' War as well. But who was this stocky fellow? Charlie had no idea, but if he had known Shaw, then perhaps he was connected to the Sinclair Station or the dogfights or even to stock-car racing, since that was Shaw's other big interest. Charlie decided he would have to learn more about the stock-car racing, but it would have to wait until he had been to the Y. Nothing today could interfere with his swim.

Unfortunately, Charlie missed his swim after all. When he climbed the stairs to his office, he found the Albany private detective, Blake Moss, waiting outside his door.

"Mr. Bradshaw," said Moss, shaking Charlie's hand, "how about it? I'm giving you one last chance to head up my Saratoga office."

Charlie unlocked the door, then entered. It struck him as unlikely that this was the reason for Moss's visit, and he remembered him the previous evening at the dogfights eagerly cheering on one of the dogs.

"Did you win last night?" asked Charlie, walking to his desk. His green backpack with his swimming suit, goggles and towel was on top of the file cabinet. Charlie told himself that all he had to do was pick it up and walk out the door.

"Pardon me?" asked Moss. He was unbuttoning his overcoat with his right hand as he held his hat in his left. His expression indicated that he didn't know what Charlie was talking about and Charlie thought he was lying.

"The dogfights," said Charlie. "I saw you there last night. I was just wondering if you'd won any money."

"I wasn't betting, Mr. Bradshaw. I was there on a case."

"You seemed pretty excited."

Moss had sat down in the visitor's chair and was rubbing his chin. His round face and short blond hair made him look boyish, despite his forty-odd years. "Well, I couldn't just stand around," said Moss. "I had to appear involved."

"Do you go there often?" asked Charlie.

"Not at all. How about yourself?"

"That was my first time."

"Were you on a case?"

"Nope," said Charlie, sitting down on the edge of his desk. "I just went for the gambling."

"Did you win much?"

"No again. One of my friends got sick and we left after the first fight. He couldn't take the blood. But I hope to go back. When's the next one, do you know?"

"I haven't heard," said Moss. Then he shook a Marlboro out from its pack and lit it. The sweet smell almost made Charlie want to smoke again. Moss glanced around Charlie's office. He wasn't as critical as he had been on his first visit. Indeed, he seemed defensive.

Charlie looked at Moss thoughtfully and wondered if he was telling the truth. He was certain that Moss had seen him at the dogfights and equally certain that Moss had come today to find out what Charlie had been doing there. But he couldn't guess the reason for his interest.

"Do you know that guy Bagley who runs those fights?" asked Charlie.

"I've met him."

"Is that how he earns his money or does he do something else as well?"

Moss appeared to become angry. "I didn't come here to be grilled by you, Mr. Bradshaw. I came to see if you had thought anymore about my offer—twenty thousand a year to run the Saratoga office of the Moss Security Agency, plus benefits. I'll even throw in a pension plan."

"I can't do it, Mr. Moss," said Charlie. "I just can't work for anyone but myself."

"Actually, I think I could make it twenty-two thousand."

"The answer's still no."

"Well, I'll keep trying," said Moss, getting to his feet. He smiled affably and stuck out his hand. "Maybe I can get you to change your mind."

"I doubt it," said Charlie, shaking his hand, then following him to the door. "By the way, how'd you make out on the Super Bowl?"

Moss turned around. "The Super Bowl?"

"Yeah, you said you were backing the Eagles and I wondered if you'd made a killing."

"A few dollars," said Moss with a tight smile, "possibly twenty-five at the most."

"Well, that's better than nothing," said Charlie, wondering why Moss was lying again.

After Moss had left, Charlie walked over to his green backpack and stared at it hard before he gave up the idea of swimming altogether. Then he sighed, blew his nose and put on his overcoat. He'd drive over to the Sinclair station to see what he could learn about Shaw.

18

"Did you ever think, Charlie, that maybe your mother had the right idea?" asked Victor.

Charlie glanced briefly at his friend, then turned his eyes back to the road. There was still snow on the Northway and the Renault had slid several times. On his CB radio static-filled voices discussed fender-benders. "What are you talking about?" asked Charlie.

"About investing in racehorses. I mean, for years she slogs along as a waitress, saving her pennies and investing in fractions of horses and finally it pays off. Bingo, she's got a big hotel and spends the winter in Paris, hobnobbing with artists at the cafés and going to the opera. You ever been to an opera?"

"I saw part of one once on TV," said Charlie, tapping his brake so he wouldn't get too close to the tractor-trailer truck ahead of him. His windshield wipers were doing little more than smearing the salt around.

Charlie and Victor were on their way down to the Harrison Speedway south of Albany, where Bobo Shaw used to work as a mechanic and had owned a garage not far from the track. Charlie had talked to four men at the Sinclair station and the existence of the Harrison Speedway was the one new bit of information he had learned. It had been hard even getting that since two cops from Albany had been at the garage for most of the morning irritating everybody. Charlie had also asked if Shaw had had a friend or acquaintance who was stocky and a little short and in his late thirties, but nobody had known anything, or at least that's what they said.

"The thing about opera," said Victor, "is that it's full of culture in the same way that chocolate is full of calories. That's how your mother, this ex-waitress, pulls off being the great lady. She's fuckin' absorbed those operas till she just shimmers with culture. I mean, if you started listening seriously to operas, you'd be wearing a top hat in no time."

"I don't want to wear a top hat," said Charlie.

"It's just a figure of speech," said Victor. "Why d'you have to be so literal?"

Charlie was having trouble following what Victor was saying and driving in the snow and ice at the same time. The opera he had seen a piece of had had this old guy carrying his dead daughter around in a bag. How did that have anything to do with culture?

"These two guys who robbed your party," said Charlie, "why don't you describe them to me again?"

"For Pete's sake, Charlie, I already done it a dozen times."

"Yeah, but you might have forgotten something." A new Buick had slid off the road up ahead and Charlie slowed to take a look. The car was nose down in a snowy ditch with the driver standing beside it looking depressed.

"First of all, they knew the special knock." Victor reached forward and rapped on the dashboard—one, pause, two-three, four.

"Bobo Shaw must have told it to them," said Charlie.

"Then they had these ski masks that made them look like cats, dark yellow with black around the mouth and eyes. And one guy had a shotgun."

"Which one?" asked Charlie.

"The heavyset one."

"That's probably the same shotgun that killed Shaw," said Charlie. "You say he was heavyset, was he fat?"

"No, just heavy, sort of brick-shaped."

"And he was short?"

"Shorter than the other guy. Maybe he was five foot ten or so. I didn't get a chance to get out my measuring stick."

"What else about him?"

"Nothing, except that he didn't like the taller guy talking so much."

"What were they wearing?"

"I told you, brown coveralls."

"And on their feet?"

"I don't remember."

"Try."

"Jesus, Charlie, you're just like a beaver—chew, chew, chew. The chunky guy with the shotgun was wearing cowboy boots."

"How do you know?"

"Because he kicked me with them, that's how—an old pair of brown cowboy boots."

"And he had a mustache?"

"No, that was the taller one. I could see it through the mouth of his ski mask. A big brown mustache."

The Harrison Speedway was in a southern section of Albany just north of the Turnpike. Surrounding it were a lot of garages, junkyards, automotive supply places, two Chinese restaurants and about half a dozen shabby houses covered with asbestos shingles. And there seemed more wires than most places—more electricity and telephone wires, thick black wires with a little snow clinging to them. Around the track was a green wall, corrugated metal in some places, wood in others. Charlie pulled into the lot behind the grandstands where about twenty other cars were parked. The grandstands were uncovered but up at the top was a press box and an enclosed area for the judges and other track officials. To the left under the stands was a large corrugated metal building which seemed to be a garage. Charlie and Victor climbed out of the Renault and walked toward it. From the track itself came the high roar of one car apparently going round and round. Charlie moved forward almost eagerly through the snow and slush. On the far side of the parking lot he had seen Leonard Graham's big Ford Bronco and he was curious to know what Graham would say about being at the dogfights the previous night.

A clanging noise came from the garage as someone kept hitting one piece of metal against another over and over. Charlie pushed the door open and Victor followed him in. About six cars were being worked on, all banged up and without glass or headlights, fitted with roll bars, and several had elaborate air scoops. They reminded Charlie of cars in the movie *Road Warrior,* which Victor still said was his favorite movie of all time. Several men were standing around a desk on the right side of the garage and Charlie made his way toward them, stepping over the legs of a man half under a souped-up Dodge. The clanging noise continued without pause. Then a hot-air blower on the ceiling came on, and its roar and vibrating rattle joined with the clanging to create a sort of awful music.

Charlie stopped at the desk and the three men turned to look at him. All wore dirty blue coveralls and had grease marks on their faces and hands. One was bald and the other two were in their twenties and looked enough like each other to be brothers, maybe even twins. The bald man was chewing on an unlit cigar.

"I'm looking for someone who knows Bobo Shaw," said Charlie. He had to shout because of the noise.

"Shaw's not here," said the bald man.

"I know, he was murdered last night."

The three men looked interested but not particularly smitten with grief.

"Shit," said one of the younger men, "he owed me fifty bucks."

"You a cop?" asked the bald man.

"Private detective." Charlie showed them his ID. Next to him he noticed Victor kneeling down and looking at people's feet. At first he couldn't imagine what he was doing, then realized he was looking for cowboy boots.

"I'm trying to find out who his friends were," said Charlie. The heater suddenly cut off and Charlie found himself shouting. "His friends were," he said more softly.

The other young man sucked his teeth. "He didn't have any friends. He owed money to everybody. I used to work for him. I never even got my last two paychecks."

"A hotshot gambler," said the bald man. "He'd bet on anything. Who killed him?"

"Some guy with a shotgun," said Charlie. "Wasn't there anybody he spent more time with, maybe someone he gambled with?"

The bald man glanced around the garage. "No one in here," he said. "You couldn't even trust him working on a car. He'd pawn his tools. Shit, he even pawned mine."

"What about that driver?" said one of younger men. "That guy he played cards with."

"They weren't friends," said the other young man. "He just owed him money."

"Yeah, but what was his name?"

"I don't know. Butch something."

"What did he look like?" asked Charlie.

"Just a regular guy," said the young man.

"Thin, fat, tall, short?"

"Maybe he was a little chunky."

"How tall?"

"Average. You know, a regular guy."

"He wasn't as tall as me," said the other young man, "and I'm six two."

"Did he wear cowboy boots?" asked Victor.

"Yeah," said the young man, "he wore cowboy boots."

Charlie and Victor talked to the other men in the garage but learned little that was helpful. No one seemed to have much use for Shaw, who had had a mean temper and owed money to everybody. Although they heard of a couple of other men with whom Shaw gambled, the one named Butch who wore cowboy boots seemed the person to look for first.

"I wouldn't call him fat," said one mechanic, "but he's like, you know, square."

"Like a brick?" suggested Victor.

"More like a cinder block," the man said.

Even though Butch occasionally raced cars at the track, none of the men could remember his last name. The bald man, however, assured Charlie that he could get it from the office, which might be open later that afternoon or might not.

Before leaving the garage, Charlie asked about the Ford Bronco parked out in the lot.

"That's Graham's car," said the bald man. "He's out there right now freezing his ass off. Not even racing. Just going round and round. He says it soothes him. Let me tell you, Buster, there's a lot of crazy people in this business."

"Any business," said Victor.

"You better believe it," said the bald man.

Charlie and Victor left the garage and continued under the grandstand. The roar of the stock car circling the track reverberated through the enclosed area and made Charlie's teeth vibrate. Walking up the ramp to the seats, they saw a blue Mustang without fenders or doors and spouting great clouds of gray exhaust as it rushed along the outside of the track. Charlie and Victor walked down to the fence. The track had been plowed but there were still patches of snow and ice. More snow was piled on the seats where they weren't protected by the overhang of the press box and judging booth. At the other end of the bleachers was a small coffee shop in what looked like a red railway caboose. The Mustang wasn't going particularly fast, maybe about sixty. The driver was just a blur, someone in black goggles, black leather cap and a black leather jacket. Charlie stepped out on the edge of the track and began waving to him.

"You watch he doesn't run you down, Charlie," said Victor.

The Mustang passed again and Charlie stepped back. "Then you'd have to break the news to my mother," said Charlie, shouting over the noise.

The Mustang had begun to slow and as it again approached Charlie the car drew to a stop. Leonard Graham unbuckled himself and climbed out of the front seat. He looked angry.

"You follow me here?" he shouted.

Charlie smiled. "Just a lucky coincidence."

"What's so funny?" said Graham. He had pushed the goggles back up onto his leather cap and his mouth was slightly open. Charlie thought he looked like a fish wearing a leather cap— a very tall fish.

"Nothing, I just thought it was funny you should think I was following you around. You win much at the dogfights last night?"

"Were you following me then as well?"

"Did you tell Bobo Shaw I was there?" asked Charlie, taking a guess.

"Why the fuck should I tell Shaw anything?" Graham's leather jacket was old and the leather was cracked. Above the pocket over his heart the name "Lion" was embroidered with red thread.

"Because he was one of Pellegrino's customers. You knew him, maybe you were friends with him."

"Fuck Shaw."

"Anyway, he's the guy I'm interested in, not you," said Charlie. Behind him Victor had begun to whistle "The Yellow Rose of Texas."

"What do you want Shaw for?" asked Graham. He stood stamping his engineer's boots in the slush and tilting his head toward Charlie.

"I wanted to talk to him about Pellegrino and see if he could identify Lynx. Have you had any more thoughts about that?"

"Never met Lynx."

"Did Pellegrino ever say anything about him?"

"Nope, just that he was a tough guy who could protect himself if he had to."

A chill wind blew across the track. Charlie pulled up the collar of his overcoat and dug his hands down into his pockets. He had lost his watch cap the previous night and still hadn't had a chance to buy a new one. His bald spot felt cold. "Could Lynx be a friend of Shaw's named Butch, who races cars here sometimes?" he asked.

"Butch Howard? No way."

"Why not?"

"He's an Albany guy. Why should he have a bookie in Saratoga? Anyway, I hear his credit's no good."

"Butch Howard lives in Albany? You know where?" asked Charlie.

"Nope. Why didn't you talk to him last night if you wanted to?" Graham appeared less interested in the conversation and kept looking toward his car, which had steam rising from under its hood.

"Was he at the dogfights?" asked Victor. "The guy with the cowboy boots?"

"I don't know anything about any cowboy boots, but Howard was there all right, at least at the beginning."

Charlie decided to upset Graham a little. "Did you know that Shaw was murdered last night? Someone blew him away with a shotgun."

Graham didn't answer but stared into Charlie's face as if to see if he were lying. His small mouth was still open and his lips were formed into a little pout. "You making that up?" he said at last.

"Shaw left the dogfights to get away from me, went to his

cousin's apartment, maybe telephoned someone and a half hour later somebody showed up and killed him."

Graham took a step back as if wanting to separate himself from Charlie and Victor. "I don't know anything."

"What did he have to hide?" asked Charlie.

"I tell you, I hardly knew the guy."

It occurred to Charlie that Graham was frightened again. "You go to the dogfights often?"

"That was the first time."

"What about Bagley, did you know him before?"

"Who's Bagley?"

"The guy who runs the dogfights."

"I never saw him." Graham had walked back to his car and stood by the hood. He began tugging at the straps of his black-leather driving gloves.

"And what about Pellegrino's murder?" said Charlie. "Have you had any more thoughts about that?"

"No thoughts, no ideas. You going to go on asking me these dumb questions?"

"It's either me or the police," said Charlie. "Did you talk to Shaw last night?"

"Not a word." Graham's mouth was open a little wider as if he couldn't get enough air.

"How about Butch Howard?"

"Not a word."

Charlie lowered his head. He was getting angry and he took a moment to relax. It seemed obvious that Graham knew something about Pellegrino's murder and probably something about Shaw's as well. One thing about being angry, it made him forget about the cold. "I hear you have some trotters," said Charlie, trying another approach. "How many do you have?"

"About a dozen. Well, six are mine and six I train for some other guys. What's this have to do with anything?"

"You got a farm around here?"

"Out in Washington County."

Washington was the county on the east side of the Hudson River from Saratoga. "Where abouts?" asked Charlie. Victor was making snowballs and tossing them at a post, missing every time.

"Just north of Cambridge. Look, Bradshaw, this is getting us nowhere."

"When you went to Pellegrino's Sunday night, I think you saw somebody and you're scared to say who you saw."

"Fuck you," said Graham.

"You even look scared," said Charlie.

Graham got back into the blue Mustang. "I told you I don't know anything," he shouted. "Why can't you just leave me alone?" Then he started the car and revved the motor, letting it get increasingly louder. Charlie stepped back to the fence as the Mustang accelerated down the track.

Victor threw a snowball after the Mustang, then tapped Charlie on the shoulder. "You're a pushy little guy," he said, "but five will get you ten that Butch Howard is our man. He's the fellow with the cowboy boots."

"If Howard's the guy we want," said Charlie, stepping back through the gate into the stands, "then he must have seen us last night. I mean, he knows us and we don't know him."

"Just put him in a yellow ski mask," said Victor, "and I'd know him anywhere."

Charlie and Victor climbed the stands to the office, which was up at the top between the press box and judging booth. The door was shut and locked but Charlie hammered on it. Just as he was about to quit, the door opened and a small old man looked up at him angrily.

"You don't have to beat the door down," he said.

"I'm sorry," said Charlie. "I didn't think anybody was here."

"I told 'em I'd be back this afternoon. I may be slow but I'm not forgetful. What do you want anyway?" The old man continued to stand in the doorway. He wore a tan corduroy jacket with food spots on the lapels. Behind him were three old wooden desks and half a dozen file cabinets. On the walls, posters of half-naked girls advertised Snap-On Tools.

"I want the address of someone who drives here," said Charlie. "Butch Howard."

"That should be easy enough," said the old man, shuffling back into the office. "I thought you were a bill collector."

Charlie and Victor entered the office. Victor pointed a thumb at one of the pinup girls. "Va-va-voom," he said.

The old man was thin and his jacket seemed several sizes too big for him. Perched on his nose was a pair of wire-rimmed glasses. He opened the middle drawer of a file cabinet and began leafing through some papers. A large picture window looked down onto the track where Graham's Mustang was still doing laps. In the distance were the tall buildings of downtown Albany.

"Here it is," said the old man, pulling out a folder.

"You got a picture as well?"

"Sure do. Does Butch owe you money? He owes lots of people money."

"Not me," said Charlie, taking the folder. Along with papers and application forms, the folder contained half a dozen eight-by-ten glossies showing a solidly built man standing next to a racing car. He had dark hair, a round face and heavy jowls around a wide jaw. His nose was a little squashed and looked like someone had once broken it for him. Although smiling, he didn't look friendly. Charlie didn't recognize the face. Butch Howard wore a set of white overalls covered with patches advertising the manufacturers of tires and oil and gasoline. Charlie copied down the address, a number on Everett Road on the other side of Albany.

"If you'd been here twenty minutes ago, you could have talked to him," said the old man.

"He was up here?" asked Charlie, surprised.

"That's what I'm saying, isn't it?" The old man discovered a gravy stain on his lapel and began picking at it.

"What did he want?"

"We start racing again in about six weeks. He wanted to sign up for a couple of races and to do that he had to pay the two hundred bucks he owes us."

"So he paid you?"

"That's what I'm telling you, isn't it?" The old man grinned as if he had scored a couple of points off Charlie.

Victor looked at the photograph in Charlie's hand. "That guy was there last night. I'm pretty sure I remember him."

Charlie looked out the picture window and down at the track. About sixty feet away was the spot where he had been talking to Graham. It occurred to Charlie that Butch Howard must have seen him with Graham, and no doubt recognized him from the previous night. And if he had robbed the Super Bowl party, then he must have recognized Victor as well. Charlie glanced at the photograph. Howard looked nothing like a lynx, maybe a bull or an ox. Again Charlie had the sense of being a few minutes too late.

19

Victor wadded up a piece of wax paper and tossed it onto the floor of the Renault. "Tell me what you like about that little broad that cleans your teeth," he said. Then he belched and rubbed his stomach. They had stopped for burgers-to-go at a sub shop near the Harrison Speedway, eating them in the car as they drove into Albany. Charlie hadn't wanted to stop, feeling there wasn't time, but Victor had insisted.

"She's kind," said Charlie, with a faint twinge of guilt.

"You still carrying a torch for Doris Bailes, is that your trouble?" asked Victor. Doris was the woman whom Charlie had lost to Roger Phelps, the high school science teacher. He thought he had gotten her out of his system, but sometimes at night he would wake up and realize he'd been dreaming about her. She would seem so real, so much with him, then, lying in the dark, he would realize again that she was gone.

"I'm pretty much over that," said Charlie, finishing the last of his diet cola. There was a taste of onions in his mouth, and he knew he'd have it with him for the rest of the day.

"It just seems to me," said Victor, "that getting your teeth cleaned is not a reason for a relationship. Big tits, yes. Pretty face, maybe. But the fact that this girl scrubs your choppers seems a little kinky."

"She's kind," repeated Charlie.

"You mean she pats your forehead and says, 'Poor thing'? Shit, if that's what you want, I'd be happy to oblige."

"I like her," said Charlie. "I really like her."

"Yeah, but she doesn't knock your socks off."

"I'm fifty," said Charlie. "I can't afford to have my socks knocked off."

"Never stopped me none," said Victor. "I'm always missing a sock here or there. What do you talk about?"

"Well, you know," said Charlie, embarrassed.

"You mean you talk about teeth?"

"Among other things."

"That's what flicks your switch, talking about teeth?"

"Not necessarily," said Charlie.

"Hey, you're my buddy, you gotta drop this dame and let me introduce you to a red-hot mama."

"The last red-hot mama you introduced me to left deep scratches on my back."

"That," said Victor, "is what red-hot mamas are all about."

Charlie looked straight ahead out at the snow and said nothing. They were crossing Albany on Central Avenue. It was getting toward rush hour and traffic was heavy.

"So when are you seeing Lady Teeth again?" asked Victor.

"Her name's Grace," said Charlie, "and I'm seeing her tonight."

"Rinse and spit," said Victor, "rinse and spit."

Butch Howard lived in a large and battered-looking apartment house on the north side of Albany. He wasn't at home. Charlie roused the super and learned that Howard lived alone, had few visitors and kept to himself.

"As far as I know," said the super, "the guy could be a monk or the king of Siam."

"Monks don't wear cowboy boots," said Victor.

The super looked at Victor suspiciously. He was a flabby middle-aged man in gray work pants and a sleeveless T-shirt. On his right shoulder was the tattooed silhouette of a collie and under that was printed the name "Irma." "If you want to make jokes," said the super, "then why don'tcha go on the TV?"

"Do you know where Howard works?" asked Charlie.

"No idea."

"Does he have any friends in the building?"

"No idea."

They were standing in the lobby by a pair of elevators. "You mind if we take a peek at his apartment?" asked Charlie.

"You want me to call the cops?" said the super.

"What about his neighbors?" asked Charlie. "Perhaps they'd like to talk to us."

"Fat chance," said the super. Then he glanced down and saw that Charlie was holding a twenty-dollar bill. "But," he added, taking the bill, "you can always give it a try."

Butch Howard lived on the fifth floor. There were seven other apartments on the floor but only three people were home— one at the opposite end of the hall from Howard, one next door and one across the hall. The woman down the hall had no idea who Charlie was talking about. The man across the way said he'd only spoken to Howard once all year. He'd wished Howard a Merry Christmas and Howard had said the same in return. The woman next door said that Howard sometimes played his TV late at night, also that he usually got in late. She didn't think he ever had any visitors, at least she'd never heard anybody. She had no idea where he worked.

"What's to say he's got a job?" she asked. The woman was dark-haired and in her thirties, and from inside her apartment Charlie could hear a baby crying. "I mean, he comes and goes at all hours. If he's got a job, it's sure not from nine to five. Maybe he's a private detective or something like that."

"Maybe," said Charlie.

She had never spoken to Howard but sometimes they'd nod

in the hall. "It's not like he's rude or anything. He just keeps to himself."

As they waited for the elevator after leaving the woman, Victor said, "Maybe he really is a monk."

"He's a loner," said Charlie. "He's a loner and he gambles and he robbed your party and maybe he killed Bobo Shaw and now and then he races stock cars." The elevator arrived and they got in. Written in red Magic Marker on the rear wall were the words "Albany sucks."

"So now what are we going to do?" asked Victor.

"We're going to take a look at the place where they had the dogfights last night."

"Are you going to tell the cops about Howard?"

"Not yet."

By now it was getting dark, although it was only about four o'clock. Charlie drove down to the river looking for the warehouse. He didn't know Albany very well and kept getting messed up with one-way streets.

"What was Butch Howard doing at the dogfights?" asked Charlie.

"Betting," said Victor.

"No, when you saw him what was he doing?"

"Just standing around."

"Did he seem eager or excited?"

"No, that's what struck me about him. He didn't look like anything, not interested, not uninterested."

"Was he watching the people or watching the dogs?" asked Charlie.

Victor had begun cracking his knuckles, methodically working his way up one hand and down the other. "I don't know, I mean, he was just a guy I noticed."

Charlie parked in front of the warehouse and got out. He felt chilled from the lack of heat in his car. Stamping his feet, he pulled up his collar and buried his chin in his scarf. "I wonder if they need detectives in Florida," he asked.

"Nah," said Victor, "they don't mind crime down there. I seen it on the TV. It's a kind of sport."

Charlie opened the side door of the warehouse and went in. Stacked on the floor where the dogfights had been were boxes of air conditioners. At first Charlie thought he might have come to the wrong place, but then he recognized the pattern of pipes on the ceiling and a pair of big sliding doors in back.

An older man in green work clothes approached them. "You lookin' for someone?" he asked.

"Ralph Bagley," said Charlie. "Has he been around?"

"What's he look like?" asked the man.

"He's about fifty, blond wavy hair, a little taller than I am, likes cowboy clothes, wears about half a dozen rings—flashy ones." A forklift started beeping as it backed up carrying a load of boxes.

"Nobody like that around here." The man seemed relaxed and not very interested. He had one of those big noses that looked spongy, as if one could sop up water with it.

"What about Butch Howard?" asked Charlie.

"Don't know the name."

Charlie unrolled Howard's picture and held it out. The man studied it for a moment, then shook his head. "Nope, don't know him."

"Could they have been around here without your knowing?" asked Charlie. The forklift turned and carried the load of boxes toward the rear of the warehouse.

"I'm foreman," said the man. "It's not very likely."

"When did these air conditioners come in?" asked Charlie.

"Just today."

"And what was here yesterday?"

"Nothing, the place was empty."

"And the day before?"

"More air conditioners."

"You notice any dead dogs around here this morning?" asked Victor.

The foreman looked at Victor as if trying to determine if he was joking or crazy. Then he scratched his nose and looked away. "You boys got anything else you want to know?"

Charlie thanked the man, and he and Victor returned to the Renault. "Somebody must know about those dogs," said Victor. "I mean, those people last night didn't just break in, have a bunch of dogfights, then sneak out again."

"But it wasn't the foreman," said Charlie, starting the Renault. He drove down the street and turned left at the corner. It wasn't quite dark enough for his headlights but he turned them on anyway. The district had a lot of small warehouses, garages and body shops, little groceries and a few tenements. The snow on the streets was already dirty, and there were great piles of it at the corners where it had been pushed by the plows. Charlie realized he had turned a block too soon in order to get back to the expressway, and he turned right at the next corner. Glancing into his mirror, he noticed a car turning behind him. Perhaps he was lost as well. Some slush had hardened under the Renault's left front fender, and the tire rubbing against it made a gentle whirring noise.

"We sure ran all over these streets last night," said Victor. "I thought I'd bust a gut."

Charlie glanced again in the rearview mirror at the other car, then turned left at the corner just to see what would happen. The car turned after him. It was a dark, late-model Pontiac with its lights off. Charlie sped up, then turned right at the next corner. The Pontiac continued to follow him. It occurred to Charlie that it was a Pontiac that had been seen driving away from the Lincoln Grill after Bobo Shaw was shot.

"You givin' your car a little exercise?" asked Victor.

"There's a car following us," said Charlie. "Don't turn around."

Charlie drove another two blocks, wondering what to do. If the Pontiac had followed him from the warehouse, perhaps the driver was somehow connected to the dogfights. But maybe it had followed him from Butch Howard's apartment house or even from the speedway. Had he been paying attention? He couldn't be sure. Abruptly Charlie swung the wheel left and gunned the motor, then at the next corner turned left again, still accelerating. The Renault fishtailed around the corner.

"Attaboy, Charlie," said Victor, putting on his seat belt, "if you crack us up, then he won't be able to follow us anymore."

"Be quiet," said Charlie, taking the next right turn. He had seen two tractor-trailer trucks parked across a side street a few blocks away and he wanted to get back to them. The Pontiac was still following but now it had dropped half a block behind. Charlie took the next right, swinging wide and fishtailing up the street through the snow. The Renault made a high whining noise as he kept it in second gear. He barely avoided a UPS truck as he skidded sideways into the next right turn. The driver's face had been a startled moon shape. Charlie gunned the motor again. The Pontiac was now almost a block behind. Straightening the wheel, Charlie saw the two semis pulled halfway across the street. He swerved left to get around the first, swerved right around the next, then accelerated and pulled up on his emergency brake at the same time, swinging the Renault into a tight circle.

"Cut this out!" shouted Victor. "I've got a delicate stomach!"

The Renault came to a stop beside the second tractor-trailer truck. Charlie flicked off his lights, put the car in reverse and backed up against the wall of a warehouse just as the Pontiac came sliding by. When he saw the other car, Charlie turned to follow it. The driver was just a dark shape.

"You got your gun?" asked Victor.

"It's back at the office."

"What about your spare?"

"It's home."

"You going to throw the rest of your burger at the guy? Maybe smack him with your road map?"

The Pontiac turned left and Charlie turned left as well. He didn't think the man in the Pontiac knew he was behind him.

The driver kept slowing at the intersections to look down the cross streets. He turned right at the next corner and Charlie turned after him.

"He's going to catch on pretty quick," said Victor. "And Charlie, these tough guys don't like being toyed with."

"I don't like being tailed," said Charlie.

But then the man in the Pontiac realized he was being followed and the rear end of his car made a little shimmy on the ice as he accelerated. Charlie pressed down on the gas and the Renault jumped forward. "Hold on," he said.

The Pontiac turned left and Charlie turned left as well, staying twenty feet behind the other car. Banks of snow lined the road. A pickup coming toward them pulled to the side to get out of the way. Charlie missed it by six inches. Again he was aware of a startled face, this time a black one. At the corner the Pontiac braked and turned left. Charlie noticed that the driver's window was open. Then he saw a hand holding a gun.

"Watch out!" he shouted, hitting the brake and ducking down behind the wheel. Charlie had begun blowing the horn so he didn't hear the gun shot, just a smacking noise as the bullet went through his windshield. The Renault was sliding at an angle across the intersection and Charlie kept pumping the brake. Above him he could see a streetlight going on, then the roof of a building. He kept his head ducked down and hung on. The Renault still must have been going about fifteen miles an hour when it hit the snowdrift. As Charlie was thrown forward, it occurred to him that he should have been wearing his seat belt. His shoulder banged against the wheel and his knee was jammed against the console. The Renault came to a stop and there was a sensation of total silence, as if he had suddenly gone deaf. Looking at Victor, Charlie saw he was slumped over in his seat.

"Victor, you all right?"

"I got bumped, that's all. How come you like to get people mad?"

"I like to see what they'll do," said Charlie. His shoulder

hurt but he didn't think anything was broken. The front of the Renault and the windshield were buried in the snowdrift and the interior of the Renault was dark. Victor stretched and began rubbing his arms.

"I wasn't bumped hard," he said, "but I was bumped all over."

Charlie's knee hurt as well but he told himself the pain would go away. He put the Renault in reverse, then listened to the tires spin. "Can you get out and push?" asked Charlie.

Victor tried to open his door. "It's jammed against the snow."

"Mine, too," said Charlie, heaving against it. "I was sort of hoping the guy in the Pontiac would think we were cops." He began climbing into the backseat to try the rear door.

"What cop in his right mind would be driving a Renault Encore?" asked Victor.

With some shoving, Charlie managed to open the back door. The Pontiac was nowhere in sight. Standing in the middle of the street, Charlie flagged down another car and with the help of the two men inside he was able to push the Renault out of the snow drift.

"Just lost control," he told them. Both his knee and shoulder hurt.

"Fuckin' snowplows do a lousy fuckin' job," said one of the men.

The right headlight of the Renault was smashed and the front was dented. Worst of all, the windshield was all cracked and starred. It would have to be replaced before they drove back to Saratoga. Below the rearview mirror was a hole about the size of a dime. In the window of the rear right door was the exit hole. Charlie wondered if his insurance would take care of it.

One of the men told Charlie of a garage two blocks away that specialized in auto glass. Charlie thanked him, then he and Victor got back in the Renault. Charlie tried to remember if Jesse James had ever had any horses shot out from underneath him. Driving to the garage, he had to keep his head out the window in order to see, and soon his ears were freezing. The first chance he got, he told himself, he was going to buy himself a new watch cap. The manager of the garage was just closing up, but he agreed to do the job for an extra twenty bucks.

"Doesn't look like a pebble," said the man. "Looks like somebody took a shot at you."

"How odd," said Charlie.

As Charlie and Victor waited for the windshield to be replaced, Charlie said, "Did you get a look at the guy who shot at us?"

"I saw his hand and I saw his gun, then I ducked."

"Nothing else?"

"You're going to tell me he was wearing cowboy boots."

"No, he had a mustache," said Charlie, feeling pleased with himself.

"Him and ten thousand other guys," said Victor. "So what are you going to do after we get out of here?"

"First I want to talk to Artemis, then I've got to get my teeth cleaned."

Behind Artemis's small house was a barn that had been rebuilt to make a great open space where she could work with her horses, galloping around and around in a circle. She was doing this now as Charlie sat in a straight chair in the middle of the circle, trying not to turn his head but rather to wait for Artemis to come around again, satisfying himself with only seeing her half the time. Hanging from the crossbeams were four large lights. A gas heater rattled noisily against the wall but otherwise it wasn't very effective. Charlie felt cold. It seemed he'd been cold for days.

The large pink horse slowly galloped by again with Artemis on his back. The horse's name was Phillip and he was Artemis's prize possession. Charlie thought this might be because Phillip was the only horse shaped like a giant tea cozy. For the past five times around Artemis had been balancing on her head with her feet straight up in the air. She wore a bright green outfit which was somewhere between a body stocking and a jumpsuit. It had spangles on the arms and legs which glittered in the overhead lights. She seemed thoughtful.

"An acquaintance, Charlie, is someone with whom you have no emotional connection. You wish the person well, but often you prefer their absence to their presence. My relationship with Leonard Graham is like that. Also he is a borrower. Didn't your mother warn you about those?"

"Never a borrower or a lender be," said Charlie, turning in his chair to follow Artemis around the ring. He had arrived half an hour earlier to ask Artemis if she knew Leonard Graham. Even since Graham had told him that he had a farm north of Cambridge, Charlie had thought that he and Artemis might live fairly near each other. As it turned out, Graham's farm was about a mile away.

"Exactly. Mr. Graham is always running out of items and coming to me to be rescued."

"What sort of items?" asked Charlie.

"Lawn mowers, fertilizer spreaders, bags of feed, a few bales of hay."

"Does he return them?" asked Charlie. His shoulder still hurt from where he had bumped it when his car hit the snowdrift, but his knee was feeling all right.

"Yes, but not promptly and once I had to ask. I found it disagreeable." Artemis flipped herself up in the air and did a split onto Phillip's back. Watching her do it made Charlie's legs ache.

"Is he good with his horses?" asked Charlie.

"Not particularly. Leonard is a man who dabbles in many areas hoping to find the one thing that will save him. He is a mediocre trainer and has a mediocre string of trotters."

"He's also a gambler," said Charlie.

"That doesn't surprise me," said Artemis, rising from her

split to do a handstand. "The trouble with that point of view is that you are always looking to be saved by something outside of yourself. I find it safer to do things for myself. I know what I have to do and I do it, or try to, and I never expect to be bailed out by good fortune. The trouble with depending on good fortune is that it so quickly turns bad."

"Do you ever buy lottery tickets?" asked Charlie.

"Once, just to see how it worked. I didn't win."

"Do you play cards, shoot dice, bet on horses or football or basketball games?"

"I'm afraid that world is a great mystery to me," said Artemis, lowering her feet so that she was bent like a croquet hoop. "I don't feel particularly moralistic about it, but neither am I interested."

"I could get into that world without much trouble," said Charlie. "My father was a crazy gambler and ended up shooting himself when he got too far behind. I still remember the house being full of policemen."

"That must have been terrible for you."

"I don't remember anything but the policemen and they were pretty nice."

"If the odds are always against the person placing the bet," said Artemis, "then it's certain that he'll eventually fall behind."

"They figure they can beat the odds," said Charlie.

"That seems a sad sort of expectation. It's a way of trying to be special but doing nothing to earn it, expecting the gods to recognize your specialness and let you win, thereby proving your superiority."

Charlie was having trouble both following the conversation and watching Artemis go round and round. "Does Graham have any friends near here?" he asked, hoping not to offend Artemis by changing the subject.

"Not that I know of, although last year he sold off fifty acres of his farm to another man who's built a house there. They seem to be friendly."

Charlie had a mental image of these crimes and problems and questions as forming a giant puzzle from which many pieces were missing, like a huge map of the United States with Texas gone and New England lost. As Artemis spoke he felt that a piece of the puzzle—one of the bigger pieces—was about to be presented to him.

"And do you know the person?" he asked.

"No, but he has the most awful little dogs. People are afraid to go by his property."

"Pit bull terriers?" asked Charlie. He realized that Graham had lied to him, had been lying to him all along.

"Precisely," said Artemis, again standing on her head.

"Is the man's name Ralph Bagley?"

"That's the very man."

That evening Charlie didn't get to Grace Washburn's apartment until ten. He kissed her cheek and she led him into the kitchen. She was not happy that he had arrived over an hour late, even though he had called; and she got to work cleaning his teeth with scarcely a hello, pushing his head forward and back and telling him to open wider. Her blond hair had been fixed in tight little curls that reminded Charlie of his ex-wife in a way that he didn't like. Over her blue dress she wore a white apron.

Why am I doing this? Charlie asked himself. As he leaned back in the chair, he kept thinking of Ralph Bagley and whether or not he looked like a lynx. He didn't think he did. On the other hand, he wasn't exactly sure what a lynx looked like. He imagined someone with cat's eyes, blondish, pointy ears, a round face, sharp little teeth. It didn't sound like Bagley. Charlie had driven by his property. The house was a modern ranch-style set back about a hundred yards from the road. There had been no lights on, although a mercury vapor light had been burning out by the barn. Bagley's yard and the area around the barn were surrounded by a high chain-link fence. Charlie had stopped his car and rolled down the window but he hadn't heard any barking.

"Rinse," said Grace.

Charlie rinsed.

"You don't seem very interested in this, Charlie," said Grace, standing over him.

"You just did it the other day."

"Clean teeth have to be kept clean, you know that."

"Sometimes I forget," said Charlie.

"Open wider," said Grace.

Charlie opened wider. Grace fastened her fingers on his jaw and began scraping at a rear molar with a metal pick. Charlie looked into her hair. Had it always resembled Marge's? That was a frightening thought.

Afterward they went out to eat at a steakhouse on Broadway which was in an old firehouse. Charlie preferred eating at Hattie's Chicken Shack but Grace said there was never anyone there, by which she meant people of standing in the community. At the steak place Charlie saw his cousin Robert and his wife, Lucy, and with them was Charlie's oldest cousin, James, and his wife, Peggy. James had his back to Charlie but Robert was facing him and pretended not to see him. It occurred to Charlie that instead of his relationship with his cousin becoming better because of the help he was giving him, it would get worse. Charlie now knew that Robert was a gambler and he didn't think his cousin would forgive that. To needle Robert, Charlie told the waitress to send them over whatever they were drinking, which happened to be a pitcher of Coke. They turned and nodded to Charlie and he nodded back. James had started out his adult life as a carpenter whom everyone called Jimmy. In his dark suit and tie, his serious, self-important expression, there was no trace of that Jimmy left. Robert was trying to smile at Charlie, but his face was so frozen that Charlie thought he had seen nicer smiles on the dead.

"I like to see you keeping up your relations with your cousins," said Grace.

"It's the least I can do," said Charlie.

After dinner they went back to Grace's house and watched

Ronald Colman in *Lost Horizon* on the VCR. After that they made love. Charlie didn't think Grace was very interested in the process. What seemed to interest her most were teeth and cleaning them and polishing them and talking about them. Kissing her on the forehead, Charlie rolled over to his side of the bed.

"I liked that," he said, wondering if he had.

"I'm glad," said Grace, rather tonelessly. Then she got up and went into the bathroom. Charlie read for a while, a book which claimed that Pat Garrett hadn't killed Billy the Kid after all. Charlie was rather shocked by it. Grace came back and went to sleep while he was still reading. She slept on her back and at one point Charlie turned and saw that her mouth was open. Guiltily, he leaned over and looked inside. How dark it was and how sharp her teeth looked. Charlie decided that he didn't like it. He thought of the times he'd kissed her and decided he didn't like that either. Finishing his chapter, he quietly got out of bed, got dressed, sneaked out of her apartment and drove home. Out on the road to the lake he felt strangely exuberant, like he was free of something or had just been let out of school early.

20

Janey Burris stood back as Charlie wiped his feet and entered the hall. "Andy Clamper is unhappy with you," she said.

"Why is that?" asked Charlie.

"He says you turned him into the police about those car radios."

Charlie took off his new blue watch cap, purchased that morning, and unbuttoned his overcoat. "That's true enough. Did he say anything else?"

Janey shoved her hands deep into the pockets of her red terry-cloth robe. It was a man's robe and reached her ankles. "He made a few rude remarks about your height."

"Anything else?"

"I can't remember."

"At least he didn't say I was overweight," said Charlie.

"Maybe I forgot that part," she said, then added, "You don't seem so overweight." She had a cigarette in her mouth, and as she leaned against the wall she tilted her head to the left to keep the smoke out of her eyes. Her eyes were a dark brown that reminded Charlie of chocolate.

"It's a congenital weakness," said Charlie. "So you've seen him?"

They began walking down the hall toward the kitchen. "I took him some cigarettes last night. He wanted me to go bail for him, but my kindness stops at cigarettes."

The morning sun through the kitchen window reflected off the yellow Formica of the counters and the white enamel table. Tacked to the wall next to the refrigerator was a large poster of sunflowers in a yellow vase. Charlie liked all the colors and didn't see why he didn't have more pictures in his own house. "I want to talk to him this morning," he said. "And I thought you'd have some suggestions as to how I might soften him up."

"So you don't want any whiskey?" asked Janey, leaning against the counter. Her short dark hair hadn't been brushed and was pointing in a thousand directions. She wasn't beautiful but Charlie found it hard not to look at her. Her face had lots of light in it somehow. Charlie couldn't explain it.

"Too early for whiskey. Anyway, my cold's better."

"How about coffee?"

"I'll take a cup."

Janey filled a blue mug with coffee from the stove and handed it to him. Then she poured a cup for herself. "You want anything in it?"

"I'm fine."

"Why do you want to soften Andy up?" asked Janey.

"A guy he worked with was shot and killed. Andy might be able to tell me about some of the people involved."

"Take him some Kit-Kats and *Easy Rider*s," said Janey. She sipped her coffee, then blew on it.

"Pardon me?"

"Kit-Kats and *Easy Rider*s. The first's a candy and the second's a motorcycle magazine. Other than gambling, those are Andy's only passions."

"I'll try it," said Charlie. He sipped his coffee. It was still too hot to drink. He glanced around the kitchen. A stuffed bear, a small locomotive, plus some dolls and other toys were scattered across the floor, along with the tennis balls. They created a comfortable sort of confusion.

"You're pretty quiet today," said Janey.

"I was wondering if you'd go out to dinner with me next week. Like Tuesday."

Janey put her mug on the counter. At first Charlie thought she was offended, but then she gave him a wink. "You plan to start courting me?" she asked.

"Maybe," said Charlie. "I mean, at least since you don't think I'm so fat."

"What if Dumkowski comes back?"

"Who?"

"My husband."

"He can come, too," said Charlie.

"That's all right," said Janey, picking up her coffee again. "I'd prefer to have you to myself."

Chief Peterson was not happy about Charlie bringing Andy Clamper a CARE package, as he called it.

"This guy's been terrorizing cars around here for six months and you want to mollycoddle him?"

"How come he's not out on bail?" Charlie asked.

"He couldn't raise the money." They talked in Peterson's office with Charlie standing in front of the chief's desk. Peterson leaned back in his chair with his fingers linked behind his head and his elbows pointing out to either side. It made his head look like something stuck to a plaque.

"I want to ask him about some stuff down in Albany. It has nothing to do with you." Sometimes it frightened Charlie how easily he could lie.

"No more than ten minutes, all right?"

"You bet."

As Charlie was led downstairs to the jail, he kept thinking that he had spent twenty years working in this building. It seemed like an entirely different life. Who had he been back then? The guard stopped at Clamper's cell, unlocked the door and pulled it open. Charlie stepped inside.

"I brought you a little present," he said.

Clamper was lying on his belly on the cot, his bare feet sticking over the end. He was dressed in jeans and a white T-shirt. Turning his head to look at Charlie, he cleared his throat and spat onto the concrete floor. "I don't want anything from you," he said.

Charlie kept holding out the bag and after another minute Clamper sat up and took it with one of his large whoopee-cushion hands. He seemed torn between looking inside or throwing it back at Charlie unopened. After a moment he looked inside. "Who told you I liked Kit-Kats?" he said.

"A little bird," said Charlie.

"And an *Easy Rider*." Clamper began to tear the red paper off the Kit-Kat.

"It's the new one, it just came out," said Charlie. "I figured you hadn't seen it yet."

"I hadn't," said Clamper, biting into the Kit-Kat. "You must have a lot of stuff you want me to tell you." Staring at Charlie, Clamper chewed the candy. He had a long, pinkish face and Charlie wondered what sort of name Pellegrino would have given him. Charlie decided he had a face like a goat, a pinkish goat. A drunk in another cell was shouting in his sleep—something about dogs biting his ankles.

"Not necessarily," said Charlie. He leaned back against the wall. It was a narrow cell with a cot, a toilet and a small sink. It was warm, even stuffy, and Clamper had thrown his two blankets on the floor. "You know Bobo Shaw was killed night before last?" asked Charlie.

"I figured there was trouble when we saw the cops." Clamper ate the candy and began leafing through the magazine. A strand of long dark hair fell forward across his face.

"You don't seem to care much."

Clamper looked up as if surprised. "It wasn't as if we were friends or anything. He bullied me a lot. Besides, I still owed him a chunk of money." Clamper finished his first Kit-Kat and began ripping the paper from the second, dropping the paper onto the floor. It occurred to Charlie that he had never eaten a Kit-Kat. They looked like chocolate-covered wafers. He found himself wanting one but he hated to ask.

"You know a guy named Butch Howard?" asked Charlie.

"I seen him at the dogfights. And he races cars, too."

"You know anything about him?"

Clamper took a large bite out of the second Kit-Kat. "Not really. He's a tough guy. The kind of person who bumps into you, then looks into your face like he's saying, 'So what.' He's friends with the bartender who works for Bagley."

"You remember his name?"

"Frankie Leach."

"What's he look like?"

"He's in his late thirties, brown hair, maybe six feet."

"Does he have a mustache?"

"Yeah."

"I remember him," said Charlie. "He spilled my whiskey on purpose." He tried to remember if many men at the dogfights had had mustaches. Down the hall a radio suddenly began to blare rock and roll, then it was turned down.

"He's got a temper," said Clamper. "They both got tempers, like they like getting mad a lot." He again began flipping through the magazine, then held up the center page which showed a naked girl sprawled across a black motorcycle. "How d'you like that?" he asked.

"Fantastic," said Charlie. "Was Shaw friends with Howard and Frankie Leach?"

"They hung out together some, but I wouldn't call them friends."

"You know where I could find Howard?"

"No idea. Maybe the Harrison Speedway." Clamper was still staring at the nude girl on the motorcycle.

"What about Leach?"

"Maybe he's with Howard or maybe Howard's with him. Like I been telling you, I see them at the dogfights and maybe once or twice at the Speedway. They make a lot of bets and quarrel with a lot of guys. I try to stay out of their way."

"Could they be the men that Shaw gave the picture to?"

Clamper looked up from the magazine, squinting at Charlie through the lock of hair which had fallen over his eyes. It was clear that he disliked being distracted from his reading. "Could be. He didn't say."

"Could they have robbed that Super Bowl party?"

"Sure, why not?" Clamper began turning the pages of the magazine, then stopped at a picture of bikers drinking and their girlfriends pulling up their T-shirts to show their breasts.

"What do you know about Bagley?" asked Charlie.

"Nothing, except that he runs the dogfights."

"And some of those dogs are his?"

"That's right. He's got five or six of them, maybe more."

"And he bets his dogs?"

"Sure, that's the whole point," said Clamper, still studying the party pictures. One of the girls was standing on the seat of a motorcycle and had pulled her T-shirt up to her neck. From where Charlie stood her breasts looked like little bald heads.

"How's he do?"

"Pretty well."

"Does he ever lose big?" asked Charlie.

Andy Clamper looked up from the magazine. "Matter of fact, he lost bad a couple of weeks ago. He had this dog that won about ten fights. A guy came up from the Bronx with a smooth-looking little dog, no scars or nothing. Bagley's dog was the easy favorite and a lotta money went down. That little dog killed Bagley's dog in about two minutes. I lost five hundred dollars."

"How much did Bagley lose?"

"I don't know, but I heard he was hurting."

"What do you know about Leonard Graham?"

"Nothing." Clamper began leafing through the magazine again. In another cell someone began singing off-key to the radio. Charlie couldn't recognize the song. Maybe it was the Rolling Stones, maybe it was the Beatles. The voice reverberated off the stone walls.

"Graham races cars at the Speedway and looks like a fish," said Charlie.

"Yeah, I know who you mean, but I've never talked to him."

"Do you know Blake Moss?" asked Charlie.

"What's he look like?"

"He's tall, a little chunky, short blond hair, a round face, about forty. He looks like he spent a lot of his life in the army. He was at the dogfights the other night. I talked to him the next day. He said it was the first time he'd ever been there."

"You're kidding," said Andy Clamper, putting down the magazine again. "He's there all the time."

"You sure?"

"Look, I'm there all the time and whenever I'm there, this guy's there, too." He began opening his third Kit-Kat. Charlie had bought him ten. By now Charlie had decided to buy one for himself the moment he left the jail.

"Is he friends with Howard and Leach?"

"Not so you'd notice, although he must know them."

"How about with Bagley and Leonard Graham?"

"He's fairly friendly with Bagley, at least as much as anybody is. I've never seen him with Graham."

Charlie asked a few more questions but Clamper had reached a whole section of motorcycle party pictures and didn't want to be bothered.

"You ever been to one of those parties?" asked Charlie.

"Not yet," said Clamper. "I just hope they don't stop having them while I'm in jail. It'd be a bummer."

Charlie made his way back upstairs to see Peterson. He wanted to learn if Peterson had discovered anything new in the Pellegrino murder. Afterward he wanted to find Graham and confront him with his various deceptions. It seemed that if he could get Graham to talk, he would have a good idea who had killed Pellegrino. Then he could track down Butch Howard. For a moment Charlie again worried that Howard had seen him talking to Graham. If Graham really knew something about the murder and Howard was involved, well, Charlie hated to think what might happen if Howard had seen them together. Once more he urged himself to hurry. Time was slipping from him.

Peterson was still leaning back in his chair with his fingers linked behind his head. Charlie had the sense he had been frozen in that position since he'd last seen him twenty minutes before. The walls of his large office and almost every available surface were covered with medals, awards, testimonials, photographs and little statues paying tribute to Peterson's involvement with Irish setters: breeding them, raising them, training them, showing them. He was, as Victor had once said, the patron saint of Irish setters. The dogs were Peterson's primary passion, as if he found in them all the innocence and goodheartedness lacking in human beings.

"Junkies, Charlie, or some first-time crook with a nervous trigger finger, or maybe even a kid. The guy got scared and just blew Pellegrino away."

"What kind of gun?" asked Charlie.

"A regular thirty-eight. Now I don't want you to keep bothering me about this business. A case like this could take months to solve. You know that Pellegrino once spent a couple of years in Attica? He had an armed-robbery conviction nearly forty years ago. Knocked over a bunch of gas stations."

"That seems unlike him," said Charlie. He stood in front o. Peterson's desk and watched the police chief's large stomach—covered by a blue vest—move calmly up and down as he breathed.

"Pellegrino was the driver. He was just a kid then. But what if he met somebody in prison, somebody who didn't like him and who's been in jail all this time? Maybe somebody like that killed him."

"I find that hard to believe," said Charlie. It seemed that

Peterson was always searching for solutions that required little or no effort on his part.

"Maybe so, but we've both seen it happen." Peterson looked pleased with his theory, and he stretched a little and yawned.

"Do you know someone named John Oates?" asked Charlie. "He owns an antiques shop up in Glens Falls."

"What's he done that I should know about?"

"Nothing in particular. Do you know him?"

"Never had the pleasure."

"What about Butch Howard?"

"Never heard of him."

"Frankie Leach?"

"Ditto."

"What about Ralph Bagley?"

"Doesn't ring a bell. What are you up to, Charlie?"

"What about Leonard Graham? He's got a small horse farm out toward Cambridge, raises and trains trotters."

Peterson slowly lowered his arms and put his hands before him on the desk. He looked at Charlie as if Charlie might be pulling a trick on him. "Now Graham I've heard about," he said. "In fact I've heard about him in the past half hour. He was found dead on his property, some kind of hunting accident. It came over the radio."

"You're kidding me," said Charlie softly.

Peterson again linked his hands behind his head. "Jesus, Charlie, why would I kid you? The state police and the Washington County sheriff's department are handling it. Don't you think I got better things to do than trade jokes with an ex-cop?"

21

As Charlie drove out to Leonard Graham's farm, he again had the sense that he was moving too slowly. He shouldn't have gone out with Grace Washburn the previous night. He shouldn't have visited Janey Burris. He shouldn't have eaten or slept or looked out the window. He should have been pushing forward, searching for Butch Howard, following Leonard Graham, talking again to John Oates and even to his own cousin. He wondered if Blake Moss was one of those ultraprofessional detectives who move through their cases like a train moves along its track. Or Jesse, when had Jesse James ever dragged his feet?

It was a sunny day and Charlie wore his dark glasses as he drove along Route 29 toward Cambridge. The rolling hills were painfully bright, and in the distance the Green Mountains resembled white pillows. He kept thinking how pretty they looked and how lucky he was to see them. Then he determinedly lowered his visor and went back to thinking about Leonard Graham. He had known that Graham was hiding something, that he most likely had seen another car that night at Pellegrino's—a car he had recognized. Why had Graham remained silent?

Possibly he was afraid. Possibly the person he saw was a friend. Possibly they had some business connection which Graham hadn't wanted disturbed. Could his death really be an accident?

Despite his hurry, Charlie stopped at the Grand Union in Greenwich and bought a couple of Kit-Kats—crisp, chocolate-covered wafers. They were pretty good but he couldn't see how they might develop into an addiction. Chiding himself, he drove on toward Cambridge, driving too fast and sliding on the patches of snow.

He arrived at Graham's farm around eleven, just as Graham's body was being loaded into the ambulance—a mound on a stretcher covered with a red blanket and a pair of worn hiking boots with Vibram soles sticking out from one end. About ten state police and sheriff's deputies were standing around in the snow, plus two men from the Cambridge police department. It was cold and the various policemen were all trying to shrink themselves into their greatcoats. The ambulance was parked back by the horse barn about a hundred yards from the house. A youngish woman in a red mackinaw stood by the door of the ambulance. She was crying and kept wiping away the tears with a blue mitten. Charlie guessed she was Graham's wife and he felt sorry for her. The police seemed to be just finishing up. Charlie knew several of them, including a state police lieutenant from Salem, Jack Shepherd, who appeared to be in charge. Charlie walked over to him.

"How you doin', Charlie?" said Shepherd, shaking his hand. "You still pushing this private racket?" Shepherd wore a blue overcoat and a sheepskin trooper's cap with the earflaps up. He was a husky fellow of about forty-five and his features were red from the cold. He was smoking a pipe and he kept one hand cupped over the bowl to warm it.

"Pretty much," said Charlie. "What happened to Graham?" They stood by the corral fence about fifteen feet from the rear door of the ambulance. The two barns and several sheds were bright red; the house was a white colonial with two wineglass elms out in front. Without leaves, it was impossible to tell if they were still alive. So many had died throughout the county.

"Shot," said Shepherd. He blew out a small cloud of smoke and glanced toward the ambulance. "Maybe it was a hunting accident."

"Why maybe?"

"Whoever did it didn't hang around. You know any reason why somebody should have killed him?"

Charlie hesitated. The rear doors of the ambulance slammed shut and the two attendants climbed in the front.

"You must have driven out here for a reason, Charlie," said Shepherd. He tapped his pipe against a post, sending the ashes into the snow, then put the pipe in his pocket.

"A guy named Shaw was killed in Albany night before last," said Charlie. "He had some stolen property that I'm trying to recover. Graham knew Shaw so I thought I'd ask him some questions. Where was Graham killed?"

"He was out at the edge of the pasture," said Shepherd, pointing past the corral. "Whoever shot him was in the woods about fifty yards beyond. We found his tracks in the snow. They led back to the road on the other side of the woods. Then we lost them."

"You don't think he was a hunter?" asked Charlie.

"No way. Hunters wander around a lot. This guy walked directly through the woods and took up his stand by a big maple. He waited quite awhile; at least long enough to smoke a few cigarettes. Then Graham came out and he shot him right through the chest. Graham's wife found him a little later, maybe fifteen or twenty minutes. She'd heard the shot around nine but didn't think much of it."

"Did this hunter have a car?" asked Charlie.

"It might have been parked out on the road. It's impossible to tell from the tracks. Or maybe he had it someplace else and walked there. How was this guy killed in Albany?"

"A shotgun," said Charlie. "How was Graham killed?"

"Can't tell for sure. Maybe a thirty-thirty."

A gray-haired woman arrived in a rusty Toyota, parked it by the barn and hurried to Mrs. Graham and embraced her. They began walking toward the house. The ambulance made a U-turn and drove out of the yard. One of the state cops was telling a story about a pickpocket to two men from the Sheriff's Department. All three were grinning. Off in the barn a horse began whinnying.

"What kind of shoes was the guy in the woods wearing?" asked Charlie.

"Cowboy boots, I think. At least they had pointed toes. You think this shooting might be connected to the one in Albany?"

"I don't know," said Charlie. "A lieutenant by the name of Boland is handling it." Charlie disliked the situation he was in. The theft of the painting, the robbery of Victor's party, Pellegrino's murder—he couldn't talk to the police about any of them. Beyond that, all these people had false fronts, false personalities that made them seem different from what they were. Pellegrino appeared to be a grocer but was really a bookie. Charlie's cousin appeared to be a real estate agent but was really a gambler. Graham, Shaw, Howard, Bagley—they all had other lives connected to their gambling and criminal activities. Nothing was as it seemed.

Graham had noticed something at Pellegrino's and as a result he had been shot. Because of the cowboy boots, Charlie guessed the killer was Butch Howard and again he thought how Howard must have seen him talking to Graham at the Speedway. Possibly it was Howard whom Graham had seen on the night Pellegrino was killed. It seemed such a mix-up. At first Charlie had thought that Bobo Shaw was the key to the entire case. Then Shaw was killed. Next Charlie had thought Graham was the key. Then Graham was killed. And now it seemed that Butch Howard was the key, and a dangerous key at that.

The man whom Charlie still hadn't spoken to was Ralph Bagley. Supposedly he had bought fifty acres from Graham and had built a house on it, although Charlie doubted that money had changed hands. Most likely it was another gambling debt. Charlie decided he had to talk to Bagley and learn what he had to say about Shaw and Graham, and if he knew anything that might lead to Butch Howard. As he spoke with Lieutenant Shepherd, he began to walk back toward his car with an eye to breaking off the conversation and driving over to Bagley's house. Charlie felt hopeful that Bagley could help him. After all, Bagley seemed to know all these people.

As it turned out the opportunity to talk to Bagley happened far more quickly than Charlie could have expected. He had almost reached his Renault and had paused to shake hands with Shepherd when one of the troopers came hurrying over to them.

"Lieutenant, a man's been killed by dogs on the next farm. He had a rifle with him."

Two state police and two sheriff's cars drove the half mile to Bagley's farm and Charlie followed last of all in his Renault. The sun reflecting off the new snow made the air sharp like a knife, and the distant farmhouses and barns scattered across the hills seemed so clear and precise that Charlie had the sense he could reach out and touch them. Bagley's house was up the hill from Graham's and on the other side of the woods. It was a long ranch house set well back from the road. Behind it was a large corrugated metal barn and a kennel. A high chain-link fence surrounded the house and other buildings. A sheriff's deputy stood at the gate and waved the cars through.

Two men stood back by the barn—one was another deputy and the second was Ralph Bagley in a green down jacket and a white cowboy hat. Charlie parked next to the police cars by the side of the house, then followed Lieutenant Shepherd along the driveway. Glancing toward the house, Charlie tried to see inside but the drapes were closed. The house had brick on the bottom half and white clapboard on the top. On each window were green shutters and on each shutter was a gold initial: B.

From the kennel came the barking of several dogs. It was a crisp sort of noise, eager and abrupt.

When Charlie saw Howard's body, he thought he recognized him from his photograph but he couldn't be sure because of the damage done by the dogs. Howard's throat had been torn. Part of his face was chewed and he was missing an ear. He wore jeans, cowboy boots and a short black leather jacket which had been badly ripped. He lay on his back in the snow, which was spattered with blood, great red splashes against the white, looking like red continents on a white map. Surrounding him were hundreds of pink pawprints, showing where the dogs had tracked the blood. Ten feet away lay a .30–30 rifle. Charlie and the half dozen policemen stopped near the rifle, letting Lieutenant Shepherd approach the body and talk to the deputy and Ralph Bagley. There was something horrifying about the pink paw prints, as if the dogs had been dancing wildly around Butch Howard as they killed him.

"I was gone all night," Bagley was telling Shepherd. "When I returned an hour ago, I found Mr. Howard. I have no idea what he was doing here." Bagley's green down jacket made his body look like a barrel. His tall rubber boots were half buried in the snow. He showed no nervousness in the presence of the body. Actually, he hardly seemed to notice Butch Howard at all.

"Do you usually let your dogs run free?" asked Shepherd. He had begun to stuff his pipe from a leather tobacco pouch which he had taken from the pocket of his blue overcoat.

"There's a high fence and there are signs," said Bagley. "I'm often away and I have a lot of valuable property. Only a fool would climb the fence."

"He had a rifle but he didn't shoot," said Shepherd. "Why didn't he, do you think?" He lit his pipe and Charlie caught the smell of his tobacco. In a pine tree behind the kennel a whole bunch of crows were cawing like crazy.

"The dogs are quick and there were three of them. Perhaps

he didn't have the chance." Bagley had his hands in the pockets of his down jacket. As he spoke he removed them and abruptly struck his fist into his other palm, making his rings sparkle in the sunlight.

Shepherd knelt down beside Howard to look more closely at his throat, which appeared to have been ripped out completely, leaving a red open wound. "Where are the dogs now?" he asked.

"I returned them to the kennel."

"Why didn't they eat him more?" asked the deputy.

Bagley looked scornful. "They're not driven by hunger. They were protecting my property. Once they had taken care of the threat, they became perfectly docile."

"This is a human being," said Shepherd, somewhat roughly. He stood up and drew on his pipe, sending a small cloud of smoke back over his shoulder.

"I realize that, Lieutenant. I'm terribly shocked by what happened." Bagley glanced over at Charlie. If he recognized him, he gave no sign of it, but he looked at Charlie for several moments. He had a heavy rectangular face, a broad nose and thick blond eyebrows. His cowboy hat was pushed back on his head and several wavy blond strands of hair fell across his brow.

"Do you have any idea what this man wanted?" asked Shepherd.

"Not in the least."

"How well do you know him?"

"We'd met several times. I knew him as a race driver. The fellow I bought this land from also races cars and I'd met this man at his house. Then I'd seen him race in Albany."

Although Bagley was obviously lying, it seemed to Charlie that he couldn't say more without revealing the existence of the dogfights. But why had Howard come here and where was his car? If Howard had indeed been the key to the entire case, that key was now gone. Perhaps his friend Frankie Leach knew something. On the other hand, if Howard had killed Pellegrino, then with Howard's death perhaps everything was over and done with. But who was Lynx? Certainly not Butch Howard, who looked more like a bull. Nor did it seem to be Frankie Leach or even Bagley. Charlie couldn't decide what Bagley looked like. Maybe one of those African antelope creatures— a kudu. In any case, Charlie felt he had been pushed back to the beginning. Where, for instance, was the painting? An ambulance from Cambridge drove up to the gate and the deputy let it through.

"Did you know that Leonard Graham was shot and killed this morning?" asked Shepherd.

Bagley tilted his head, then shook it slowly. "I had no idea," he said. He seemed mildly surprised, but mostly Charlie was struck by how little emotion he exhibited. Nor did he show much curiosity or ask any questions about the killing. He was polite but disinterested, and seemed only waiting for the police to leave and take Butch Howard's body with them. Again Charlie found Bagley's eyes on him, but his face bore no expression other than faint interest. Charlie found it disquieting.

"Were you friends with Graham?" asked Shepherd.

"I'd known him for some years but we weren't particularly close. He didn't like my dogs and I felt he regretted selling me this piece of land."

"How'd you get along with him?"

"Perfectly amicably but without much warmth. Leonard Graham was a passionate gambler. It made up his entire conversation. I have little interest in the subject and so we didn't have much to talk about."

Again Charlie felt that Bagley was lying. Wasn't he, too, a gambler? At least he bet on the dogfights. Charlie glanced again at the house and wished he could see inside it.

"Can you think why anyone should have wanted to kill him?" asked Shepherd.

"Not in the least," said Bagley. Then he stepped back as the two ambulance attendants waded past him through the snow with a stretcher. "Do you think Howard shot him?"

"We'll have to wait for ballistics and to check his boots against the tracks in the snow, but it seems like a good chance. What I don't understand is why he wasn't able to defend himself against your dogs."

"As I say, they are very fast and they probably came at him from different directions."

"Why wouldn't the dogs fight each other?"

"They've been trained as guard dogs."

"Why do you have these dogs? Do you fight them?"

"I breed them and sell them. They have many admirable qualities. Only a very wicked person would fight them."

Bagley uttered the lie so smoothly that Charlie at first thought he hadn't heard him correctly.

"And you like these dogs?" asked Shepherd.

Bagley smiled. "Yes, they can be very loving, very warm and affectionate."

Before Charlie drove back to Saratoga, he stopped by Artemis's farm to tell her about Graham and Butch Howard. He found her in the barn exercising Phillip, or perhaps Phillip was exercising her because as Phillip slowly galloped in a circle, Artemis stood on his back doing calisthenics. Even though it was cold in the barn, Artemis was dressed only in a black leotard. Charlie kept pacing back and forth and slapping his arms to his body to keep warm as he told her about the two deaths.

"I was really tempted to speak to Bagley," said Charlie, "but I didn't want Shepherd to know that I knew him."

"What would you have said to him?" asked Artemis.

"First of all, I would have called him Mr. Lynx just to see what he would do."

"But he doesn't look a thing like a lynx," said Artemis. She lay down on Phillip's back and began doing sit-ups.

"I guess you're right, but then who is Lynx?" Charlie stood in the middle of the ring as Phillip galloped around him. He tried not to keep turning but seemed unable to and in no time he was dizzy.

"There's a faint chance it's Frankie Leach," continued Charlie, answering his own question. "I mean it's either Leach or Howard who's blackmailing my cousin. And if it's Leach, then I'll find out tonight. The trouble is that even though I don't remember his face too well, I'm sure he doesn't look like a lynx."

"Do you think it's either Leach or Howard who has the painting?" asked Artemis as she continued her sit-ups.

"Possibly. Lieutenant Shepherd is contacting this cop in Albany and they'll be searching Butch Howard's apartment. The thing is, neither Howard nor Frankie Leach seems like the sort of guy to hang onto a painting, even a painting of a famous racehorse. That's why I wanted to see inside Bagley's house, but he wouldn't even let me use the phone."

"Could you sneak in when he wasn't there?" asked Artemis, standing up again.

It had always struck Charlie how willing Artemis was to forgo the legal for the illegal. He guessed it was one of the things he liked about her. Then, with some surprise, he wondered what that said about him. "He's got that huge fence. And even if you got over it, then how do you handle the dogs? Seeing that dead guy was pretty unnerving."

"What about through the fields?"

"There must be over two feet of snow out there."

"Horses don't mind the snow."

"And the dogs?"

Artemis flipped herself over so she was standing on her hands. "Dear Phillip's back is about six feet above the dogs. Besides that he's a good kicker."

Charlie decided that Artemis was joking. Personally, those dogs terrified him.

22

Charlie's cousin Robert looked as out of place in the bar of the Bentley as a socialite in a coal mine. Dressed in his regulation tweeds, he appeared ill at ease and skittish, as if afraid that somebody would see him and tell somebody else and that person might tell a third person and suddenly an insurance deal might fall through or he might lose a sale on a house. It amazed Charlie that he had ever allowed himself to be pushed around by his cousin's moral bullying.

"Would you like a whiskey," said Victor, "just to cheer yourself up?"

"I don't drink," said Robert.

"What about a Shirley Temple? Sweet on the tongue, soft on the belly."

Robert refused to answer. The three men were sitting at a table waiting for Eddie Gillespie. The bar was closed, but every now and then someone would come to the outside door and knock. Each time Victor would look stern and shake his head. And each time Robert would duck and cover his face with his hand. Charlie kept thinking how many times he had heard his cousin revile all gamblers, how he had expressed scorn for Charlie's father and disapproval for the way Mabel Bradshaw had raised the money to buy the hotel. As Robert sat chewing his thumbnail, Charlie kept wanting to call him names and to quarrel with him, but in fact he wasn't particularly angry. He felt freed from his cousin. What a jerk he was.

Robert left off chewing his thumbnail, then stared at his thumb as if it, too, had disappointed him. His long horse face looked unhappy and doleful. "I don't have a lot of confidence in your plan, Charlie," he said.

Charlie didn't answer. His .38 was stuck in his belt and the butt kept digging into his ribs.

"What choice do you have?" asked Victor.

"But the suitcase is empty."

"So what? Does the blackmailer know that? What's he got, X-ray eyes? He'll stop his car and that's all that counts." Victor sipped a whiskey and glanced at Robert as if he were unusually stupid. He had never had any patience with Charlie's relatives.

The plan was for Robert to drop the suitcase off on a dirt road about a mile from Marin Avenue near Lake Lonely. There was a vacant house and Robert had been told to put the suitcase next to the mailbox at nine-thirty. If Robert tried to interfere in any way, letters would be mailed to Chief Peterson and the *Daily Saratogian* explaining Robert's involvement with Pellegrino. Robert had a copy of the letter and it frightened him. It detailed his wins and losses, mostly losses, over the past year—losses totaling about $80,000. It also said how he had been at Pellegrino's on the night of the murder and how he stood to benefit from Pellegrino's death—particularly that he wouldn't have to cough up the $30,000 for his Super Bowl loss. The note seemed to indicate that the blackmailer had arrived at Pellegrino's after Robert left, had found his scarf, put it by the body and then spent some time hunting out incriminating papers. Again Charlie felt that the original blackmailer must have been Shaw.

"What kind of car do you have?" Charlie asked his cousin.

"A Toyota Camry. Why?"

"Did you ever take it to that Sinclair station on Broadway that works on Japanese cars?"

"What has that to do with anything?"

"Did you take it there or not?"

"Well, yes, they were cheap and . . ." Robert acted as if Charlie was being tiresome on purpose.

"Did you know a mechanic there, Bobo Shaw?"

"I know no one named Bobo," said Robert rather huffily.

"A smallish man, round face, stringy black hair. He looked like a monkey."

"I never talked to any of the mechanics, just the woman in the office."

Charlie dropped the subject. Even if Robert hadn't known Shaw, there seemed a good chance that Shaw had known him.

Victor had been studying the note from the blackmailer. Clearing his throat, he tossed it back to Robert. "This is a real piece of literature. He spells 'sorry' with one 'r' and 'punished' with two 'n's'. How can you be scared of a guy who can't spell?"

And Charlie had wondered what sort of speller Jesse James had been, or Dillinger or the Sundance Kid.

Eddie Gillespie arrived at nine, slapped Robert on the back, then left with Charlie and Victor almost immediately. Charlie was driving his Renault. Gillespie had borrowed an old tow truck with big wooden bumpers and a CB radio. Each would park about a mile on either side of the mailbox. Charlie would wait in the driveway of a house belonging to an ex-burglar he knew and Eddie would wait in the parking lot of a tavern called The Fisherman's Rest. Although Charlie couldn't be sure what kind of car the blackmailer would be driving, he thought it might be the dark late-model Pontiac he had tried following in Albany the previous afternoon, the one driven by the man with the mustache who might or might not be Frankie Leach. In fact, Charlie was certain it would be Frankie Leach, and he kept trying to remember the bartender at the dogfights and if that was the same face he had briefly seen in the window of the Pontiac. Had the man looked like a lynx? Somehow the mustache didn't fit.

As they drove, Charlie asked Victor, "What sort of animal do you think Pellegrino would have called you?"

"An oyster. He would have called me Mr. Oyster."

Charlie glanced at his friend and the car swerved on the snow. "Why an oyster?" he asked.

"Because people used to think oysters were aphrodisiacs and I like that. Maybe he would have called me Mr. Oyster, maybe he would have called me Mr. Spanish Fly."

"But you don't look like those things," said Charlie.

"Yeah, there's always a wrinkle somewhere." Then, after another moment, Victor said, "You think this caper is going to do your cousin any good?"

"What do you mean?" The headlights on the snow reflected back toward them and gave Victor's face a ghostly pallor.

"Will he go on being an asshole who thinks he's a pillar of the community?"

"Probably." Charlie tried to imagine his cousin entering a monastery or dedicating his life to working with the poor.

"Then maybe it would be better to let Peterson know about him, let the papers expose him or whatever."

Charlie drew up by the driveway of the ex-burglar, then backed in. The house was dark as Charlie knew it would be. Like any sensible person the ex-burglar spent part of each winter in Florida. At least the driveway had been plowed.

"But if that happened," said Charlie, "everyone would learn that Pellegrino was a bookie. Then the tax people would come down on his wife. Anyway, I thought you wanted this guy. He's almost bound to be one of the men who robbed your party." Charlie flicked on his CB radio, then turned the knob to his channel.

"And the guy with the cowboy boots got eaten by dogs, right?"

"Killed, not eaten."

"Not a chummy way to die."

"What is?" asked Charlie. It was cold in the car and Charlie tried to pull his overcoat across his knees.

"Maybe humping a coed," said Victor. "You know, there you are in the very act of amour and you pop an aorta. You'd be smiling all the way to heaven."

"Or the other place," said Charlie.

Robert's Toyota Camry drove past the driveway at exactly nine twenty-five. Charlie and Victor hunched down in their seats and waited. The Renault was parked near the house about twenty yards from the road. In the space of fifteen minutes Robert's was the first car to drive by. Up at the corner where Robert had made the turn off Marin Avenue were a streetlight and several houses. Down the dirt road were a couple of farms. It had begun to snow lightly and every so often Charlie flicked on his windshield wipers so they could see. Charlie's feet were numb and he imagined freezing to death before anything happened. Then, ten minutes later, a second car turned off Marin Avenue.

"It's that same Pontiac," said Victor.

Charlie didn't answer. He felt pleased with himself. He started up the Renault and slowly drove out of the driveway, keeping his lights off.

Victor picked up the microphone on the CB radio. "Heart's Blood to Riff-Raff," said Victor, "the party just went by: a dark blue Pontiac with one person. Over."

After a moment Eddie Gillespie's voice came through the small speaker. "Riff-Raff to Heart's Blood, I'm moving to intercept. Ten-four."

"How come you got such a silly name as Heart's Blood?" said Victor.

"I like it," said Charlie, slightly offended. "I read it in a poem."

"You're impossible," said Victor.

Charlie was still driving without lights, increasing his speed until he was going about thirty-five. Up ahead he could see the taillights of the Pontiac. He kept thinking of the bullet that had been fired at them the day before and he slid his .38 out of his belt. Then he saw the Pontiac's brake lights go on. He guessed it would take Frankie Leach about ten seconds to stop the car and pick up the suitcase. Charlie hoped to collar him before he could start up again.

"Get ready," said Charlie.

"You bet," said Victor cheerily. He had a small .32 that Charlie didn't like him to carry, mostly because Victor knew nothing about guns and had only gotten his license a few years before when he started working with the detective agency.

"Try not to shoot that thing," said Charlie.

"Shit, Charlie, you always say that."

The Pontiac had stopped. Charlie pressed his foot on the gas. He no longer felt cold. In fact, even without gloves his hands were sweating. Somewhere up ahead Eddie Gillespie was coming toward them in the tow truck. Charlie was still a hundred yards from the Pontiac, when suddenly it shot forward, fishtailing a little in the snow. Even at that distance they could hear the roar of its motor.

"He must have heard you," said Victor.

Charlie flicked on his lights and pushed the gas pedal to the floor. The Renault skidded and straightened out. Then, about half a mile ahead, another pair of headlights flicked on coming toward them.

"There's Eddie," said Victor. "I don't know why you don't have more faith in the boy."

The Pontiac began weaving, aiming for a way around the tow truck. On either side of the road were high snowbanks. By now the driver would have realized that the other cars weren't police cars, or at least they didn't have lights and sirens. Charlie remained hunched down in his seat. The Renault was bouncing badly over the potholes and chunks of ice on the road. Charlie wondered why he kept buying these small fragile foreign cars. He needed a 4 X 4 like a Jeep or Graham's Bronco. He hoped Leach wouldn't shoot, if only because Charlie didn't want to repeat the bother of getting a new windshield. Almost as an afterthought he put on his seat belt.

Victor rolled down his window. "You want me to take a shot at him?"

"Don't even think of it," said Charlie.

They were gaining on the Pontiac, which seemed practically on top of the tow truck as if trying to scare Eddie out of the way. Charlie felt a twinge of sympathy for the driver of the Pontiac, who had no way of knowing that Eddie Gillespie lived for moments like this and was probably happily chuckling as he prepared to ram the Pontiac head-on. Abruptly the Pontiac veered to the left. The truck turned as well and the Pontiac shot up into the snowbank. Charlie touched his brakes and began to slide. He started pumping them lightly. The rear end of the Renault began swinging to the right. Charlie accelerated to come out of the slide and the Renault straightened out. When he looked again, the Pontiac was buried up to its windows in the snow and he was about twenty feet from the tow truck stopped in the middle of the road. Charlie pressed down more firmly on the brake, slowly slid, and at last hit the wooden bumper of the tow truck at about two miles an hour.

"Quick," said Charlie, unhooking his belt and jumping out of the car. "Remember he's got a gun." He ran toward the Pontiac with his .38 held slightly above his head in his right hand. Off to his left he was aware of Eddie and Victor running as well. It was snowing harder, big flakes that looked like fragments of white cloth. Charlie found it hard to keep his balance on the slippery roadway. He saw someone trying to push open the door of the Pontiac, which was blocked by the snowdrift. The person kept pushing, heaving himself at the door with dull thuds, then managing to squeeze himself halfway through. The lights from the Renault and the tow truck made long shadows across the snow.

"Stop where you are!" shouted Charlie.

The driver was wearing a dark pea jacket and a red ski cap. Charlie saw the man twisting his body, trying to turn toward him. He also saw the gun in the man's hand. Charlie was about five feet away. Instead of shooting, he leaped forward and brought the barrel of his gun down hard on the man's wrist.

"*Yow!*" shouted the man. He dropped the gun, which disappeared in the snow. Charlie grabbed the man's coat collar and pulled him out of the car. They both staggered back through the snow to the road. Once they were on firmer footing the man took a swing at Charlie and missed. Charlie kicked out, hitting the man's knee so that he stumbled back and fell. He wanted to avoid shooting since almost certainly somebody nearby would call the police. Anyway, he had to talk to this person, not shoot him. Charlie took a deep breath and tried to stop being angry. Such feelings were a nuisance.

By now Eddie and Victor had run up behind the man and, when he tried to get to his feet, Eddie pushed him down again. Victor was waving his small pistol above his head like a Fourth of July sparkler. Its shiny chrome shimmered in the light.

"Stay where you are," said Charlie. "You're Frankie Leach, aren't you? I want to talk to you."

"Who the fuck are you?" said Leach. He stared up at Charlie, who stood clearly outlined in the lights from the tow truck. "Shit, you're that private dick from the dogfights! You wrecked my car."

Charlie considered the animal qualities of Leach's face. It looked nothing like a lynx. His face was long, angular and had oversized features. With his mustache, he looked a little like a sheep. "Listen," said Charlie, "I could arrest you for blackmailing, I could arrest you for the murder of Joe Pellegrino, and I could arrest you for that robbery at the hotel during the Super Bowl. You either talk or go to jail."

"I never killed Pellegrino," said Leach more uncertainly. He tried to get up again but Eddie Gillespie pushed him down.

"You have information about Pellegrino's death," said Charlie. "That makes you an accessory."

"I wasn't there. Shaw knew about it."

"And you can also be arrested as an accessory in Shaw's murder. Weren't you driving the car? Maybe you even shot him."

"No, honest! I had nothing to do with his death." Leach's voice was getting too loud and Eddie tapped his ribs with his boot.

"But you knew about his blackmailing, right?" said Charlie. "You wangled all that stuff out of him before he got shot."

"He told us, he told us!"

"Who's us?" asked Charlie.

Leach turned his head away and seemed to be staring at the tow truck. Victor stood by his feet, still fiddling with his .32.

"And what about yesterday?" continued Charlie. "You put a bullet through my windshield. That's attempted murder. You're in a lot of trouble, Mr. Leach."

Frankie Leach turned back to look at Charlie. He didn't say anything but he appeared angry, and maybe frightened as well. He pushed back his red ski cap. Snowflakes were getting caught in his mustache.

"You know that Butch Howard was killed this morning?" asked Charlie.

Leach jerked up his head. "You're lying to me."

"He was killed on Ralph Bagley's farm," said Charlie. "The dogs got him. Bagley said it was an accident."

Frankie Leach kept staring at Charlie but he didn't say anything. His anger seemed to change to confusion and fear, even grief. It made his face seem softer.

"You drove him out there, didn't you?" asked Charlie. "You took him out to Bagley's first thing this morning."

"Maybe I did," said Leach more quietly.

"Bagley claimed he hardly knew Butch Howard," said Charlie. "Is that true?"

Leach was silent a moment, then said, "Butch worked for him. He did lots of stuff for Bagley."

"Like what?" said Charlie. Leach turned away again, refusing to answer. Charlie found himself growing irritated, then stopped himself. "Like killing Leonard Graham?" he asked. "You know that Butch Howard shot him this morning? Then he walked over to Bagley's and the dogs killed him."

Leach was still looking away, but whether he was refusing to answer or grieving for his friend, Charlie couldn't tell. "What happened to that painting of Man o' War that Shaw gave you and Butch?" asked Charlie.

Leach's anger seemed to be coming back, but it wasn't directed at Charlie but at Ralph Bagley. "Butch gave it to Bagley. How'd Bagley say it was an accident?"

Charlie ignored the question. "Why did Shaw give you the painting in the first place?"

"Shaw owed Butch some money."

"And Butch owed Bagley some money?" asked Charlie.

"Sure. How'd the dogs kill Butch?"

"Bagley said that Butch climbed the fence when he wasn't there and the dogs attacked him."

"Why'd he do a dumb thing like that?"

"I don't know. He'd just shot Leonard Graham with a thirty-thirty. Maybe he was after Bagley as well."

"Jesus," said Leach. "Fuckin' dogs. Jesus." He kept blinking and looked up at Charlie, then Victor, then Eddie Gillespie as if he had been somehow tricked or cheated. His nose was long and broad and again Charlie thought he looked like a sheep, maybe a ram.

"Why'd you drive Howard out there this morning?" Charlie repeated.

"He asked for the ride. Bagley wanted him."

"What did Bagley want?"

"I don't know."

"Did he want him to kill Graham?"

"I don't know."

"Okay, stand up," said Charlie. Leach stood up and Gillespie handcuffed him. Then they walked him back to Charlie's car. Charlie wanted to get away before anyone else drove down the road and started asking questions.

"Did Shaw tell you and Howard about that gambling party at the hotel?" asked Charlie.

"That's right. You going to arrest me for that? I'd like to see you try." Leach's anger was back again. It seemed to grease all his actions and needed to be kept at a certain level, like the oil in a car.

"How would you like a hole in your head?" said Victor, pushing Leach up against the side of the Renault. He reached down and took Leach's wallet and began leafing through it. Charlie saw a wad of money.

"Hey!" said Leach.

"Shut up," said Victor, waving his pistol. He bent down by the headlights and began counting the money. "You must of hit it big, Frankie, there's over three grand here. I'll leave you fifty for car fare."

"You can't take that," said Leach furiously.

"Why not?" asked Victor. "You got ten grand from us. What's wrong with my getting a little back?"

"And just remember you owe us seven thousand more," said Eddie. "Damn, if you weren't wearing handcuffs, I'd bust your face!"

Leach didn't say anything. Eddie Gillespie shoved him roughly into the rear seat of the Renault, then started back toward the tow truck.

"I'll meet you at my office in ten minutes," said Charlie, getting into the front.

Starting the Renault, Charlie waited for Eddie Gillespie to back up, then drove around him and headed toward Saratoga.

"Where're you taking me?" said Leach.

"Where's Bagley?" asked Charlie.

"He's down in Albany. He's got some fights tonight."

"Same place?" asked Charlie.

"No, another place."

"You know where it is?"

"Maybe."

"You know why Bagley should want Graham dead?"

"I don't know nothing," said Leach. He cleared his throat and made a spitting noise.

"Hey, cut that out," said Victor.

Charlie felt unhappy with himself. He wanted to put Frankie Leach in jail, but then too much secret knowledge would become public knowledge. "Were you friends with Butch Howard?" asked Charlie. They were just entering Saratoga near the harness track. It seemed to be snowing harder.

"He was my buddy," said Leach tonelessly.

"Then what do you care about Bagley?"

"I don't care shit for him."

"I'll take you down to the dogfights," said Charlie. "But if you say a word about this blackmailing business, you'll go straight to jail. If I was still a cop, I'd take you there anyway. You know about too many murders."

23

It was snowing even harder and the wind had picked up so that not only was the Northway itself a solid blanket of white but even the air seemed palpable, as if they were driving through a white wall. Charlie had to hunch over the steering wheel in order to see, although really he was guessing more than seeing. It was almost 11:00 P.M. and there was no other traffic going toward Albany, not even trucks. Victor sat in the front with Charlie. Eddie Gillespie and Frankie Leach were in the back. Leach was still handcuffed and didn't like it. He didn't speak but he kept grumbling and muttering to himself until Eddie told him to shut up. They had stopped briefly in Saratoga to put the $3,000 in Charlie's safe and to pick up Eddie after he had dropped off the tow truck. Charlie had also called his cousin and told him not to worry.

"How can I not worry, Charlie," Robert had said, "when I know my secret is not secure?"

Charlie had rolled his eyes and tried to sound consoling.

Glancing in the rearview mirror, Charlie noticed Frankie Leach staring sullenly out the window. For the hundredth time Charlie wondered what to do with him. Mostly Charlie wanted the chance to confront Ralph Bagley and test out a theory he'd been working on. But then what? He didn't worry that Leach would contact Chief Peterson about his cousin because Eddie had already explained he would then make it known around Albany that Leach had robbed the Super Bowl party. That prospect had frightened Leach, and for a moment he had stopped his muttering and grumbling to swear he would keep his mouth shut. Charlie in fact knew he would have to let Leach go, but first he wanted Leach to take him to the dogfights just so Bagley could see them all together.

"Maybe it will light a little fire under him," Charlie had told Victor.

"You mean make him mad?"

"Well, sure."

"Charlie, you're a detective. You're supposed to use your keen intellect. You think Sherlock Holmes just went around making people mad?"

"Sometimes you use what you've got," said Charlie.

Once they reached Albany, Leach directed them to the warehouse where the dogfights were being held. It was also near the river and about five blocks from the warehouse they had gone to before.

"How many warehouses does he have?" asked Charlie.

"Maybe four or five," said Leach. "He talks around the owners, gives them a percentage of the take."

Charlie parked a block away. After they had gotten out of the car, Victor took off Leach's handcuffs. It was snowing so hard that they were all covered with big flakes in no time.

"What are you going to do with me?" asked Leach.

"I'll let you go," said Charlie. "My business will be pretty quick. If you interfere with it, it'll just make more trouble."

"I won't say anything," said Leach.

The insincerity in his voice was so great that Charlie found it hard not to smile. Leach was angry about his friend's death and would most certainly make a noise about it. Depending on whether or not the death was accidental, Bagley's reaction could be quite different.

"I know you're upset about your friend," said Charlie, "but don't make a scene."

"I won't," said Leach, rubbing his wrists.

"Jesus, Charlie," said Victor, "how can you trust a crook like this?"

Charlie didn't answer. Pulling up the collar of his overcoat, he began trudging through the snow toward the warehouse. Frankie Leach followed him, and Victor and Eddie Gillespie trailed behind.

"I'm looking for Bagley and another guy," said Charlie. "Try to make sure I don't get jumped."

"Who's the other guy?" asked Eddie.

"You don't know him. His name's Blake Moss."

Outside the warehouse were a couple of men standing in the doorway to keep warm. Charlie guessed they were guards. They nodded at Frankie Leach and he nodded back, then they stepped out of the way. The door was unlocked and Charlie pushed it open. People were shouting inside. A fight was going on. The air was smoky and smelled of straw and sweat. Two of the bouncers from the other night turned toward them as they entered, but when they saw Frankie Leach they seemed to lose interest. Charlie walked up to them.

"I'm looking for Blake Moss," he said. "Have you seen him?"

"He's over on the other side," said one of the men.

"I want to talk to Bagley, too," said Charlie. "Go find him and tell him that I just showed up with Frankie." Charlie gave the man one of his business cards but hardly paused as he kept walking across the floor, forcing the two bouncers to follow him. At least a hundred men and women surrounded the portable fence, shouting and make bets with one another. Beneath the noise, Charlie could just make out the growling of the dogs. One of the bouncers went off into the crowd to look for

Bagley. He was a tall man and kept raising himself up on tiptoe to see over people's heads. It was at that moment that Frankie Leach decided to hurry off in the opposite direction. Realizing something was wrong, the second bouncer started after him.

"Hey," said Victor, taking the bouncer's arm and removing something from his pocket. "I bet you never seen one of these. It's a pornographic Easter egg. You look through this little hole and you see two rabbits doing dirty." He held up a pink plastic egg to the bouncer.

Charlie kept walking, making his way around the fence. There was a lot of noise and the ring of people watching the fight was packed solid. Charlie had gone about twenty feet when he saw Blake Moss on the other side of the warehouse. Moss was leaning over the fence shouting at the dogs and his face had gone all red. Charlie pushed his way through the crowd. People were shouting and jostling one another. A skinny woman with bright pink lips kept shouting, "His throat, get his throat!"

Charlie came up to Moss from behind. In the ring one pit bull had the other by the rear leg and was dragging him backward, while the other had twisted around and was chewing on a portion of the first dog's ear. Then they rolled over and there was a little cloud of dust and spray and blood. Looking across the ring, Charlie saw Ralph Bagley with the bouncer, and at that moment, Bagley looked up and stared at Charlie. Even his eyes looked sharp and pointed. Charlie stepped behind Blake Moss and took hold of his arm.

"I want to talk to you, Mr. Lynx," he said.

Moss turned quickly. He seemed confused, then he looked afraid. "What was that?"

A round blond face, small ears, short blond hair—sure he was a lynx.

"You're Mr. Lynx. Isn't that what Pellegrino called you?"

"Get away from me!" said Moss, giving Charlie a shove, then pushing past him.

Charlie staggered back, bumping into several people before regaining his footing. Glancing across the ring, he saw Ralph Bagley still staring at him. Then he saw Frankie Leach pushing through the crowd toward Bagley. Charlie turned and hurried after Moss, who was running back toward the dog cages. Charlie ran after him, ducking and weaving around the men and women watching the dogfight and oblivious to anything else. The shouting reminded Charlie of the shouting at the track when the horses were in the home stretch—a confused roar, a fierce intensity. Ten feet ahead was a door beside the cages and Moss ran through it. Charlie followed him. As he passed through the door, the dogs barked and lunged, banging against the metal mesh. The door opened onto a long hall and he hurried down it. Charlie kept telling himself that Eddie Gillespie was the great runner, while he was just a quick trotter. Where was Eddie when he needed him? Moss was about twenty feet ahead. Reaching another door, Moss pulled it open, then glanced back at Charlie as he disappeared through it.

Charlie tried to make himself run faster and could almost hear the muscles in his legs making little yelps of protest. His heavy overcoat was still buttoned and it encumbered him. Stuck in his belt, his revolver chafed against his skin. Charlie ran through the door at the end of the hall and into a large storage room. Moss was already on the other side, tugging at another door. The door appeared to be locked. Moss smashed his shoulder against it, but it wouldn't budge. Hardly pausing, Moss turned and ran back toward Charlie, bending low, getting ready to leap. Charlie had no time to unbutton his coat and pull out his gun. To his left was a desk and a swivel chair. He stepped toward them, grabbed the chair and shoved it into Moss's path. Moss tried to turn but he was off balance and there wasn't time. The chair hit him across the knees. He went sailing across it and tumbled to the floor, sliding on his shoulder into a pile of empty cardboard boxes. Charlie managed to unbutton his coat and pull out his .38. He hurried after Moss and pushed him down again from behind. Yanking back Moss's head, he shoved the barrel of the .38 into his left ear.

"We're going to talk, Mr. Lynx," said Charlie.

Charlie patted him down for a gun but Moss was unarmed. Then Charlie stepped back several feet. Moss sat up and stared angrily at Charlie. Again the image of a lynx appeared in Charlie's mind.

"Stay where you are," said Charlie. "You were Pellegrino's fifth customer, the new one, the tough guy whom Pellegrino thought he could count on if there was trouble. Instead you betrayed him." Charlie heard his voice rising with anger and he paused to get control of himself. Around them brown cardboard boxes were piled to the ceiling. "You told your friend Bagley that Pellegrino was an easy mark, that he was holding forty to fifty thousand of Super Bowl money and it would be easy to rob him. Did you tell him to kill Pellegrino as well? What happened, did you owe Bagley money? How much was it?" Charlie took a step forward and lightly kicked one of Moss's black shoes.

"Twenty thousand," said Moss. He didn't seem angry now. His whole body sagged and looked lumpish, as if constructed from meal sacks.

"So for twenty thousand you told Bagley he can kill Pellegrino. And Bagley, too, needs the money, right? One of his best dogs had just gotten whipped. He came to you for his twenty thousand and you told him about Pellegrino, right?" Charlie kicked Moss's shoe again.

"I didn't tell him to kill him," said Moss quietly. He was leaning against the pile of boxes with his legs straight out in front of him. He wore a brown sport coat, khaki pants and a light brown turtleneck. Dirt and dust from the floor had left cloudy patches on his jacket.

"Well, he did," said Charlie, sticking his revolver back in his belt. His watch cap was still on. He took it off and shoved it in his pocket. He told himself he should feel glad to have figured out this business but instead he felt depressed. "Bagley shot Pellegrino four times with a thirty-eight. But when he was leaving, he had some bad luck. Either he or his car was seen by Leonard Graham, whom Pellegrino called Mr. Grouper. Graham owed Bagley some money as well and was afraid of him. Bagley thought Graham would keep his mouth shut, but then he heard that Graham had been talking to me and that changed everything. You know that Graham was murdered this morning? You've got some responsibility for that one, too."

"I hadn't heard." Moss's smooth blond face bore an expression of fear and exhaustion. It, too, was sagging, as if all his skin was sliding downward.

"Butch Howard killed Graham with one shot from a rifle, trying to make it look like a hunting accident. It was stupid and Bagley knew it was stupid. When Howard went back to Bagley's farm, Bagley set his dogs on him, killing him. And now there's you, you're the last person who can connect Bagley to Pellegrino's murder. What do you think Bagley's going to do with you? He knows I'm here. He saw me with you."

"Bagley's a crazy man," said Moss, still speaking softly. "He'll kill me."

Charlie didn't answer. The certainty in Moss's voice had slightly shaken him.

"What do you want?" asked Moss.

"I want to get Bagley and take him to the police where you'll make a deposition. You're supposedly a detective, you know what has to be done. Bagley's got to go to jail. To hell with the rest." Charlie was almost surprised at his words, but he was tired of keeping everything secret. It didn't sit well with him. If Bagley had truly killed these people, then he had to be punished.

Moss slowly got to his feet. "He's got guys here. He's dangerous."

"Either you help me or you end up in jail yourself."

Moss stared at Charlie, looking from one eye to the other.

He was bigger than Charlie yet seemed uncertain of him. "Let's go," he said.

Blake Moss walked back down the hall to the main part of the warehouse. Charlie stayed several feet behind him. He felt that with the help of Moss, Victor and Eddie Gillespie he could arrest Bagley and Frankie Leach as well. Actually, as he had to remind himself, he wasn't a cop so he couldn't arrest them, but at least he could drag them down to police headquarters and start yelling for Lieutenant Boland, who must still be working on Shaw's murder. Frankie Leach could probably tell him a lot about it and Leach would be lucky if he weren't arrested as an accessory or at least charged with conspiracy. But could the four of them really grab Bagley and get him out of here? What about the bouncers and even Leach? What about that huge crowd of people? And Charlie worried that he was again deluding himself, that there was no easy way to get Bagley and that if he didn't watch it he could wind up dead in a ditch.

Another dogfight was going on. Back by the cages an earlier winner was being patched up, while an earlier loser was being wrapped in several black plastic garbage bags. A young man in a black T-shirt was standing over the winning dog, winding white gauze around its head and shouting, "You did it! You did it!" as the dog wagged its stub of a tail.

Charlie looked around for Victor and Eddie Gillespie, but couldn't see them. For a moment he wished he were half a foot taller. Moss was being extremely docile and Charlie didn't trust him. More people had arrived and there were well over a hundred people in the room, mostly pressing against the portable fence. The air was musty and full of cigarette smoke. Near the bar Charlie saw Ralph Bagley talking to Frankie Leach. Charlie steered Moss away from them. "I need to find my friends first," he said.

He pushed Moss toward the fence, meaning to circle around it. The noise of the shouting was deafening in the enclosed space—waves of yelling that grew louder and louder. Again, as a faint counterpoint beneath the shouting, was the growling and snarling of the two fighting dogs. It occurred to Charlie that the crowd sounded far more ferocious. He made his way around to the right, keeping Moss ahead of him. Glancing between several men and over the portable fence, Charlie saw two dogs rolling over and over in a compact heap with blood and saliva spraying from them. On the other side of the fence, he saw Victor, not looking at the fight but staring away at the door as if suddenly startled.

Something was wrong. Charlie gave Moss a shove forward. "Get moving!" he said.

But then there was the sound of a sharp whistle from the other side of the room. For the briefest second everything went still, and all that could be heard was the growling and whining of the fighting dogs. Then people began pushing and running in all directions as everything fell into confusion.

"It's the police," said Moss. Immediately he hurried forward through the crowd and before Charlie could respond four or five running men pushed between them.

"Wait!" shouted Charlie. But either Moss didn't hear him or chose not to. Charlie ran forward but people kept shoving him and blocking his path. A woman in a blue dress and stiletto heels had fallen down and other people kept tripping over her. Charlie paused to drag her to her feet, then looked to where he had last seen Victor, but he was gone. On the other side of the room were at least a dozen police and men from the A.S.P.C.A. Three men had climbed over the portable fence and were trying to separate the fighting pit bulls. Charlie kept getting jostled and pushed. He looked for Moss but couldn't see him. Another door was open on the far side of the warehouse and people were running through it into the snow.

"Everyone stand where you are!" shouted a voice through a loudspeaker.

Charlie pushed his way toward the wall, then climbed onto one of the metal dog cages to get his bearings. Beneath him a tiger-stripe pit bull kept hurling himself upward at Charlie's shoes so that the cage shook. Even though the dog was barking there was so much other noise that Charlie could barely hear it. Twenty policemen must have been in the room, plus A.S.P.C.A. officials. The police were grabbing people and herding them inside the portable fence. Charlie could see no sign of Victor or Eddie Gillespie. Then he saw Moss over by the bar. With him was Ralph Bagley, who seemed to be holding onto Moss's arm. Charlie jumped down from the cage and began to push his way toward them. There was a door behind Bagley and he seemed to be forcing Moss in that direction. People were running, looking for a way out, shouting to one another. A middle-aged woman in a red dress had rushed at one of the policemen and was kicking and screaming. Another policeman grabbed her from behind, picked her up and carried her toward the portable fence.

It struck Charlie that Bagley could have easily called the police himself when he learned that Charlie was looking for Blake Moss. But was that really likely? He pushed his way toward the place where he had last seen Bagley, while trying to avoid the police and the people who kept running into him. Then he saw the two bouncers hurrying toward him. With them was Frankie Leach. Charlie turned back toward the hallway where he had chased Blake Moss earlier. The shouting and barking, whistles blowing, the sound of feet tramping across the wood floor—all this felt like a heavy weight against Charlie's body. One of the bouncers had begun wrestling with a policeman. The second one, the bigger of the two, was almost on top of Charlie. The man took a swing at him and missed. Charlie swung back, hitting him in the chest, then was hit in the jaw in return. He couldn't waste time like this. He closed with the man and kneed him in the groin. Then he shoved the man in front of Frankie Leach and ran toward the open door of the hallway.

There were two doors at the end. One led to the storeroom

where Charlie had earlier talked to Moss. He hoped the other would lead outside. Maybe he could catch Bagley as he was leaving the warehouse. Three other men were in the hallway as well, pushing through the door into the storeroom. An older woman in a purple ankle-length down coat sat on the floor covering her head with her hands. Charlie ran past her.

As he ran down the hallway, Charlie realized that Leach was still chasing him. He pulled his gun from his belt and turned around, kneeling as he did so. Then, with a kind of nervous exasperation, he saw that Leach had a gun as well. The woman in the down coat saw the guns and began to scream.

"You're a dead little rat!" shouted Leach. He fired at Charlie and missed. The bullet ricocheted off the wall with a whine. The woman screamed again and pressed herself back against the wall. At almost the same instant Charlie aimed low at Leach's feet and squeezed the trigger. He kept telling himself he had never killed another human being, and he felt angry with Leach for putting him in this position.

The pistol shot in the enclosed hall made his ears ring. Leach shouted and stumbled forward, landing on his belly. His pistol fell from his hand and slid across the floor. Charlie picked it up. Leach was holding his leg and rolled back and forth groaning. Blood was spurting from his shin. Charlie reached into his back pocket, took out his wallet and found his identification. He was going to need it. Two policemen appeared in the door. Charlie dropped both pistols and held up his hands.

24

The Albany radio station was predicting the worst storm of the
season, and already the announcer had begun to list events that
had been canceled for the following day: lectures, Contra
dances, beanos, a church supper in Cohoes. Charlie imagined
hearing about the cancellation of his own investigation: All
work on the case of the stolen painting or the murder of Joe
Pellegrino has been postponed until the onset of warm weather.
Charlie would heave a sigh of relief. He would go home and
go to bed. At the moment he was driving out to Ralph Bagley's
farm in Cambridge. Charlie was alone and it was past two
o'clock Sunday morning. Victor was still being held by the
police and Eddie Gillespie had disappeared.

Charlie had nearly spent the night in jail as well, but at last
he had convinced the police to call Lieutenant Boland, who
had been very happy to receive Frankie Leach, wounded leg
and all. Leach, on his part, seemed ready to tell Boland all he
knew about Butch Howard in hopes that the police wouldn't
take his shooting at Charlie with an unregistered revolver very
seriously.

"I didn't kill the guy," Leach had argued, adding, "I always been a lousy shot," as if poor marksmanship had been the major stumbling block of his criminal career.

Before Leach was taken away in the ambulance, Charlie had had a few words with him. Leach wasn't sure where Bagley had gone, but he thought Bagley had driven out to his farm and that he had taken Blake Moss with him. Leach was almost friendly, as if glad his arrest had put their relationship on a different footing. He had lain on the stretcher covered with a red blanket and sipped a Coke while dogs barked in the background. Charlie asked Leach why he had decided to help Bagley, considering that Bagley had killed his friend, Butch Howard. Well, he had owed Bagley money and Bagley had said he'd wipe the slate clean if he'd only stop that little detective. Charlie understood. After all, gambling debts came first. Leach apologized for calling Charlie a little rat and urged him to keep quiet about his attempt to blackmail Robert. Even without a blackmail conviction it seemed certain that Leach would spend a few years in jail. Charlie hemmed and hawed and appeared to drag his feet, but at last he promised.

Driving up Route 2 toward Cambridge, Charlie felt pleased with himself. Here he was, fifty years old, and he had wrestled with Bagley's bouncer and fought a gun duel wounding his attacker in the leg. Even Jesse James would have been proud of him. Even Wyatt Earp. These successes had led him, perhaps rashly, to decide to pursue Bagley out to his farm by himself; that is, if the snow allowed it. Although the plows had been through several times, there was still about eight inches covering the road and the Renault kept slipping on the hills. If it weren't for the tracks of a truck that had passed sometime earlier, Charlie wouldn't know where the road ended and the fields began. Even so, the great white flakes formed a curtain that reflected his headlights, making it almost impossible to see.

It was nearly two-thirty by the time Charlie drove slowly past Bagley's farm. He had his windows rolled down and liked how the snow made his car so silent. The mercury vapor lights were burning back near the barn and Charlie saw a black Ford Taurus parked by the house. There was very little snow on the car's windshield and Charlie decided that Bagley had just recently arrived. The gate was shut and appeared locked. The tall chain-link fence stretched off in either direction, its metal posts topped with little caps of snow. From somewhere Charlie heard the sound of barking. He kept driving and took a right at the next corner. A quarter of a mile up the road was Artemis's horse farm. Charlie felt uncertain about waking her. But hadn't she said how her horses didn't mind the deep snow? Anyway, Charlie still had his gun tucked in his belt and the important thing was to get Bagley before he killed Blake Moss.

Charlie pulled his car a few feet into the snowdrift that was Artemis's driveway, then waded through the snow toward her front steps. Although he was wearing boots, the snow was above his knees and he walked slowly like a stork, lifting each foot above the surface. It was impossible to hurry. The house was a large shingled bungalow with a long covered porch or veranda surrounding it on three sides. Charlie hammered on the front door. He wondered if he was wrong about Moss. Perhaps he had been in league with Bagley all along. Perhaps he had gone with Bagley of his own free will. In that case Charlie could be nastily surprised even if he got past the dogs. But it wasn't just Bagley and Moss, there was also the painting of Man o' War to think about. He imagined it over Bagley's fireplace in his living room or maybe over his bed or even in the dining room. And then he imagined Mr. Whitman's expression of surprise when he lugged the darn thing into his office. Charlie hammered on the door again.

But then here was Artemis, opening the door. She gave Charlie an inquiring look. "I hope, Charlie, that this isn't purely a social call." Artemis wore a white nightgown under a white robe. With one hand she brushed her dark hair back from her eyes. She wasn't exactly angry, but neither was she pleased.

"I need a back way into Bagley's farm," said Charlie, stamping the snow from his feet. "He's got a man in there and I think he's going to kill him."

Artemis pushed open the door. "Why didn't you explain right away," she said. "Just let me get dressed."

Charlie brushed the snow from his pants legs, then sat down on a bench in the hall to wait. All four walls and even the ceiling were covered with garish circus posters showing clowns, elephants and acrobats, as well as equestriennes like Artemis doing handstands and flips over the backs of prancing horses. The posters made Charlie dizzy just looking at them. He wondered how he was going to feel riding a horse through the snow. He took out his .38 and put another bullet in the chamber. He thought of all the jobs he might have taken: schoolteacher, baseball manager, shop clerk. He couldn't see himself in any of them. Then he thought of Janey Burris, with whom he had a date for Tuesday night. They'd go out to dinner. They'd talk a long time. His anticipation made him short of breath. He hadn't even told Victor about her, not wanting to be teased. He'd call Grace Washburn in the morning if he wasn't eaten by dogs or in the hospital. No more teeth-cleaning. No more rinse and spit.

Artemis reappeared in the doorway, wearing white leather pants, a leather jacket and a short white leather cape. "Do you like my outfit?" she asked. "It will help me blend with the storm."

Charlie wondered if she had any sense of the danger. "What about your horse?"

"Dear Phillip is a pinkish color. He'll just have to pretend he's part of the night itself. Perhaps a very large snowflake."

"Do you realize how dangerous all this is?" asked Charlie, standing up.

"Of course I do. Shall we depart?"

They waded through the snow out to the barn. Charlie had his watch cap pulled down to his eyebrows and could hardly see through the thick flakes. The snow in his boots had melted and his feet were wet. He had started coughing again and had to eat several handfuls of snow in order to stop. At least they would each have a horse. Charlie was pleased to the extent that it meant he would have a western saddle, which would allow him to hold on. Artemis herself would ride bareback.

"This is Roger," said Artemis, introducing Charlie to a large palomino that stuck its head toward him over the door of its stall. "Roger is very gentle and if he throws you it will mean nothing personal."

"Is he good at kicking dogs?" asked Charlie.

"Of course," said Artemis. "Horses love kicking dogs. It's in their blood."

Artemis saddled the palomino and they led the horses out of the barn. Their hooves went *clop-clop* on the barn floor, then became silent as they passed into the snow. Holding a stirrup, Artemis helped Charlie into the saddle. He didn't like how high up he was. The leather creaked and Roger twisted his head around to look at him. Charlie felt that the horse didn't trust him.

"Artemis, are you sure you realize how dangerous this is?" repeated Charlie.

Artemis made an exasperated snorting noise. "Do you think I would have let you rouse me out of a sound sleep if it wasn't? Let's go." She jumped onto Phillip's back and stood there for a moment, looking grand in her white leather suit. Then, much to Charlie's relief, she sat down in a more or less normal fashion. In her right hand, she held a coil of rope. Turning Phillip toward the open field, she trotted off.

Charlie jounced after her. The snow rose above the horse's knees. Charlie pulled his watch cap farther down over his ears and tried to hang on, gripping the reins and pressing down on the horn of the saddle so he wouldn't bounce on top of it in a nasty way. He took his revolver out of his belt and stuck it in the pocket of his overcoat. In the other pocket, he carried a large flashlight. By standing up in the stirrups Charlie found he could somewhat alleviate the bouncing. He wanted to ask Artemis if he was doing something wrong but she was about ten yards ahead. Charlie wanted to make Roger move faster but he wasn't positive how to do it and, besides, he didn't want him to hurry too much. He made a tentative clucking noise and Roger stepped forward more briskly, just as he was supposed to. Charlie felt a little more comfortable. At least the horse appeared responsible. They moved across the snow-covered field in the midst of the storm and soon Artemis's farm was invisible behind them. Nothing could be seen in front. Charlie kept looking for the lights by Bagley's barn, but there was just the mass of gray flakes in the darkness. Charlie made another clucking noise and Roger drew up beside Phillip and Artemis.

"How far is it?" asked Charlie.

"Not far, less than a quarter of a mile. There's a back gate. Perhaps Phillip can tug it open. He enjoys simple chores."

"Have you ever thought of going into police work?" asked Charlie. He was struck by how the snow muffled their voices.

"I don't like their outfits," said Artemis. "Besides, if I did it for a living, it would soon become dull. Better to have a valuable friend who can occasionally amuse me with it."

"I just hope we don't get killed," said Charlie.

"Don't be downcast. Think of your heroes and feel reassured."

"Even Jesse James would have found this foolish," said Charlie.

In five more minutes Charlie began to make out the glow from the lights by Bagley's barn, and several minutes after that they came to the chain-link fence. Artemis turned left, looking for the gate. It was at the corner and closed, with about three feet of snow piled against it.

"Shall we have Phillip pull it open?" asked Artemis.

"Be my guest," said Charlie.

Artemis tied one end of the rope to the gate and the other around Phillip's neck. "In a previous life," said Artemis, "I believe dear Phillip was a tow truck."

It took about a minute of pulling before Phillip could drag the gate open through the snow, but he seemed to do it without even getting out of breath. Unfortunately, the process hadn't been entirely silent and there was a screech of bending metal. Then, as Charlie rode through the gate after Artemis, he heard the sound which had frightened him more than anything else that evening. It was the bark of a dog, followed by another and another—they were brisk, eager little barks and appeared to be getting closer. Charlie wiped the snow from his eyes, then took out his flashlight and pistol. He was pressing his knees against the palomino so tightly that his legs hurt.

"Here they come," he said unhappily.

Artemis rode ahead, sitting astride Phillip, but with her arms around the horse's neck and bending over so that her mouth was close to his ear. Charlie found it difficult to hold the reins, the gun and the flashlight while sitting on the horse with any degree of confidence, especially if the horse meant to do some serious plunging and kicking. He regretted momentarily not being a six-armed creature like one of those Buddhist or Hindu gods and was distracted by that thought until Artemis called to him.

"Charlie, turn on the light!"

Charlie flicked on the light and pointed it ahead past Artemis. At first all he could see were swirling snowflakes and a white expanse, but then he saw something which made him think of moles, two moles burrowing toward them. At least he saw their burrows advancing and then he saw the animals themselves as they kept leaping up, trying to get above the snow. But they weren't moles, of course; they were Bagley's pit bull terriers, all white and snow-encrusted except for their pink and panting mouths.

They plowed through the snow, leaping and pushing, muscling it aside, snarling their way forward, while their tracks trailed behind them like long white snakes. They ran directly at Artemis's horse, which suddenly snorted and reared up and began to kick, began leaping and plunging as the dogs tried to fasten onto his legs, tried to bite and hang on and bite again. The dogs never hesitated or seemed frightened of the plunging hooves, but ran among them, leaping up toward Phillip's belly, growling and snarling, then falling back into the snow. Watching, it was all Charlie could do not to gallop away. His own horse was nervous and kept prancing and rearing up, making it hard to hold on. It was impossible to shoot at the dogs without hitting Phillip. It was impossible to help, other than keeping the flashlight focused on the dogs. Artemis lay flat on Phillip's back with her arms around his neck and her white leather boots pressed to his flanks. And it seemed that in seconds she would be unseated and thrown into the snow where she would be attacked.

But Phillip kept rearing and plunging, almost dancing as he kept the dogs away from his legs. He clipped one dog and it tumbled away, leaping back seconds later. Both dogs were entirely snow-covered. They didn't bark, just kept leaping and dodging the horse's hooves. But then Phillip kicked the other dog hard with his rear hooves, sending it flying and yelping through the air. And before the dog could return, the horse whinnied and came down with his front hooves on the back of the first dog, then kept trampling it, burying its body in the snow, which slowly turned pink in the light of the flashlight. The other dog ran back but more slowly and, before it could lunge, it was again kicked. Then Phillip pursued it, not letting it scramble to its feet, and the horse trampled this dog as well, stamping and stamping until there was no more than a red mess in the snow which the falling snowflakes immediately began to cover.

Charlie swung the flashlight around in a wide arc, looking for other dogs. There were none to be seen. He felt rather ineffectual but was glad to have been left out. It would have been impossible to hang onto his horse if the dogs had attacked him. They reminded him of those piranhas that were always plaguing South American explorers in the movies of his youth.

Artemis had jumped to the ground and was inspecting Phillip's legs. "That was rather nasty," she said.

"Is Phillip all right?" asked Charlie.

"A few scratches. Let's hope the creatures weren't rabid. Do people make pets of these things?"

"Some people," said Charlie.

Artemis washed the scratches on Phillip's legs with snow, then jumped up onto his back. "Promise there will be no more of them. It would have been humiliating to fall. I haven't fallen in public for twenty years."

"It would be worse to be eaten," said Charlie.

"No," said Artemis, "professionally speaking, it would be worse to fall."

They moved forward again. Charlie flicked off the flashlight and for a moment he could see nothing. Then he made out the mercury vapor lights over Ralph Bagley's barn.

"Let's go see if we can rescue this fellow," said Artemis. "Is he a friend of yours?"

"No, he's a detective who wants to open an office in Saratoga and put me in charge of it."

"And will you do that?"

"Of course not."

They were riding side by side through the snow. Charlie was feeling more comfortable in the saddle even though he didn't like the bouncing. He slipped his gun and flashlight back into the pockets of his overcoat. As they approached the barn, Charlie briefly told Artemis what he knew about Blake Moss and Ralph Bagley, and what had happened that evening at the dogfights.

"And why didn't you tell the police about Mr. Bagley?" asked Artemis.

Charlie had no good answer for that. Maybe it was because he had no real evidence, just theories and arguments. Maybe it was because of Mrs. Pellegrino and her grief. "I wanted to get him myself," he said at last.

25

The barn was a long galvanized metal structure with sliding metal doors. They were closed. At one end, however, near a mercury vapor light was a small door for hay set about a dozen feet above the ground. It was open and light shone faintly through it. Propped up against the hay door was an aluminum ladder. Charlie and Artemis reined their horses to a halt. From inside the barn Charlie could hear barking. A trough of snow-covered footprints led from the house to the ladder. There didn't seem to be any leading back. Charlie looked past the barn to the house, which was dark. The black Taurus, now blanketed by snow, was pointed toward the gate. It was still snowing hard and the lights made the flakes look yellow. The air shone with them, making it seem as if they were inside a feather bed. Charlie moved his horse closer to the ladder.

"I'm going up this," he said. "Why don't you wait here?"

"Why don't I take a peek at the house?" said Artemis.

"He might have dogs inside."

"I'll knock first."

"Artemis, this guy's dangerous." Charlie had a sudden impulse to shake her. The feeling embarrassed him.

Artemis looked solemn as if aware of Charlie's disapproval.

Her dark hair was full of snow. "Do you think he's sleeping?" she asked.

"No, I think they're in the barn." Charlie gripped the ladder, putting his left foot on one of the middle rungs as he swung himself off the saddle. Just as he was pulling himself onto the ladder, his foot slipped and he fell to the side, hanging backward with one leg dangling above the snow. Then he swung his foot back onto the ladder, drew himself up and began to climb. The rungs were icy and cold on his hands.

"Beware of dogs," said Artemis below him.

It seemed an unnecessary warning but Charlie was grateful just the same. He climbed up the ladder and over the sill. The light came from the middle of the barn, up near the sliding doors. Charlie couldn't see exactly where because of the amount of stuff piled around him. Stacked on the second floor were bales of hay, empty dog cages, dusty tables and chairs, cardboard boxes and some green canvas lawn furniture. Several ropes hung from the rafters where lumber was stored. Some dangled free and others were tied to the wooden posts that rose above him. Charlie pushed one of the ropes aside as he made his way forward. The light was dim and the loft was shadowy. Ahead of him, dogs were barking and growling. There seemed to be a lot of them—a whole pack, he thought—and the sound made his body grow cold.

Charlie reached into the pocket of his overcoat for his revolver. It wasn't there. He tried the other pocket but it held only the flashlight. In a panic he searched all his pockets. He could feel his heart pumping faster, feel himself begin to sweat. The revolver was gone. He searched his pockets a second time. The pockets were baggy and without flaps. Charlie took off his watch cap and rubbed it across his forehead. His revolver must have fallen in the snow, and Charlie again felt how the horse had kept bouncing him up and down. Right now the revolver was probably in the process of being buried somewhere out in the field. How could he ever find it?

Frightened, Charlie turned back. There was no way he could face those dogs unarmed. He kept thinking of their teeth, their fierce tenacity. He would go to the house and call the police. What a fine detective he was if he couldn't hang onto his own gun. He took a few steps back toward the ladder but then he heard voices behind him. He stopped and listened but couldn't make out the words. He turned forward again, moving very carefully. The loft had a wooden floor strewn with hay and Charlie's feet made no noise. He kept thinking of the pit bulls. He remembered how Butch Howard's throat had looked, or the red absence of a throat. Go back, he kept telling himself, go back. But he kept going forward. He passed some garden tools and picked up a spade, then felt foolish carrying it. But he kept it and it made him feel a little braver.

Charlie stopped at last by some stacked bales of hay that rose a few feet above him. Looking around the bales, he saw Bagley and Blake Moss about ten feet ahead at the edge of the loft. Bagley's back was to Charlie and Moss was sitting on the floor with his hands tied behind him.

"This is where I train them," Bagley was saying. "And they fight here too, sometimes. Private fights for friends."

"Let me go," said Moss. His voice sounded terrified, more of a whisper than a voice.

"I can't. I told you, I don't trust you. What were you saying to that detective?" Bagley wore a brown deerskin jacket with a fringe down the sleeves. He held a revolver to his side. Charlie thought it looked like a .38 and wondered if it was the same gun that had killed Pellegrino. On the floor behind Bagley was a Sony video camera.

"Nothing," said Moss. "I told him nothing." He was sitting cross-legged and looked up at Bagley. Charlie saw that just past Moss was an open space, and about twelve feet beyond that was another loft. Presumably the open space was some sort of garage down below and Bagley was using it as a pit. From it, Charlie heard the whine of a dog, then a bark. On either side of the pit were several large lights, like movie lights. One of the lights was in Moss's eyes and he kept blinking and turning his head.

"You're a liar, Blake. And soon you'll be a dead liar. The dogs will like you. You'll taste sweet. You'll make a wonderful video for me, fighting the dogs as they tear you apart—the brave end of a brave man. I'm sorry I never showed you the others." He picked up the camera and pointed it at Moss. There was a whirring noise. "Say something, Blake. My customers like to hear people talk."

Moss wore a gray tweed overcoat and he ducked his head into the collar. He was sweating and his blond hair was plastered down across his brow. "Go to hell," he said.

"Perhaps you'd like to sing something," said Bagley, still pointing the camera at Moss. "Do you know any show tunes?"

"You killed Pellegrino," said Moss. His voice sounded strained, as if he was talking with something wrapped around his throat.

Bagley lowered the camera. "Yes, but you were the one who told me he had all that money."

"I didn't know you were going to kill him."

"Just his bad luck," said Bagley. "He recognized me. I had no choice."

"And what about Graham?"

"He saw my car driving away from the grocery. I knew a lot about Graham. I could have sent him to jail. So I talked to him. He swore he'd keep his mouth shut. But then there he goes yapping to that little detective. People are so untrustworthy. And you, too, you know, you were talking to him as well." Bagley sounded personally hurt.

"Why'd you kill Butch Howard?"

"He knew too much and he had killed Shaw. They were bound to get him for that and when they did, he'd make some kind of deal and tell them about me. Besides, I needed another film."

"They'll catch you, Ralph." Moss said this almost sadly.

"I won't be here. I'll make my little video of your valiant but futile struggle, then put your body out in the snow and leave. Just as I did with Butch. You should have seen Butch fight my dogs. He actually threw one. But they were too many for him. They were all over him. But even at the end he fought. He had helped me with the others, finding actors, bums, alkies, so it was only right that he should star in his own. It made a wonderful video. My friends will be very pleased. It almost made me think well of him. Afterward, I dragged him outside. That's the nice thing about snow, don't you think? It cleans up everything. I hope you're brave, Blake. You're a strong man. You can put up a good fight."

"That detective knows about you," said Moss. "He'll tell the police."

"So you told after all," said Bagley. He sounded not so much disappointed as wounded. "I don't like you, Blake. You're dishonest. But fortunately, I'm through here for a while. I just need to pack a few things and get my money. And make my video, of course. They're quite lucrative. In an hour I'll be in Bennington and tomorrow I'll fly to Santo Domingo. They like dogs there. I'm only sorry you can't come with me. But we'll watch you. I'll sit with my friends after a good dinner and we'll watch you on the TV. Don't die too quick. Promise me?"

Charlie kept looking up at the ropes dangling from the beams above him. There was one attached to a pulley which hung from one of the beams above the open space. Then the two ends of the rope slanted down over Bagley's head to a post about five feet away where they were wrapped loosely around a spike.

"But now I have no more time," said Bagley regretfully. "You can either fight my dogs with your hands tied or with them free. Which do you prefer? It makes a much better video with the hands free."

"Ralph, for the love of Christ . . ."

"No whimpering, Blake," said Bagley sternly. He sounded

like a teacher or strict parent and he stamped his foot. "Just tell me what you want."

"Untie my hands."

"Then you must do something for me," said Bagley, again in a friendly voice. "Swing your legs around so they hang over the side."

Blake Moss crawled around, managing to sit up and hang his legs into the open area so that his back was to Bagley. The dogs began barking and snarling.

"No tricks now," said Bagley. "Butch tried to grab me when I freed his wrists and I had to hit him. It didn't give him as good a chance when he fell." Bagley picked up his camera. "Just let me get a shot of you sitting there," he said. The video camera began to whir.

Both Bagley and Blake Moss had their backs to Charlie, who was sweating and so frightened that he could barely make himself move. He kept thinking of his revolver someplace out in the snow. Maybe he had dropped it when he had swung onto the ladder. He wanted to look but there was no time. He had never been so terrified, but he couldn't just stand and wait for Moss to be killed. Slowly he crept over to the post where the two ropes were looped around the spike.

"Sit right up at the edge," said Bagley helpfully. His voice was quite cheerful, and Charlie thought he must be crazy. "See the dogs, how enthusiastic they are? Roughneck's the biggest, he's the tiger-stripe with the torn ear. Then Shiloh, the brown one. Then Temper with the black front paws and Butcher with the white mark on his chest. And Spanky, the small one. He's always hungry."

By now all the dogs were barking. Bagley was right. They seemed enthusiastic. Charlie undid the two ends of the rope from around the nail. He could feel his knees shaking and tried to calm himself but there was no time. He hated how cowardly he felt. He reached up as high as he could and wrapped the ropes around his hands. You're fifty, he told himself, you shouldn't be doing this. Bagley was bending down behind Blake Moss. Charlie ran at them, then swung.

"Moss, hang on!" shouted Charlie.

Bagley spun around. He was still holding the video camera in one hand, while in the other he held a knife. His revolver was tucked in his belt. Dropping the camera, he tried to pull out the gun but it was too late. Charlie's feet struck him in the chest and he toppled backward over the edge of the loft. He grabbed at Charlie's feet, pulling off one of his rubber boots with the shoe in it as he fell. Charlie swung out over the open area. Looking down, he saw the five dogs darting out of the way as first the camera, then Bagley, then Charlie's boot fell among them. Bagley landed on his back and rolled over. Immediately the dogs were upon him, burying him with their quick bodies. Charlie swung back but he didn't swing far enough so that he could let go of the rope and jump back onto the floor of the loft. The bright lamps made the air seem dusty and thick. Charlie couldn't stop staring at Bagley as he rolled and kicked at the dogs and struggled to his feet with three of the dogs hanging from him. Blake Moss was still sitting at the edge of the loft, staring at the dogs. Bagley was yelling.

"Stop it! Down! Down!"

But the dogs didn't pause in their attack. Somehow Bagley got the revolver from his belt, but one dog was fastened to his arm and two to his legs while the others kept leaping toward his face and neck. Charlie saw Bagley staring up at him as he fought, saw how Bagley tried to yank his arm to point the gun at him swinging back and forth ten feet above the floor of the barn. The revolver fired and the bullet crashed through the metal roof. Blake Moss jumped back from the side of the loft. His hands were free. He knelt down and looked over the edge more cautiously. Charlie clung to the rope, as he swung back and forth, wrapping it around his feet. His hands burned and his arms ached. Bagley was still trying to get another shot, but then the dogs dragged him down. He fired once more and one of the dogs yelped and jumped away and began madly gnawing at its hip. Then Bagley was buried among the remaining four dogs in a writhing fur mass and suddenly there was a great spurt of blood and Bagley's legs began twitching frantically, beating against the wooden floor with a loud drumming sound.

Charlie turned away and looked at Blake Moss, who was still staring into the pit. When Charlie looked back again, Bagley was lying motionless. Two of the dogs had backed away from him and were looking up at Charlie. The other two were still tugging at Bagley's deerskin jacket which was torn and soaked with blood. The dogs' paws kept leaving red prints around the body. One dog had gripped Bagley's wrist and was shaking it, worrying it like a rat and making Bagley's rings flash in the light. The last dog lay still in a corner in a small pool of blood. Charlie slowly swung back and forth. The two dogs beneath him began barking at him, barking and leaping. Then a third dog left Bagley's body and joined the others beneath Charlie, whose feet hung down about two yards above them. Then the fourth dog joined them. They kept leaping and Charlie could feel their warm breath on his one bare foot.

Moss stood watching Charlie from the edge of the loft. "You're in a real pickle, aren't you?" he said.

"Get me down from here," said Charlie. His hands were sore and his arms felt stretched and painful.

Blake Moss didn't say anything but kept staring at Charlie. His eyes had narrowed, making him look even more like a lynx. Other than that his face bore no expression. About six feet separated the two men.

"Moss, get me down from here!" repeated Charlie. He wondered how long he could hang on. An hour? Two? It must now be three-thirty in the morning. When would anyone be coming to the farm? He imagined Moss turning and walking away, feeling that with Charlie dead no one would know of his involvement.

"Moss . . . ," Charlie began.

"Charlie!" called Artemis from somewhere back in the loft. "Are you all right? I found your gun."

"I'm over here," called Charlie. "I need some help."

Moss shook himself like someone coming out of the water. "What do you want me to do?" he asked.

An hour later Charlie and Artemis were riding back through the snow toward Artemis's farm. They had left Blake Moss, who was preparing to call the police. Before going, Charlie had managed to retrieve his boot from the garage area of the barn with a long pole as the dogs had barked and leaped at him. The boot had been badly chewed but Charlie didn't mind. He would keep it as a souvenir.

Charlie had given Moss the case. He was just as glad to be out of it and to avoid answering questions. He had erased all mention of Pellegrino from the video in the barn, while the video of Butch Howard's death, which they had found in the house, was enough to keep the police from asking about Pellegrino or anything else. And Moss would appear as a minor hero. Charlie didn't really care, even though Moss had been willing to let the dogs kill Charlie as well.

"Just one thing," Charlie had told him as they were about ride off. They had been on horseback by the house and Moss had been standing nearby in the snow.

"What's that?" Moss had asked.

"Forget about an office in Saratoga, Mr. Lynx. I know too much about you."

Charlie had expected Moss to look embarrassed, but his face showed no expression. After a moment, Moss had shrugged. "What did Pellegrino call you?" he asked.

Charlie tried to hold a straight face, but then he grinned. "He called me Mr. Owl," he said.

Riding back, Charlie kept his flashlight pointed at the snow. Their old tracks were nearly covered and by the time the police arrived there would be no tracks to be seen. But Charlie wasn't thinking much about the police or Moss or Bagley or his own bravery but of something that Artemis had found in the house. It was the picture of Man o' War, which had indeed been hanging in Bagley's living room. Charlie was now carrying it wrapped in a garbage bag. He wished he could see himself riding Artemis's palomino as he held the picture of Man o' War under his arm. He wished he had a photograph of it, even a video— he and Artemis, riding side by side with the picture of Man o' War and the snow falling all around them. He would give copies of the photograph to Mr. Whitman and maybe to Chief Peterson and Janey Burris. Even Jesse James would have been amused.

Artemis stood up on Phillip's back and stretched. "What do you keep chuckling about?" she asked.

"I'm just glad to get this picture back," said Charlie. "It's been a real nuisance."

26

Monday morning around ten Charlie and Victor were having breakfast at the Spa City Diner on Broadway at the edge of Saratoga. Victor was plowing through a double order of French toast with maple syrup and bacon, while drinking a large glass of orange juice—"Fresh-squeezed," as he had told the waitress, "none of this frozen junk." Charlie had ordered poached eggs without toast because he didn't want to gain weight. But he envied Victor his French toast, and the sight of it made his poached eggs taste like dust in his mouth. They sat in a booth near the door, and the bright sun pouring through the big windows felt hot on Charlie's neck. The restaurant was full and there was a constant clatter of dishes and the sound of people talking. Waitresses in white hurried back and forth.

"You mean you had another gambling party last night?" Charlie was saying. He was not pleased.

"That's right, although really it was the continuation of the first party, except without the football. We watched a Celtics game but it wasn't the same." Victor spoke without looking up from his plate, but whether from embarrassment or hunger, Charlie couldn't tell. Most likely it was hunger. As Victor ate, his frizzy gray hair bobbed to the movement of his chewing.

"And the same people came?" asked Charlie.

"All fourteen of them. We gave back the money each guy had had before that last hand was so rudely interrupted by Butch Howard and Frankie Leach. Then we began again. We played till eight this morning, as a matter of fact. That's why I'm a little pooped." Victor wore his three-piece gray suit and appeared the picture of health. He looked so distinguished that several times Charlie had noticed people staring at Victor as if thinking they had recognized him from TV.

"But where'd the money come from?" asked Charlie. "You only had the three thousand you got from Leach." He couldn't tell if he was being dense or if Victor was confusing him on purpose. Breaking the yolk of one of his eggs, he watched the yellow ooze across the tines of his fork. Then he glanced again at Victor's French toast. How good it looked.

"Eddie got it from the dogfights."

"You mean he won it?" Eddie had shown up mysteriously the previous day with no explanation as to why he had disappeared. He hadn't been picked up by the police like Victor. Instead, he had spent the night in an Albany hotel, then come back to Saratoga in a cab. He had looked flushed and pleased with himself.

"No," said Victor, "he swiped it. He saw where the money was being collected and that's when he called the cops."

"Eddie called the cops?"

"That's what I'm saying, isn't it?"

"I thought Bagley called the cops."

"Nope, it was Eddie. He called them and told them all sorts of stuff including a little bit about illegal dogfights. The dogfight part was true, the rest he made up."

"But why did he call the cops?" The word "nonplussed" popped into Charlie's mind and he guessed that was what he was feeling.

"He wanted to create a distraction so he could get the money. Then, when the police barged in, he just swiped it, although I guess he had to belt somebody."

"But that's theft," said Charlie, shocked.

"Yeah, I guess it is." Victor lowered his head and tried to look solemn. Then he took a bite of bacon and chewed it noisily.

"So he got exactly seven thousand?"

"I gather he got a little more, but seven K is what he returned to us. He said the rest was for expenses and we didn't argue."

"But I told you I didn't want any more gambling at the hotel," said Charlie. He couldn't decide how he felt, whether amused or depressed. Perhaps he felt a bit of both. He pushed his eggs away and sipped his coffee. At the next booth two men whom Charlie occasionally saw at the Y were also eating French toast. He was struck by how happy their faces looked.

"It was just this last time," said Victor. "It won't happen again."

Charlie rather doubted that. "So how'd you do in the game?"

"I won about fifty bucks and of course I got a percentage of the pot. Tubbs won pretty big. Other guys, you know, some won, some lost. And I got this for you." Victor handed Charlie an envelope.

Charlie opened it. Inside were fourteen one-hundred-dollar bills.

"That's for getting our money back," said Victor.

"Seems you and Gillespie did that by yourselves," said Charlie, putting the money in his coat pocket. It occurred to him that he now had a lot of money. He could travel to Argentina with Artemis, see a whole other world, be warm day after day. Winter in Saratoga could take care of itself. He began to look around for the waitress. He needed some real food.

"Yeah, but you found out who stuck us up. Did you see any of that video that Bagley shot of the dogs killing Butch Howard?" Victor snapped his teeth together several times, then made a wincing face.

"Only a minute or two. It was pretty unpleasant." As a matter of fact Charlie had only been able to stand about ten seconds, just long enough to see the dogs leap at Howard and to see his terrified expression.

"And guys pay to see things like that?"

"I guess so." Charlie again waved at the blond waitress. She nodded to him, but then walked on by. He found himself thinking about beaches and palm trees and sultry women dancing tangos. For some reason these images were not as alluring as he felt they should be. He thought again of Bagley and his snuff videos. Maybe those horrors were still too fresh in his mind to allow him to enjoy anything else. "That's why Bagley took Moss back to his farm," Charlie continued, "just so he could shoot that tape. He had a couple of other tapes like that besides the one of Howard. Like he'd killed two other men the same way. And there was evidence he had made even more. Howard would help him round up people that no one would look for, bums for the most part, people without homes. There's no telling how many he made."

"What a great guy," said Victor. "Too bad you couldn't have shot a tape of him getting eaten."

"I was otherwise indisposed," said Charlie. A second waitress walked by without stopping, despite Charlie's upraised hand. Couldn't she see he was starving? The woman was trim and athletic, reminding him of Janey Burris. For the thousandth time he told himself that he was taking her out to dinner the next night. Each time he thought this the news came as a surprise. It made his heart beat fast.

"And you got your money from Whitman?" asked Victor.

"That's right, I took him the painting first thing this morning. He hadn't even had time to take off his coat."

"What happened?"

"Not much," said Charlie. "I took the painting into his office and put it on his desk. He stared at it. Then he wrote me out a check for five thousand."

Charlie remembered how Whitman had looked—his pale face, gray hair, a three-piece pin-striped suit. The sun had been pouring through the bay windows of his office and had shone on the chestnut coloring of Man o' War. And now Charlie had $6,400. He could go anywhere. Why didn't he want to?

"Did he say anything?" asked Victor.

"As a matter of fact he did," answered Charlie, feeling pleased with himself. "He said, 'You surprise me, Mr. Bradshaw.' "

"You bet your ass, Charlie. What a devil you are, baby face and all. I bet he's surprised. I bet he's sitting there right now with his mouth open, saying, 'How in the world did it ever happen?' "

But Charlie wasn't paying attention. The trim waitress had stopped at their booth. Again she reminded him of Janey Burris and again he felt the beating of his heart. It was Janey who had made Argentina suddenly less interesting. He imagined sitting with her and talking to her and touching her skin. Was he really one of those emotional jerks who could stumble so easily from infatuation to infatuation? But perhaps this time it was more than that. He had a mental image of all the chartreuse tennis balls spread across her kitchen floor and how comfortable he had felt there. Once more the future was full of promise.

But in the meantime the waitress was looking impatient. Time was passing; the morning getting late. "I'd like some French toast too, please," said Charlie. "And don't forget the bacon."

FOR THE BEST IN PAPERBACKS, LOOK FOR THE

In every corner of the world, on every subject under the sun, Penguin represents quality and variety—the very best in publishing today.

For complete information about books available from Penguin— including Pelicans, Puffins, Peregrines, and Penguin Classics—and how to order them, write to us at the appropriate address below. Please note that for copyright reasons the selection of books varies from country to country.

In the United Kingdom: For a complete list of books available from Penguin in the U.K., please write to *Dept E.P., Penguin Books Ltd, Harmondsworth, Middlesex, UB7 0DA.*

In the United States: For a complete list of books available from Penguin in the U.S., please write to *Dept BA, Penguin,* Box 999, Bergenfield, New Jersey 07621-0999.

In Canada: For a complete list of books available from Penguin in Canada, please write to *Penguin Books Canada Ltd, 2801 John Street, Markham, Ontario L3R 1B4.*

In Australia: For a complete list of books available from Penguin in Australia, please write to the *Marketing Department, Penguin Books Australia Ltd, P.O. Box 257, Ringwood, Victoria 3134.*

In New Zealand: For a complete list of books available from Penguin in New Zealand, please write to the *Marketing Department, Penguin Books (NZ) Ltd, Private Bag, Takapuna, Auckland 9.*

In India: For a complete list of books available from Penguin, please write to *Penguin Overseas Ltd, 706 Eros Apartments, 56 Nehru Place, New Delhi, 110019.*

In Holland: For a complete list of books available from Penguin in Holland, please write to *Penguin Books Nederland B.V., Postbus 195, NL–1380AD Weesp, Netherlands.*

In Germany: For a complete list of books available from Penguin, please write to *Penguin Books Ltd, Friedrichstrasse 10–12, D–6000 Frankfurt Main 1, Federal Republic of Germany.*

In Spain: For a complete list of books available from Penguin in Spain, please write to *Longman Penguin España, Calle San Nicolas 15, E–28013 Madrid, Spain.*

In Japan: For a complete list of books available from Penguin in Japan, please write to *Longman Penguin Japan Co Ltd, Yamaguchi Building, 2-12-9 Kanda Jimbocho, Chiyuoda-Ku, Tokyo 101, Japan.*

FOR THE BEST IN MYSTERY, LOOK FOR THE

FOR THE BEST IN MYSTERY, LOOK FOR THE

☐ **MURDOCK FOR HIRE**
Robert Ray

When he is hired to find a dead man's missing antique coin collection, private detective Matt Murdock discovers an international crime ring that is much more than a nickle-and-dime operation.
256 pages   *ISBN: 0-14-010679-0*   **$3.95**

☐ **BRIARPATCH**
Ross Thomas

This Edgar Award-winning thriller is the story of Benjamin Dill, who returns to the Sunbelt city of his youth to attend his sister's funeral—and find her killer.
384 pages   *ISBN: 0-14-010581-6*   **$3.95**

☐ **DEATH'S SAVAGE PASSION**
Orania Papazoglou

Suspense is killing Romance, and the Romance Writers of America are outraged. When a fresh, enthusiastic creator of the loathed hybrid, Romantic Suspense, arrives on the scene, someone shows her just how murderous competition can be.
180 pages   *ISBN: 0-14-009967-0*   **$3.50**

☐ **GOLD BY GEMINI**
Jonathan Gash

Lovejoy, the antiques dealer whom the *Chicago Sun-Times* calls "one of the most likable rogues in mystery history," searches for Roman gold coins and greedy bird-killers on the Isle of Man.
224 pages   *ISBN: 0-451-82185-8*   **$3.95**

☐ **REILLY: ACE OF SPIES**
Robin Bruce Lockhart

This is the incredible true story of superspy Sidney Reilly, said to be the inspiration for James Bond. Robin Bruce Lockhart's book tells the thrilling story of the British Secret Service agent's shadowy Russian past and near-legendary exploits in espionage and in love.
192 pages   *ISBN: 0-14-006895-3*   **$4.95**

☐ **STRANGERS ON A TRAIN**
Patricia Highsmith

Almost against his will, Guy Haines is trapped in a nightmare of shared guilt when he agrees to kill the father of the man who will kill Guy's wife. The basis for the unforgettable Hitchcock thriller.
256 pages   *ISBN: 0-14-003796-9*   **$4.95**

☐ **THE THIN WOMAN**
Dorothy Cannell

An interior designer who is also a passionate eater, her rented companion who writes trashy novels, and a rich dead uncle with a conditional will are the principals in this delicious thriller.   242 pages   *ISBN: 0-14-007947-5*   **$3.95**

FOR THE BEST IN MYSTERY, LOOK FOR THE

☐ CAROLINE MINUSCULE
Andrew Taylor

Glittering diamonds and a medieval script prove a lethal combination when a leading authority on the Caroline Minuscule style of script is murdered.
234 pages   ISBN: 0-14-007099-0   **$3.95**

☐ THE PENGUIN COMPLETE FATHER BROWN
G.K. Chesterton

Here, in one volume, are forty-nine sensational cases investigated by the high priest of detective fiction, Father Brown, whose cherubic face and unworldly simplicity disguise an uncanny understanding of the criminal mind.
718 pages   ISBN: 0-14-009766-X   **$9.95**

☐ APPLEBY AND THE OSPREYS
Michael Innes

When Lord Osprey is murdered in Clusters, his ancestral home, with an Oriental dagger, it falls to Sir John Appleby and Lord Osprey's faithful butler, Bagot, to pick out the clever killer from an assortment of the lord's eccentric house guests.
184 pages   ISBN: 0-14-011092-5   **$3.95**

☐ THE BODY IN THE BILLIARD ROOM
H.R.F. Keating

The great detective and lovable bumbler Inspector Ghote is summoned from Bombay to the oh-so-English Ooty Club to discover why there is a dead man on the very billiard table where snooker was invented.
256 pages   ISBN: 0-14-010171-3   **$3.95**

☐ STEPS GOING DOWN
Joseph Hansen

Frail old Stewart Moody is found one morning strangled with the oxygen tube that was keeping him alive, in this powerful tale of obsessive love and the tawdry emptiness of evil.
320 pages   ISBN: 0-14-008810-5   **$3.50**